STOLEN SECONDS

TETHERED FATES
BOOK TWO

GHEETI NUSRATI

Editing by Emma Jane of EJL Editing
Cover Design by Daniela of Ever After Cover Design

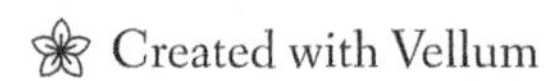

AUTHOR'S NOTE

Stolen Seconds contains mature and graphic content that is not suitable for all audiences. Reader discretion is advised.

I trust that you know your triggers.

PLAYLIST

"Video Games"—Lana Del Rey
"Do I Wanna Know?"—Arctic Monkeys
"remedy"—Alexa Cirri
"Cinnamon Girl"—Lana Del Rey
"Shameless"—The Weeknd
"Love in the Dark"—Adele
"I love you"—Billie Eilish
"Black Friday"—Tom Odell
"Constellations - Piano Version"—Jade LeMac
"High"—Stephen Sanchez
"making the bed"—Olivia Rodrigo
"Swim"—Chase Atlantic
"Born To Die"—Lana Del Rey
"The Color Violet"—Tory Lanez
"Falling In Love"—Cigarettes After Sex
"Where's My Love"—SYML

For those who suffer.
And come out stronger.

PROLOGUE
IRINA

One Year Ago

Appearances were a deception. One could alter it and hide what was inside. Emotions were the same. It was easy to manipulate and control them, swallow them into the depths of your soul.

Feeling had only ever caused me pain and the only way I avoided it from consuming me was to let it die inside of me, in the hollowness of my chest where it yearned to be fed.

Over the years, it became easier to bear, yet I sensed the strain chip at me bit by bit.

"Are you almost done?" My best friend's soft voice filtered through the door. "You never take *this* long getting ready."

With one last glance in the mirror, my hair pin straight and face marked with makeup, I pinched out a smile and exited the bathroom.

"Oh, yeah?" I cocked an eyebrow at her. "How would you know now that we live miles and miles apart?"

Aurora scowled at me, green eyes narrowing in distaste. Although she knew my joke was lighthearted, it was a bitter one.

My partner in crime had the misfortune of dealing with circumstances she couldn't avoid or change. Hence, why she moved back to her hometown in Italy, married to a made man, no less.

It was my first time in the colorful country and when I arrived a week ago, tension I had thought would diminish from seeing her, only intensified with the horrible situation she was in.

"Too far?"

"Miles and miles," she sighed.

It was my last day with her before I flew back home to New York and I intended to make the most of it.

Home hadn't been the same since Aurora left. She was a constant in my life and possibly the only one capable of stitching that hollowness inside my chest. And as soon as I understood that, I held on in hopes of one day waking up to feel *normal*.

"Well, I'm ready for the spontaneous day ahead of us." I linked my arm with hers. "Shall we?"

Aurora huffed incredulously, trying and failing to appear annoyed, but I spotted the slight grin stretching across her face.

She patted my arm. "The only thing that bastard of a man did right was allow you to visit."

Bastard of a man, being her husband, Roman Mancini. *Don* of the Cosa Nostra.

That would've scared an ordinary person, but I truly gave zero fucks about who he was. Besides, I knew of Aurora's upbringing, her past, and family. I was only sorry that she was sucked back into this world that she worked hard to escape.

"Key word being bastard."

The morning and afternoon were spent stuffing our faces with Italian delicacies and shopping at luxurious boutiques.

Italy was utterly breathtaking; the landscapes of the cities and ancientness of its architecture were awe inducing.

It was how I ended up dragging Aurora to a private event. It beckoned me to have a peek inside.

The white building was ethereal, enticing me with its gold detailing to enter.

"Irina, we can't cut in line!"

Aurora never took risks unless I forced her into it. Considering where she was at this point in her life, a small act of mischievousness would do her good.

I admit, adrenaline gave me a high that I constantly chased. It grounded me, allowing me to block the impending spiral of chaos. Every fix left me wanting more, eager to numb the empty space between my ribs.

"Sure, we can," I retorted. I usually got my dose from less respectable places, but this would do.

However, the hostess in front seemed to have caught sight of it with the attitude she presented.

"Can I help you?" the pristine hostess asked with a tone that had me opening my mouth to serve her the same *generosity*.

"We're here to attend the event," Aurora blurted out, her attempt at trying to diffuse an impending argument.

She knew I hated disrespectful people and one day, my tongue would be my downfall, but until then, I'd continue to reciprocate.

"My name is Aurora. Aurora *Mancini*."

The dark-haired woman's eyes widened slightly as she glanced down at the list in front of her before looking pointedly at my best friend. "Do you have identification on you to prove that?"

I couldn't blame the woman for being difficult. I knew it had everything to do with me cutting the long line of people who were *actually* on the guest list.

"You're holding up the line, Alicia. What seems to be the problem here?"

The voice was a deep timbre that touched me deep into my bones.

Alicia—the hostess—wasn't the only one who stiffened. I too stiffened behind Aurora from the sheer power of the stranger's masculine tone.

"Sir, these ladies want to enter, but they're not on the list. One of them is even claiming to be a Mancini," she mocked as her face turned a shade of beetroot red.

I bit my tongue before I said something that would surely dig us into a deeper hole. This man was undoubtedly the owner and with it being my last night in Italy with Aurora, I didn't want it to end with us in jail.

Not sure how her husband would react to that, either. Perhaps ban me from the country itself.

Aurora tensed. "We were leaving, actually." She laughed uncomfortably.

Did she know him?

I might've agreed to leaving if it weren't for the hostess smiling at us with arrogance.

Peering over Aurora's shoulder, I smiled back at her. "No, we weren't. . . "

The rest of my words died down when I caught sight of the beast standing near her. He was bigger and taller than any man I'd ever seen.

His hands were hidden in his pockets as his gaze flickered to me, head tilting and assessing me as if I were his own source of entertainment.

"Irina," Aurora hissed at my defiance, but I ignored her, held captive by rich caramel-brown eyes.

I realized this was a silent battle when the man's mouth curled into a smirk.

As a Russian, I was taught to never break first in all aspects of life and I sure as shit wouldn't start now.

The man had a perfect appearance, freshly shaven, sandy-brown hair trimmed and styled, and a black leather jacket that clung to his biceps as if it were tailored for his body.

Raising a brow at him in challenge, I waited.

The male species always referred to themselves as dominant and superior compared to a female.

Me? I was out to knock down their pedestal till they were on their knees before me.

"Let them in, Alicia."

I thought so.

The hostess hesitated before she moved aside.

My gaze locked with his as Aurora and I moved past them. Something untamed flashed across his features, his jaw clenching tightly.

A literal creep.

I clasped Aurora's hand and led us inside.

It was an art museum, a magnificent one, with exquisite art pieces decorating the walls and a few statues standing tall along the center.

The environment was spacious, lit up by chandeliers as guests softly murmured to one another and admired the view.

The further we walked around, the more my stomach turned into knots.

These art pieces were erotic. Displays of sensual desires and pleasure.

The one in front of us, in particular, was a skewed painting of vibrant colors. An intimate clashing of bodies and dimension.

"Anyone could create this." I felt a knot twist in my gut. "What's so artistic about two people *ravishing* one another?"

Aurora glanced at me with pinched lips, and I hated that my expression must've told her I regretted dragging us in here.

It was the smell of musk and spice that hit me before *his* words. "What unfortunate thinking, *piccola ribelle.*"

I refused to give his unwanted presence attention as I stared at the painting, hoping he would go away from the lack of it.

And when his scent continued to invade my space, I did what I do best. "You're part of the male population; of course, you'd think that way. And I don't speak Italian, *mudak*."

When I felt his breath, warm against my ear, I stiffened. My hands clenched into fists, hard enough to draw blood as my nails dug into my palm.

"Your tongue will get you in trouble, *piccola ribelle*." He dragged those two words, unfazed by my earlier statement. "The next time you call someone an asshole, be aware of who's on the receiving end of it."

With that, he stalked off. His physical presence might've been gone, but his words and scent clung to me as if they were staking a claim.

I exhaled harshly, unaware that I had even held my breath when he was near. And something strange happened.

This wasn't the fix I expected, and yet it happened unintentionally.

Nausea flooded my senses.

It couldn't have been because of him, could it?

I refused to believe that a strange man invoked a rush of adrenaline in me.

"What did he say?" Aurora whispered beside me, bringing me away from my turmoil.

"*Nothing*," I grumbled. "Now, let's go." *Before that creep came back*. "This place wasn't as great as I thought."

She turned, heading toward the exit. "Mhm."

CHAPTER 1
LUCA

One Year Later

The worst part of winter? Blood drying on your sweaty skin.

I was unfazed by the body fluid, but washing it off was a hassle I'd rather not inconvenience myself to.

Thank "I don't have all day." I caressed the side of Rocco's face with the tip of my knife. "What happened to the shipment?"

He coughed up blood, saliva mixed with it as it dripped down his chin. I waited for the remorse to hit, but it never did.

And it never would when I barely held more than superficial relationships with everyone outside of my circle.

I leaned down, resting my hands on my knees. "Do you want me to prolong your suffering?" I gestured to his mangled body and the damage I had already created. "Perhaps if you answer my question, you can leave here without further. . . consequences."

"I don't know *anything!*"

"Oh, but you do," I retorted.

When I got the call from Roman this morning that the drug shipment hadn't been received by the Russian Mafia, I knew we were fucked.

I had always been particular about the process of when, where, and how shipments were sent out to avoid any possible obstacles.

Yet, here I was, interrogating one of our men on the location of the goods because I hadn't been at the exchange myself.

I couldn't trust anyone, never had and never would, but I slipped up, and it wouldn't happen again.

"I have a family." Rocco groaned in pain—probably from the crimson color leaking from the side of his ribs. "Please, Luca."

I straightened myself, sighing. Every single interrogation ended the same exact way. The traitor begging for their life because of their family. The same family they didn't think of when betraying their *Don,* knowing we would find them and dish out their punishment.

A punishment that sent them on their way to God.

"Prolong suffering it is, then." I reached for him but stopped short when he spoke.

"Wait!" He was visibly shaking now, teeth chattering as if we were in the middle of a fucking blizzard. "Th-they gave a m-message."

I kept my expression neutral to the bit of knowledge he shared. "Who?"

"I d-don't know," he gritted out. "Their f-face was covered."

"What was the message?"

"*Y-you're* out of t-time."

Clarity shifted the situation. There was only one person who'd been hellbent on time and position when it came to me.

"That wasn't so hard, now was it, Rocco?"

His brown eyes widened with hope, a feeling that would drift away as soon as it rooted. "N—"

In one fluid motion, I flicked my wrist, the end of my knife sliding along his throat.

His eyes widened further; except this time, it was from fear, choking on his own blood. The seamless line widened as blood gushed down the column of his neck.

It took less than a minute for the sound of his gurgling to cease.

The dreaded part of killing someone was the aftermath of having to clean up the bloody mess.

It was a tedious process I had done countless times. I often wondered how it was so easy to get away with murder and hide the body as if it never existed.

Grabbing the cigarette pack from my jean pocket, I took a stick out before pulling out my phone and dialing Nicolai's number.

"Good morning, Luca," he answered.

The little shit had become a soft spot for everyone since Roman saved him years ago.

"Must you always answer formally, Nico?" I chuckled. I swear, the kid was an old soul trapped in a body of a twenty—two year-old.

"I think the term you're searching for is respectfully, not formally." I could practically picture him pushing up his glasses with the tip of his middle finger. "You and the others lack basic manners."

"And you lack the understanding of when to shut up, but here we are."

"My apologies," he drawled snidely, his snickering coming through the line.

As I said before, I had a soft spot for the little shit.

"I need you to come down to the Fort and cleanup for me." I lit the tip and inhaled a drag of smoke. "I have somewhere to be."

I didn't need to say what the cleanup was because, as young as Nico was, he was far more intelligent and lethal than most of our men. This wasn't his first time getting his hands dirty, either.

"Can't you call Ric? I'm busy."

"Busy with your nose buried in some book. I'm sure Shakespeare will still be there when you finish your task."

"Maybe if *you* picked up a hobby such as reading, you'd get rid of your morbid one."

I barked a laugh. He had one hell of a sense of humor. "Killing isn't morbid, it's art. Now, get your ass here."

With that, I hung up and made my way to my bike.

The Fort was in a discreet and secluded part of the city, hard to find and longer to reach. A good hideaway destination from outsiders.

Roman had connections with higher authorities to turn a blind eye to our business, but that didn't guarantee our immunity.

Crushing the cigarette beneath my boot, I climbed

atop my black Harley-Davidson and fastened my helmet before reviving the bike to life.

The drive to my next destination would give me time to cool down my temper.

Did he think I was stupid? If it wasn't obvious before on who sabotaged the plan, it was when Rocco told me of the threat he was given.

Winters in Italy were a charmer, the lively atmosphere was contagious to a fault, and it never surprised me when tourists roamed through the country during this time of year.

I breezed through the streets until the view of the mansion peeked through the trees, greenery surrounding the ostentatious architecture.

I neared the property, the gates immediately opening for me, and inviting me to my own personal hell.

Riding past the fountain path that led to the front of the house, I parked my bike in the roundabout and cut the engine.

"Luca!"

The sweet voice of my baby sister drifted through the air.

I swear to fuck she had a sixth sense that told her whenever I set foot on the premise.

Before I had a chance to hop off, she tackled me, crushing me into her delicate form.

"When did you get so strong, Eva?" I joked, wrapping my arms around her.

Her hold became firmer, along with the guilt that gnawed at me.

My sister and I had fifteen years between us. One of

us heir to the Changretta and the other a Mafia princess waiting to be wed to the most suitable bachelor. An absolute travesty.

I wasn't around anymore as much as I used to be, and I knew Eva loathed me a fraction for it. It didn't matter that she knew our father was the reason why. In her eyes, it was as if I abandoned her.

I ruffled her sandy-brown hair affectionately. "Forgive your asshole of a brother. He's trying."

She loosened her hold and stepped back, hurt evident in her green eyes as she stared at me. "Are you here to stay?"

I pursed my lips. She knew I would never come back willingly, yet she asked anyway. Every. Single. Time.

Before I had a chance to spew the same reply I always did, she turned on her heel and walked away.

Usually, I'd go after her, but I had to deal with the menace of a human—our father—first.

I walked up the steps to the arched double doors and pushed them open.

The moment I stepped foot inside, I stilled. The house had kept its distinct smell. Even though that smell belonged to my dead mother, who'd been gone for years.

The urge to turn back and never set foot in this cursed house again was intense. Instead, I closed the door and walked through the foyer to the hall on the left.

I knew security was watching my movements as I maneuvered through the house, alert and ready to tame me if I acted out. Not that they'd get to lay a finger on me before I snapped their necks.

My father wished he could see that part of me, only to

remind me how alike we were—ruthless and unapologetic. A monster.

He was wrong. In every sense of that word, he was.

I would've never killed my wife like he had.

As I neared the waxed oak door to his office, I picked up my pace. The sooner I talked to him, the faster I could leave.

I walked in without knocking, sat my ass on one of the black leather chairs, and put my feet up on his desk.

If the old man was triggered by my actions, he hid it skillfully.

Zeno Canaveri was one of a kind, truly. With a thirst for violence, it wasn't surprising why the fucker always had security with him. The minute he was alone, his head would be on a stick.

Even now, a burly man occupied one corner of the well-furnished room, staring at me as if I stole his favorite toy.

"Leave," I ordered him.

The man gaped at my father, who was more focused on the paperwork in front of him.

"Don't look at him, look at me." His thick neck moved as he swallowed before he settled his attention back to me. I nudged my head to the side. "Get the fuck out and close the door."

That's the irony of respect. It's not earned by being civil. No, it's by asserting your power and getting rid of anyone who questions it.

Everyone in this manor knew exactly what kind of fucker I was. They could all appear unfazed, but we all knew they ate from the palms of my hands like dogs.

When the door clicked shut, I relaxed further into the chair.

"You're in no position to order my employees."

My father finally looked up; his hazel eyes boring into me.

I could deny any internal similarities between us, but the physical traits were always there to remind me exactly whose son I was.

"And you're in no position to sabotage my operations, *Father*."

"*Yours?*" he enunciated by widening his eyes. "Nothing is yours, boy."

I gritted my teeth, knowing exactly the direction this conversation was taking.

"You could have all of this." He raised his arms, gesturing around himself. "Yet you choose to work for Roman as if you aren't a Canaveri."

My lips spread into a smile as I regarded the man in front of me. "And I bet that drives you insane, doesn't it? Knowing I'd rather associate myself with the Cosa Nostra instead of the Camorra."

His eye twitched, a tell that it did in fact drive him crazy that I willingly chose another over my family, and he couldn't do anything about it.

The Cosa Nostra was held in the highest regards when it came to the Italian Mafia and no one questioned Roman, not even my father.

"Continue your futile attempts at getting me back and Roman might overlook that you're my father."

He slammed his fist on the desk, the sound echoing around us. "You are my *heir!* You *will* take your rightful position as the leader of the Camorra. I won't let our legacy die because of you, boy."

His words fell on deaf ears. I had heard them before, and it became less and less effective over the years.

Setting my feet down on the marble floor, I stood. "For that to happen, you'd have to die first. And I long for that day, father."

I was halfway across the room when his voice reached me.

"Think long and hard about the decision you're making. Perhaps you've forgotten how valuable little Eva's position is as my daughter."

I clenched my fists, sensing that constant anger inside of me bubbling to the surface.

He was waiting for my reaction, and I wouldn't—

"The offers have been tempting. They prefer their brides young and—"

It was a reflex. You talk about my sister in a disgusting manner, and I'm a madman seeing red.

I felt my knuckles tear as I pounded into my father's face, the adrenaline of having him at my mercy exhilarating.

He didn't fight back, only gave me a bloodied smile. "You're exactly like me."

"I'm *nothing* like you," I seethed as I raised my fist.

"Luca! Luca, stop it!"

The sound of Eva's voice filtered through my murderous thoughts, halting my movements.

I peered over my shoulder and found her face blotchy as tears clung to her cheeks.

"Luca," she whispered, her voice shaking along with her small frame. "Please, can we just go?"

My chest burned from breathing harshly as I came down from my high.

I turned and grabbed my father by the collar. "Use my sister to threaten me again and I'll cut out your fucking tongue."

He didn't say anything as I released him, grabbed Eva, and walked out of the office.

"What offers?" Eva asked as I continued walking down the hall.

I ignored her, irritated that she'd been eavesdropping. It didn't matter what our father said, I would never let her be wed to anyone from our world.

When I reached the main door, I stopped short and closed my eyes.

This was never easy, and I wished I could take her with me, but if she was with me, she'd be a liability, a weakness that many people would use against me. I couldn't risk putting her in danger.

At least if she stayed at this house with our father, I knew she would be thoroughly guarded by security. And as a one man show, that wasn't something I could provide her right now.

"You're leaving?" she asked, her voice breaking. "After that?"

I nodded. Despite our father's tasteless ways, no harm had come to Eva since I'd left.

"I hate you."

Three words that had me turning to face her.

Her tears were flowing freely now as she regarded me with an expression that gutted me.

"Eva. . . "

"I do." She nodded furiously. "But don't worry, once I'm sold off like a whore, I won't be a burden to you anymore."

"Don't you dare, Evangeline! Everything I do is for you." The burn in my chest came back tenfold. "And how many times do I have to tell you to stop eavesdropping?"

Her lip trembled, pouting slightly like it used to when she was a small child.

I raked through my hair, frustrated that I couldn't give her what she wanted.

"Come here." I gestured to her with my hand, but she shook her head, her eyes blinking rapidly to get rid of her tears.

Stepping forward, I wrapped my arms around her, and she sobbed into my chest.

It hurt knowing I was partially to blame for her distress. I wished things were different for her. And I'd make sure it was. Soon.

"Hey. . . hey," I cooed, pulling back and cupping her face. "I'm going to do right by you."

She sniffled. "How?"

"Don't worry about that." I gave her a small smile to put her at ease.

I knew what I had to do, and I hated it.

"Now, wipe those tears. I can see your snot."

She laughed as more tears fell from her eyes before she hugged me. "I didn't mean it, you know?"

"I know."

CHAPTER 2
IRINA

I was a liar.

When my best friend asked me to come visit her in Italy for Christmas, I knew it was my only chance to find what I'd been searching for.

I couldn't disclose the reason to her and it was eating me alive. She was the only person I'd break myself into pieces for just so I could be the friend she deserved.

In the end, I wondered if she'd hate me or pity me. Both outcomes would surely disintegrate the hollowness inside my chest until I'd been bled dry.

The arch doors swung open, revealing Aurora and her broody bastard husband, Roman Mancini.

"Rina!" Aurora squealed, throwing herself at me in a bear hug.

The wind was knocked out of me as I caught her in my arms. Her cinnamon scent smelled like home, and I couldn't be happier to be in her presence after months apart.

"I've missed you, too." I chuckled, squeezing her. When we pulled apart, I took her in from head to toe. She looked the same. . . yet different. "There's something going on with you. What is it?" I demanded.

Aurora's face twisted in confusion at my abruptness. She regarded me like *I* was the one who appeared unusual.

"Is it him?" I asked, pointing to the large man behind her. "How is the bastard treating you, anyway?"

Her green eyes widened slightly as she glared at me to shut my mouth.

Roman finally stepped forward, staring at Aurora as he wrapped his arm around her waist possessively. "The *bastard* is treating her just fine," he said gruffly.

The last time I talked to Roman was on a video call when I told him I'd hoped his *dog* learned how to not answer other people's phone. The dog being the leather wearing giant who I had the misfortune of meeting once. And I hoped to avoid him during my visit.

I smirked at the affection Roman so proudly displayed for my best friend. "I expect nothing less."

Although Aurora and Roman's relationship started out rough, it was clear as day the infinite love they held for one another.

An inferior emotion if you asked me.

"Welcome to our home, Irina. I hope your stay is. . . memorable." Roman assessed me as if he was analyzing me in his head.

Did he think I was a threat? I had given him no reason to believe that, but I guess as a *Don,* you had to assume the worst in everyone and everything. And considering it was our first time meeting in person, I couldn't quite blame him.

"Let's go inside and I can show you around," Aurora interjected. "Don't worry about your bags. They'll be taken to your room."

Once we entered the house, Roman kissed Aurora's cheek and parted ways with us.

I stared as she watched her husband walk down the corridor before he disappeared around the corner.

"You really do love him, don't you?"

She turned back to me, a smile plastered on her glowing face. "What was that?"

"You love him," I stated.

And in one sentence, she summed up their unconditional tie. "He breathed me back to life."

"Poetic as ever."

She smacked my arm playfully. "Oh, shut up. The day someone tames your craziness, I'll never let you live it down."

"I don't see that happening. Ever."

Their manor was a dream. The décor was warm and inviting, which surprised me. It was luxurious but subtly done with vintage furnishings.

"Your room is here." Aurora gestured to the black oak door with a Victorian plate knob. "I'll let you freshen up before dinner."

With that, she turned on her heel and left the west wing.

My bags were already perched atop the bench at the end of the four-poster bed when I entered the room.

It could've been taken as a master bedroom with the huge pane windows and an even larger bathroom.

As I wandered through the space, I noticed the different shades of red on every surface.

A small smile curved my mouth. This had to be Aurora's doing, her way of making me feel at home.

Guilt bloomed, my chest caving in further remembering the reason for my visit. But this was inevitable.

After washing up with too many bath scents to choose from, I pulled out my phone and clicked the first contact.

"*Printsessa.*" My father's voice filtered through the line.

"*Privet, Papa.*"

There was a sort of irony to him calling me princess. I was one, yet I grew up differently than the expectations that would've tied me down.

When I was born, my parents hid me from the outside world. I lived in the four walls of our manor, longingly waiting for the day I could go beyond our property border. This was a secret within our inner circle, kept hidden from outsiders.

As daughter of the *Pakhan*, my father knew that I would be a liability to him. He knew that I'd be used against him if the opportunity arose for his enemies, and he'd rather die than put me in any danger.

He was one of the most ruthless yet loving men I had ever met. He protected me from our world without thinking of the consequences that would've happened if I was exposed.

Yet he hadn't known danger could come in different shapes and sizes.

Whether my father wanted it or not, I'd been exposed to violence since I could remember. I'd seen what happened in the west wing of our house when he held *special* meetings. I had been given strict instructions not to leave my room when they occurred, but no one ever paid me any attention, let alone the staff. Why would they when my own existence made me feel hollow?

At the age of fifteen, I'd killed someone for the first time. All it took was for a wrong touch from an employee and I hadn't hesitated to make sure it was their last.

The experience had left me jarred, and I couldn't grasp onto the reality of what I had done.

My mother had found me in my room, stock-still covered in blood and instead of consoling me as I had expected, she retrieved my father. That's when my training began.

Furthermore, he had doubled down, decreasing the number of people who were allowed past the property gates, leaving me to wilt in my room with how vacant the house had become.

When I wasn't training, I would lay in bed, longing to experience more than what I'd been molded to accept.

Even the moments that I'd shared with my parents had felt more of a chore than out of genuine interest. I couldn't even blame them with how frequently they were away for business. Nonetheless, I'd savored them in hopes of having it forever. But it was short-lived. Time went on and yet I felt stuck.

Days blended and it became harder to live in secrecy. I had been isolated, rotting in the recesses of my mind, and I couldn't handle the silence—the stillness of it all anymore.

When I experienced my first panic attack, my father was there, defeat and pain written across his face as we both knew I couldn't continue living the way that I was.

At eighteen, I left home. But I couldn't escape who I was.

I moved to America and became somewhat of a spy for him, gathering information in secret so he could gain intel on others. And as an attorney, it was easier to do so.

To this day, no one knew that my real last name was Morozov. Not even my best friend.

"Have you settled in at Aurora's?"

I sighed at the mention of her name. "Yes."

"What is it, *Irina*?" he asked, his tone laced with concern. I could picture him now, seated in his mahogany office and sipping on his vodka.

"I. . . I just feel guilty for lying to her about the reason for my visit."

I trusted Aurora wholeheartedly, but I knew it wouldn't be fair to have her keep this from Roman. If he found out, it could lead to an unwanted war, and I couldn't risk it.

She was the first person I'd ever been comfortable enough to be around when we'd first met. But my true identity was something I'd never shared with her. That was a risk I couldn't take, especially not after she'd married the *Don* of the Cosa Nostra.

"You know exactly why they can't find out your real

identity," he muttered, power ripping from his voice. "And *never* be ashamed of being my daughter. You are the gem of the Bratva and I won't let guilt chip away at you. . . or stop you from your mission."

The same Bratva that hadn't known of my existence until after I'd left Russia. It was ironic, how I'd been more valuable to them in the end than most of their other members.

I was more than capable of fending for myself. After my father found out I'd killed for the first time, he made sure I was never put in a situation that I couldn't get out of. He didn't doubt my skills, but I felt as though sometimes he'd forgotten I was his daughter and not his employee.

I couldn't help but laugh. "Mission? *Papa,* that *mission* it to bring my brother home."

Nicolai Mancini. But I knew that wasn't his last name. He was a Morozov, heir to the Bratva.

My efforts at finding information about him led to dead ends. It seemed that Roman had made it *his* mission to conceal everything about Nicolai.

The only reason we found his location was because of my cousin, Viktor, who was tech savvy to no end and our link in keeping our names clean.

"Bring him home, *Printsessa.*"

My father had an affair while on a business trip to Italy over two decades ago. An affair that gave me a brother I never knew about.

My parents had an odd relationship, fucked up, to say the least. It was a chaotic and an abnormal dynamic, but they were forced to marry for a stronger alliance, so it wasn't surprising.

They did love one another, though; I knew it when my mother passed away. I saw the way my father mourned her loss. That pain had aged him.

I wasn't oblivious about the origin of my internal issues. I once embraced hope, I once embraced love, and I once embraced sympathy. I felt it all unconditionally until it grew harder to elicit them.

When you've been a slave to your own life, it messes you up. And I think I stopped blaming my parents when the route to self-destruction became mind numbingly peaceful.

The only reason my father had the nerve to seek out Nicolai was because my mother had died three years ago and the shame of bringing in his half Russian *bastard* son would fall on him alone. And as the *Pakhan* no one would question him.

"Do you even know what happened to his mother?"

I held my breath as I waited for his answer.

"No, I stopped all contact with her when she fell pregnant."

My stomach dropped at his words. "And you just forgot them?"

"His mother was a *worker* for the club I was holding business at. It meant nothing. She refused to stop the pregnancy and. . . "

"So, you up and left," I breathed, my heart racing. Shouldn't that have made me hate my father? It should've but I couldn't hate someone who'd given me his devotion, so what did that make me? "Did my mother know about Nicolai?"

"Of course, she knew. I'm not proud of it, Irina but I had an image to uphold." The line went silent before he spoke again. "I would've terminated the pregnancy whether she had wanted it or not, but she begged me. It was the first and only time I'd ever shown mercy on someone."

He did have an image to uphold, but that was a horrible thing to have done. I felt sorry for both Nicolai and his mother. It made me wonder what happened to her and how my brother fell under Roman's protection.

It wasn't fair to ask Nicolai to take responsibility and become heir to the Bratva eventually, but our worlds had never been fair. They took and took and took.

And Nicolai deserved to know that part of himself whether he wanted to or not.

"I'll bring him home, but it'll take time."

I wanted to create a friendship with my brother first. I missed out on years of knowing him and I would execute that the way I wanted to regardless of what my father said.

He already took him away from me once and I wouldn't let him do it again.

"I'll be in touch."

Sleep wouldn't come to me. Not when I was jet lagged and had thoughts of my brother roaming around in my mind.

I huffed a sigh as I slipped on my robe and exited my room.

The halls were dimly lit, guiding me down the curved stairway.

I hadn't been able to explore the entirety of the manor and Aurora had only shown me the important areas of her home.

There were numerous rooms upstairs, and I wondered if one belonged to Nicolai or if he lived elsewhere.

The house was silent except for the crackling of a fireplace.

I hadn't checked the time before coming down, but I knew it must've been late in the night.

As I neared the living room, I heard light whispers and laughter.

Roman and Aurora were nestled together before the fireplace, cocooned with piles of blankets and pillows.

From my position, I could only see Roman's face, listening intently to something my best friend was saying.

This was the first time I had seen him candid and with the awe filled expression across his face, I knew he loved her as much as the woman in his arms did, if not more.

Aurora huddled closer to him, and he wrapped the blanket around her before looking up to where I stood.

Shit.

I backed away a step, bringing my finger to my lips, telling him to not make my presence known to her.

He raised his brows, a silent question asking me if I was okay.

That made me smile. Not because he was concerned for me but because he knew Aurora would've wanted him to ask. By extension of my best friend, I was in good graces with her husband.

I nodded, turning on my heel and leaving them.

I'd once believed in love, but the love that was true wasn't sunshine and flowers. It was heartbreaking and painful, fear of allowing someone to hold that power over you.

A love that I'd never submit myself to.

CHAPTER 3
LUCA

"Your decision is final?"

I took a drag of my cigarette as I stared out onto Roman's property.

We stood on the balcony of the third floor, the cold breeze of early morning seeping through my clothes.

"Yes."

One simple word yet it held the weight of an anchor.

Roman turned to face me, his silence louder than any words he could've said. I knew he wasn't happy with my answer with the way his lips pursed.

He knew me through and through. It didn't matter if we didn't share the same blood, we were brothers in every sense of that word.

"Don't." I leveled his gaze. "It's the only way I can protect Eva."

"And does Evangeline know that you've chosen to become the leader of the Camorra?"

Another inhale of smoke, feeling the burn in my chest.

No, she didn't, and it wasn't any of her concern. I wouldn't hide it from her, but I wouldn't explain my choices either. She'd beg me not to do this for her sake. And it'd be useless.

I had already spoken to my father last night and finalized my position.

"It doesn't matter. Her reaction wouldn't have hindered my decision."

"I see," he said, turning toward the view before us. The sun had fully risen, brightening the winter sky.

"Any advice?"

"On?"

"Being a leader."

I knew the ins and outs of our organizations but Roman was the most feared *Don* which earned him my respect. He unapologetically did as he pleased, and the other three clans followed whether they approved or not.

I had always been a one man show, bound by nothing and not giving a shit what others did either.

He didn't answer me, causing me to glance over at him. His body shook as he laughed silently.

It caught me off guard. Roman rarely *ever* laughed openly.

"You're asking me for advice on how to run a criminal organization." He chuckled, shaking his head. "Don't worry, Luca. I'll be sure to hold your hand every step of the way."

"Oh, fuck off." I threw the cigarette on the floor, crushing it under my boot.

A flock of birds chirped above, and it was only when I looked up that I caught a glimpse of pale blonde hair.

My heart thumped against my rib cage harder than before. I inched forward, clutching the wooden railing as I watched *her*.

Women either feared me or kneeled before me but this little rebel had done neither.

And what a mistake she'd made a year ago by doing that and catching my attention. It was a fucking understatement.

I ran my tongue along my teeth. "You have a guest over."

"Irina arrived yesterday," Roman confirmed. "She'll be staying with us for Christmas."

A fiery sensation ignited inside the pit of my stomach, traveling through the rest of my body. I wanted to know what else that troublesome tongue of hers was capable of.

My lips quirked up when I remembered the way she called me an asshole in Russian, thinking I wouldn't understand.

My father raised me to learn many languages. He'd said it would be beneficial to know what outsiders said when they spoke in their native tongue. It had been a useful skill during operations.

"I want you to leave her alone, Luca," Roman said, interrupting my thoughts.

"Did I say something to elicit that command?"

Aurora joined her Russian friend, carrying two mugs before she sat down inside the gazebo.

"You *are* a dog," he muttered. "Perhaps if you stopped staring at her like she was your next meal, I wouldn't have to warn you away."

A dog? The fuck did that even mean?

"She's Aurora's best friend and not one of your escapades. Irina is *off* limits."

He slid the door open and left me alone with his unwarranted order.

I wish I could head his warning, but I'd never been good at fearing them. Roman could control as many people as he wanted to, but we both knew I wasn't on that list. And what he didn't know, wouldn't hurt him.

Seeing my little rebel again hadn't been in the cards, but now that she was, I had to play the game.

Roman walked down the stone path to where his wife sat. He leaned down to kiss her and Irina averted her eyes, her head turning toward the house.

Her gaze fell on me, the sun reflecting against her blue eyes. She stilled, her full red lips parting slightly in what seemed to be shock.

I tilted my head at her unblinking stare. I'd caught her by surprise with my presence. Good.

In a split second, her face morphed into a scowl. However, the interesting part was that she didn't avert her eyes.

It seemed that I wasn't the only one who wanted to play this game. My little rebel was intrigued and who was I if not to satisfy her interest.

I winked at her, knowing the reaction I'd receive would satiate my unauthorized desire.

And as her middle finger shot up at me, I knew this woman would be one hell of a damn chase.

"Luca!" Aurora called out, pulling my attention. She beamed at me with a wide smile. "Come down!"

I nodded at her, my eyes flitting to Roman's narrowed

ones. If I was being honest, once Irina was in my peripheral, she had become my sole focus. So, if he'd seen my interaction with her, I knew he'd give me shit for it.

I walked downstairs from the balcony and through the double doors in the back.

The trail to the gazebo would've been surrounded by flourishing flowers if it weren't for the winter. The gazebo itself was a large hardtop patio with curtains—that were tied back—and a round marble table at the center surrounded by cushioned wicker chairs.

Irina tore her gaze away from me, her long hair swaying from the wind. She wore tight leather pants with a large black coat that covered the rest of her body.

"I guess introductions aren't really necessary since you two have met before," Aurora said, her cheeks turning a light shade of pink, probably recalling the time she and her friend attempted to get into my museum.

They hadn't been on the list, but I was obviously a gentleman. How could I turn down the woman who avoided my gaze as if it was her fucking job?

"And what a first impression it'd been."

"Indeed."

Fuck me. Her voice was smooth as silk. . . and grated on my nerves. How could one woman have this effect on me?

Irina looked up at me, her face fierce against her fair complexion. "I'd say first impressions tell you all you need to know about a person."

The freckles on her face appeared more prominent under the harsh light of the sun, somehow emphasizing her displeasure to my presence.

I ran my finger over my lip to hide my amusement. "Then I hope I made an unforgettable one."

Her jaw clenched, the outline of her tongue poking against her cheek. "It's difficult to say when I hardly remember the interaction." She stood from her seat, eyeing the length of me in distaste. It could've been with any expression, but my little rebel had checked me out and damn it felt good to have her ocean blues on me.

As she passed by me, I suppressed a groan from her amber scent drifting toward me. "I'll have to fix that, *piccola ribelle*," I whispered.

I sat in her seat, watching her stride back into the house before I regarded the beloved couple.

"Luca," Roman gritted out through clenched teeth, anger marring his face. "What did I tell you?"

I shrugged. The bastard was a control freak in every way, and I'd never give him the satisfaction.

"What did you tell him?" Aurora's brows furrowed as she glanced between her husband and me.

"He told me to stay away from your precious guest."

Aurora laughed, slowly at first before it grew louder. Her hand clutched the side of her stomach as we eyed her strange outburst.

"What's humorous about that, *anima mia?*" Roman asked, caressing the strands of her black curls.

She wiped the tears from the corners of her eyes and chuckled once more before composing herself. "I love you both, but you're fools. Irina can handle herself and she certainly doesn't need a man warning off others on her behalf. Nothing could break that girl."

That wasn't surprising but Aurora feeding me information on her had only made my skin buzz with curiosity and anticipation.

I wanted to be the one to break Irina, to peel back all her layers just so I could put her back together again. *Just so I could call her mine.*

That thought jarred me. I had never been fixated on anything or anyone in my life. Yet, this Russian woman had only said a handful of unpleasant words to me, and I'd been captivated.

I didn't know whether to revel in it or loathe it.

"Besides, Luca is a gentleman. He won't cross any boundaries, isn't that, right?"

I stared at her expectant face and saw how confident she was in me. I'd always liked Aurora; she was the only person who'd brought a *Don* to his knees. But her image of me was skewed. She didn't know that when I wanted something, I'd get it without so much of thinking of the consequences.

I smiled at her lazily and looked at the man who'd turned a blind eye to all my questionable actions over the years. "That's right. Although, what's the saying? A gentleman never tells."

Pushing Roman's buttons was my favorite pastime so when he shot to his feet to lunge at me, I dodged it and walked backward toward the house. "See you later, brother," I called out. "Aurora, it's always a pleasure!"

He stepped forward before a giggling Aurora tugged him back down in his seat.

My cabin was a few miles away from Roman's manor. It was atop a large piece of land, far away from everyone and everything. Exactly how I wanted it.

I entered using the keypad and kicked off my boots, feeling the weight of the day settling upon my shoulders.

Movement from my right had me pulling out my gun in a split second.

"It's Eva!" My sister appeared before me, her hands up in defense mode as her eyes widened.

"What the fuck, Evangeline?" I bellowed, my heart racing. I put my gun back inside its holster. "Never do that again."

"You gave me your pin," she whispered, letting her arms fall beside her.

"For emergencies." I glared at her. "Call me before you show up next time."

She knew better than to come here unannounced, especially when I wasn't home. I'd secured the place, but she could've been followed by anyone.

"So now I need permission to come see my brother?"

"If it has to do with your safety, then yes. You do as your told, do you understand?" I knew my words were harsh, but she had come unescorted and without her security team.

"Yes, I fucking understand! Eva, do this, Eva, do that!" Her anger was palpable, her body shaking. "I'm exhausted, *fratello*."

She walked into the living area and sank down onto the black leather couch, her frail shoulders slumped.

I looked up at the white ceiling, reining in my emotions. I often wished our mother were here to guide me on how to approach certain situations with Eva. I'd helped raise her, but I knew she missed out on that motherly bond, and I wished she hadn't.

I felt the start of a headache, remembering the reason why my mother was six feet under the ground. And I'd make sure my sister didn't meet the same fate.

I removed my leather jacket and sat beside her. She peered up at me with a sad expression and in this moment, she resembled our mother so heavily, it pained me.

"You want to talk about it?"

She shook her head subtly.

"Alright, come here." She laid her head on my lap like she used to do when she'd cry as a small child. "I'll always take care of you."

The silence stretched as I caressed the strands of her hair before she asked, "And who takes care of you, Luca?"

I didn't know how long I'd sat there, mulling over my sister's question until sleep overcame her.

I didn't need anyone to take care of me and the only person who ever had was murdered in front of me by our father.

CHAPTER 4
IRINA

"Does this look okay?" I asked Aurora, staring at myself in the full-length mirror.

I never wore anything revealing—unless it was for a mission. It made it harder to hide my weapons and with this silky red dress, I was only able to wrap my blade around my upper thigh. The only reason I had worn it was because Aurora came into my room and insisted.

She stood beside me, her emerald eyes catching mine in the reflection, matching the flowy green grown she wore. It was a bit large on her, but I refrained from commenting on it. I was the last person to tell others how to dress. "You could wear a trash bag and you'd still be stunning."

It was Christmas Day and Aurora had planned a small party at the manor. She'd said she wanted it to be intimate with her closest friends and family. And all I could think about was Nicolai and if tonight I'd meet him.

Nerves pricked at my skin, worried that he wouldn't

like me. It was a stupid thought because he had no reason to hate me. . . yet.

"When is everyone arriving?"

Socializing with others was a skill I had needed to learn after leaving Russia. It was interesting how easily people fell into manipulation. All you needed was to give them what they wanted to hear.

Yet, the hollowness inside my chest expanded, ready for the onslaught of emotions I'd shove down.

"They should be arriving soon." She handed me my lipstick. "I should head down and make sure Roman isn't yelling at the staff."

I chuckled. "I'll see you in a bit."

With a quick kiss on my cheek, she left the room.

I applied the deep red shade across my lips, relishing at how the particular color boosted my confidence.

Stepping back, I smoothed my blonde hair away from my face. All my life I had been told how beautiful I was, and while I didn't care for the repetitive compliment, my father taught me how to use it as a weapon of deception. It was pathetic how people willingly gave information to anyone remotely attractive.

The sound of a soft melody permeated the house as I exited the room.

It was as if I'd stepped into a winter wonderland. Twinkling lights were strung up along with multiple Christmas trees standing tall all over the main level. It was grandiose, over the top and festive.

I loved this time of year and the only way I could describe the feeling it gave me was warmth. A small sense of euphoria to be enveloped in a sense of reality that would end as soon as it began.

It made me recall how many holidays I missed with my parents and how we'd never be able to make up for them. Short-lived like everything else in my life.

"Was there a reason you were wandering the manor the night you arrived?"

I turned my head to find Roman standing beside me. He was dressed in all black, eyeing the garland above the fireplace with a head tilt as if there was something wrong with it.

"Doesn't it get exhausting being aware of your surroundings around the clock?"

He caught my gaze, piercing me with his nearly black eyes. "The way I see it, every single person has a tell." He stared ahead again. "Once you find it, you can exploit it."

Of course, I'd known that. I was always alert and ready to strike, if need be, in any situation. Although, allowing Roman to know that would lead him to believe there was more to my story than being Aurora's best friend.

"Noted, but I don't have a tell, Roman. You can stop being skeptical of me."

His lips twitched in what could've been amusement. "I always liked you and I can see why my wife is fond of you."

Making friends had never been appealing to me until Aurora and even then, she had become my only friend. One person you could trust was better than multiple. The more people who knew about your life, the easier it was for them to use it against you.

In my book, this was a small victory. If circumstances

were different, I think I could've befriended Roman but what was the point when I was here to take my brother home.

"The feelings are mutual."

He nodded and turned on his heel. "Enjoy the party, Irina."

As the hour droned on, guests had arrived and my palms grew clammy when I spotted Nicolai.

I had been watching him from afar, unsure of when to approach him. Not that I could when the beast dressed in leather was talking to him.

He was a brute who clearly had expected every woman he encountered to fall at his feet with the way he openly winked at me only a few days ago.

As if I summoned his attention, his eyes flitted to me, the caramel in them darkening as they trailed along my body.

I gritted my teeth, my pulse skidding angrily at the way he gawked at me as if he had every right to.

I'll have to fix that.

I remembered the words he'd whispered to my ears only. The only thing he'd need to fix was his creepy fixation.

"Sorry." Aurora diverted my attention as she came to stand beside me, breathing harshly. Her curly hair was fluffier, and the sleeve of her gown had fallen from her shoulder. "I was. . . occupied."

I pressed my lips together. Considering she had staff to make sure everyone was fed and entertained, her definition of occupied did not fall into that category.

"Roman couldn't wait, could he?" I asked, fixing her

sleeve.

Her face flushed with color, but she smirked mischievously. "Maybe *I* was the impatient one."

My head tilted back as I laughed heartedly from her unexpectedness bluntness. When I looked around to make sure no one had overheard our less than holy conversation, I found Luca still staring at me. My smile slowly dropped as my own face heated with warmth.

I'd never been shy of receiving attention from others, I was used to it but there was something about having *his* that unsettled me.

"You know Roman warned him off," Aurora said, glancing over to where Luca stood. "But I set them both straight that my best friend knew how to handle herself."

I appreciated that. I was more than capable of dealing with others, but she didn't realize this information confirmed my suspicion.

The brute wanted me for some reason and from the feral way he looked at me, I knew this was a game I'd need to play strategically to veer him away.

"Curiosity killed the cat, Aurora," I replied, narrowing my eyes at him. "He'll find out that this one bites first."

"Never doubted that." She linked her arm around mine. "Before you start *biting* though, let me introduce you to everyone else."

Roman had his whole security team around, many of them standing with watchful eyes despite the lack of danger but it made sense when their chief was Ricardo, a large man with a buzz cut who grunted more than he spoke.

Aurora's brother, Enzo, and his girlfriend Sofia were

seated at the kitchen island, whispering between themselves.

"Enzo." Aurora caught his attention before he pulled back from the redhead and smoothed his concerned expression to a gentle one as he regarded his sister. I didn't miss the way his eyes hung with tiredness. "This is Irina."

"It's finally nice to put a name to a face." I chuckled.

Enzo had been there for Aurora during a time when I hadn't been able to and for that he was in my good graces.

"I've heard nothing but great things about you, the pleasures all mine." He smiled and turned toward his girlfriend. "Irina, this is. . . Sofia."

The woman pinched out a smile that didn't seem genuine as she shifted uncomfortably.

Enzo seemed to have read her body language because he grasped her hand and set it atop his lap. She looked at where they were joined and her face morphed into puzzlement.

I knew enough from this interaction to know there was something off about Sofia.

She turned back to face me. "Hello." Her voice was husky and stronger than I expected.

"Nice to meet you, Sofia."

She stared at me for a beat longer, the green in her eyes empty as if she were in a daze.

"I'm making rounds before dinner," Aurora told them before pulling me away.

When we were out of earshot, I said, "That was interesting."

She sighed, shaking her head slightly. "Interesting doesn't even sum it up."

I'd have to ask her about them later. I had a suspicion there was a lot to unfold about that relationship.

"And this is my favorite man," she cheered before we reached my brother. "Don't tell Roman I said that."

I wouldn't dare. And the thought of Nicolai being liked among them gave me a sense of peace to know he was taken care of all these years.

"Aurora." Nicolai crookedly smiled, nodding his head in greeting at her. "How is Roman's salvation doing?"

She giggled as a blush crept along her face. I realized that was an inside joke between them.

I knew it was wrong of me to feel the pang of jealousy I did but seeing how close they were reminded me of how much I'd lost.

Someone called for Aurora, and she hurried off, leaving us alone.

"Hi, I'm Nicolai."

My head flicked to the side so fast it gave me whiplash. They were words that I'd wanted to hear all night.

My brother smiled at me, his brown eyes crinkling at the corners adorned with black glasses.

He laughed, the dimple on his cheek deepening. "There's a situation regarding Roman and the chef."

My heart beat against my ribcage, loud enough for me to hear it as I took in his features, trying to recognize the similarities between us and there were. We had the same pale blond hair and a peppering of freckles across our face.

I must've been staring in shock because his smile faltered a bit, causing me to collect myself.

"Irina." Even the smile on my face felt awkward.

"It's a pleasure to make your acquaintance." He spoke

elegantly, his voice a deep melody.

A surge of emotion clawed up my throat, the sting of it burning my nose. I hadn't expected to react this way. "Likewise."

He unclasped his hands from his back and let it rest at his sides. "You're Russian." It was a statement.

"The accent gave it away, didn't it?"

He nodded. "*And* Aurora speaks of you constantly."

Her and I both. She was truly my ride or die.

"Do you know many Russians?" The question slipped out before I could stop myself. This was not the time and place to unfold our history.

His brown eyes sparked with something I couldn't place, his lips pursing as if he were stopping himself from saying what he really wanted to. "Can't say I do."

I didn't believe him and sooner or later I'd find out his real answer. There was a possibility that his mother had told him who his father was.

Awkwardness settled over us and I cursed myself for being the reason why.

He must've noticed the mood change because he smiled at me again. "But I'm delighted to have met one now."

His respectable comment cracked a piece of my exterior, making it harder to be near him.

"Thanks," I mumbled, walking past him until I'd made my way through the back doors.

The cold wind did nothing to stop the crawling sensation rippling through my spine, slow and steady before it paralyzed me in place as I choked on air.

Invisible hands grasped at me, threatening to tear me

apart as I was plunged back into that dark place of nothing.

The episode didn't last long, but it was enough to remind me that I was still stuck in the shackles of my mind.

I gasped, inhaling a lungful of air before heaving in a fit of coughs.

I didn't think I could do this. It was hard to even be near Nicolai, let alone speak to him.

I hadn't seen him grow up and now he was a well-mannered man among people who were his opposite. Yet I was a mere stranger to him.

Suddenly, all I could think of was protecting him from anything and anyone.

It was hypocritical of me, wanting to take him away, only so he could fall into the same position he was in now.

Breathing through my nose, I let the crisp winter air ground me. That's when the smell of musk and spice enveloped me, suffocating and lethal.

I slowly slid my hand down my thigh, parted the slit of my dress until I'd found my blade and clutched it.

I told Aurora I bite first, just not with my teeth.

In swift motion, I had the knife to the brute's neck, glaring at him.

Luca loomed over me, larger than I remembered. He stared down at my hand before he set those daunting caramel eyes on my face.

He took one step forward, and I dug the blade further, not enough to draw blood but enough to warn him off.

His pupils flared as he took another step, his chest nearly crushing into mine.

The pounding of my pulse rushed to my ears as my knife nicked him, blood trailing down the column of his tattooed throat.

He fucking cut himself.

I faltered from his unexpected action, but he didn't notice, proceeding to walk toward me with purpose until he had me cornered, my back hitting the side of the house.

Under the moonlight, he looked like a nightmare come to life. Rough features, untamed hair that curled at the base of his neck and eyes that could trap someone in their depths.

His gaze flicked to my mouth, his expression one of pure savagery.

The winter air suddenly felt nice against my overheated skin as a layer of thick tension crushed me.

His hand moved toward his neck, his tattooed fingers tracing the cut, and painting them with his blood.

The faint flicker of a high coursed through me, ceasing that hollowness inside my chest and diminishing the residue of my earlier episode.

Not again.

I held my breath when that same bloody hand clutched my chin.

"What are-"

He pierced me with a vicious stare as he leisurely swept his thumb across my mouth, cutting me off.

His skin against mine elicited a sharp sensation as if he'd stung me.

My blade was still against his throat, but he seemed to be unfazed by that and the blood soaking through his white tee shirt.

A guttural sound ripped from his throat as he traced my lips, smearing his blood against them. "Made just for me."

I had seen enough craziness in my time, but I had never encountered anyone like Luca. He was clearly a psychopath, driven by delusion.

I opened my mouth to tell him exactly that when he tsked, his thumb pressing harder against my lips. "Such a pretty mouth for a viperous tongue." His face hardened, heat radiating off him in waves. "I hope this interaction was far more memorable, *piccola ribelle*."

With that, he nudged under my chin and walked back into the house.

What just happened?

I swallowed, staring at the tip of my blade, stained with his blood.

Was this how we'd play the game? Him cornering me in dark places when no one was around.

No one had ever affected me the way Luca had. No one had ever been able to evoke a high with a mere touch and I didn't know if it was fear or anger that sat bitterly in the pit of my stomach.

Maybe I was as psychotic as him because I hesitantly slid my tongue across my bottom lip, tasting the tang of metallic.

The rest of the night had passed in a blur. We'd gathered in the living area after dinner, sipping from mugs of hot chocolate.

Aurora suddenly squealed, standing in the center of the room. “I can’t keep it in anymore. I’m pregnant!”

My heart soared at the unexpected news. I knew how much she’d wanted this, especially after what she’d been through with her last pregnancy.

Cheers and congratulations erupted as everyone engulfed her in hugs and I was in awe at the way Roman watched her fiercely as if he’d remove anything or anyone that could tarnish her happiness.

“This is the best news,” I said, my throat thick from excitement. “I’m going to be an aunt!”

Aurora wiped the fallen tears from her eyes. “I’ve been wanting to tell you for four months now, but I wasn’t sure. . .”

She hadn’t needed to finish her sentence because I knew what she meant.

I squeezed her hands reassuringly. “I understand. Now let me see the belly.” I chuckled.

I knew there had been something different about her, but I hadn’t expected this and as she stretched the gown across her stomach, I saw the bump. “The doctor said some women don’t show as evidently as others but it’s growing every day,” she soothed, rubbing her stomach.

“Well, I’m so happy for both you and Roman. Although, having another Roman running around in society would be a nightmare.”

She laughed. “Agreed.”

Her husband came to stand behind her. “Is that so?” He peered down at her, resting his hands on her hips.

She leaned against his chest, setting her hands atop his. “Tis so.”

CHAPTER 5
LUCA

"You ready for this?"

Sweat trickled down my forehead as I pounded against the leather bag. "I'm always ready," I answered to Alessio, my trainer.

After a few more rounds, I let my arms swing to my sides, breathing heavily to regain my composure.

I'd occasionally indulged in the fights that the Underground Club held—a facility exclusive to high-society families. The fights kept the elites satisfied with entertainment and the money it brought in made them wealthier.

For me, it was about the reputation and blowing off steam. I'd never lost and thus created a name for myself. Bets continued to be placed on my victory and I'd never disappointed.

When you instilled fear in others by showing the sheer power of what you were capable of, it was less appealing for them to cross you.

"I don't need a trainer."

My head snapped toward the voice, an itch creeping along my fingertips at the unexpected presence.

I clenched my fists as I found Irina in conversation with another trainer. She had the tightest pair of sportswear on, black leggings that framed her legs perfectly and a tank top that molded against her waist.

I bit the side of my lip, wanting to mark her with more than just my blood on her lips.

Even now I could picture that exact moment from Christmas night. Her blue eyes that shined with anger and red lips that curled with hatred.

She had no idea that her reactions invoked my need to feast on every inch of her. To sink so deep into everything that made her until she forgot where she began and ended.

I would take from my little rebel as long as she played this game. And she was.

I couldn't pinpoint the reasoning to my sudden fascination with the blonde-haired woman who walked into every room as if she owned it, but the visceral need was there. Tangible enough for me to taste it and feel it coursing through my veins.

And I knew it was there to stay.

But what was her reason? Didn't she know, her defiance was enough to get me on my knees and crawl to her? I had cut myself to prove that exact point, needing her to understand the depth of how far I'd go to have her.

A spark of sensation ghosted against the side of my neck from where her blade had nicked me. It hadn't been deep, but it left a light scar that I relished in. I *wanted* her to mark me.

Since that night, I had wondered why she'd been

carrying a weapon, and I intended to seek out that answer on my own.

Removing my gloves, I walked toward her slowly, noting the frustration crossing her face.

"You're not understanding me. I don't need a female trainer." She crossed her arms. "I don't need a trainer, period."

A rule the Club's boxing facility had was that every member needed to be under a trainers list for authentication reasons.

I stood behind Irina, smelling her addicting amber scent as I towered over her. "She's with me."

Dante peered over her head, a silent conversation passing between us. I knew this wasn't allowed, but I also knew he wouldn't stop me. After a hesitant pause, he nodded his head and walked away.

Irina's hair slapped my chest as she spun to face me, her blue eyes narrowing. "I'm not *with* you."

A grin carved its way across my mouth, and I couldn't tell if it was from seeing her again or her attitude.

"No?" I cocked my head to the side, feigning confusion. "We'll have to fix that."

"You're delusional," she hissed, her body shaking as she took a step toward me.

Was that supposed to be threatening?

She was one raging Russian and fuck, I wanted her fury.

I leaned down, watching the rise and fall of her chest before catching her eyes. "Call it what you want, *piccola ribelle,* but you'll be mine."

Her distaste was visible as she bared her teeth, that fire

blazing brighter in her pupils. "I will *never* be yours. Not in this lifetime or the next."

She turned to walk away, but I grasped her long ponytail, pulling her back toward me.

A gasp escaped her as her back collided into my chest.

She felt so fucking soft against me, I had to refrain myself from pushing further into her.

Didn't want to scare off my little rebel if I appeared too eager.

I wrapped her silky hair around my fist twice before pulling her head back.

Her full lips parted as she glanced up at me with trepidation. It had my pulse buzzing with renewed energy.

"You're here for a reason, Irina." I rasped. "Don't tell me you're too scared to see it through."

And the most beautiful thing happened. She smiled, her straight white teeth appearing slowly.

I was in a daze, mesmerized by her beauty and she used it to her advantage, her next move catching me off guard.

She dropped herself forward as her slender leg pushed back simultaneously and swung toward my face, the force of it knocking me to the ground.

Who the fuck was this woman?

She settled on top of me, her knees on either side of my waist while her elbow dug against my throat. She leaned down and whispered in a lethal tone. "Touch me without my permission again, and it'll be the last thing you do."

Heat pulsed in the space between us, the beat of her heart clashing against mine.

"Stay in this position." I enunciated by squeezing her hips. "And I might adhere to your request."

When her cheeks hadn't flushed with color the way I expected, I knew this woman was truly created for me. Walking on earth with the sole purpose to taunt and torment me.

"I'm not sleeping with you, Luca. Get that through your thick skull."

My name on her tongue was a caress, not gentle like a lover, no. Her voice drove deep into my bones until they splintered and cracked. Until she'd ruined me completely.

Ruin me, sweetheart.

She was stronger than I expected, and I needed that. An equal. But I think my little rebel truly thought she could pin me down.

My hands slid along her waist, her curves molding against my palms as I switched our position, so I was on top of her.

She grunted from the light force as I settled between her legs, pinning her wrists above her head.

"Who said anything about sleeping?"

This close, I could see the dusting of freckles decorating her nose and cheeks. They presented an image of innocence, but she was far from it.

I watched her take shallow breaths, her angelic features turning sharp as she struggled against my hold. The more she moved, the more her scent invaded my senses. It filled me with pure dopamine.

Did she know how breathtaking she was?

My expression must've conveyed something that had

her stilling and time ceased to exist for a moment as we locked eyes.

It ended too soon as she blinked a few times, her brows lowering before her head shot up, ramming into my nose, and causing me to loosen my hold.

She slid out from underneath me and all I could do was laugh as blood gushed from my nose.

No one had ever caught me off guard and I always had a strong intuition so the fact that Irina had done it twice in the span of minutes was beyond my understanding.

Maybe this was a sign to stay away from her but the mere thought of doing that sent a dull ache between my ribs.

"Stay away from me, you brute." She grabbed her bag and walked off in a huff to the building's exit.

I let my head fall back against the floor, smiling to myself as blood continued to trickle down my nose.

And I didn't know if it made me a masochist, but I'd let her do it again.

She was *definitely* made for me.

I'd almost forgotten that I needed to give a shit about being the leader of the Camorra until this morning.

I crushed the cigarette under my boot, waiting for the Bratva's exporter.

After my father sabotaged the previous shipment, Roman handed off the entire operation to me.

Doing business with the Russians was always risky, but it had more benefits than not. And it'd establish a good rapport with my crew, even though they were loyal to my father but that was okay, I didn't trust them either. I only needed to cement into their brains that I was the one who they answered to.

A black van pulled up to the side of the warehouse and parked before a lean man stepped out.

He was alone which was surprising. We'd discussed to keep this one on one, but I didn't think he'd comply.

"Viktor." I acknowledged him with a head nod.

He was a cold man; I could tell with the way he carried himself as if every movement and reaction was mechanical. His brown hair was a contrast against his pale skin which added to the sharpness of his demeanor.

I shoved my hand into my leather jacket, pulling out another stick of death. "How long do you plan on staying in Italy, Viktor?" I asked, sticking the cigarette in my mouth.

He widened his stance, clasping his hands behind his back. "Until I'm certain we can trust the production of our partnership."

Releasing a puff of smoke, I walked toward him. It was understandable that he'd want to make sure there were no glitches in our exchanges, but I hated having a stranger in my territory.

"You understand that I'll have eyes on you?"

He smiled or what appeared to be one. It was stiff and crooked. "I don't doubt it."

I'd dealt with Russians before and I knew that they were hardheaded with a penchant for blood but as I eyed Viktor, an unpleasant taste settled on my tongue from his demeanor.

Yeah, I was keeping an eye on this fucker, alright.

I spread my arms wide, gesturing around us as I let a grin creep on my face. "Welcome to Italy." I patted his shoulder on my way out. "Don't get comfortable," I added sternly.

When I reached my bike, I texted Ric to send me a file on Viktor Morozov.

CHAPTER 6
IRINA

Rain pattered softly against the window, easing me in a state of comfort.

"When are you going to open up the office in New York again?"

My eyes drifted away from the glass and toward Aurora. She was seated in her office chair, a stack of paperwork in front of her.

A smile touched my lips at the way her brows furrowed as she focused on her task.

I stood from the window seat and made my way toward her.

She turned her chair and my eyes fell to her baby bump, which was evident now that she stopped trying to hide it in loose clothes.

"When are *you* going to stop working?" I asked, spreading my palm over her stomach.

"Don't avoid the question," she scolded. "You love working."

After Aurora moved back to Italy, I was the one who decided to end our partnership firm back in New York.

I transferred our clients to a trusted firm for the time being, but many of them stuck with Aurora due to her previous successes.

She was right though. I did love working but with the passing of my mother and the discovery of my brother shortly after, that dreaded feeling inside my chest became overwhelming and I needed a pause.

Aurora gasped—nearly giving me a heart attack—as she put her hand over mine and laughed. "Do you feel it? The baby is kicking."

There was a slight movement beneath my fingertips, and it made my heart soar. I already loved the little one, and I hadn't even met them yet.

"I feel it," I croaked out. "Am I the first to feel it move?"

Aurora shook her head, her green eyes sparking with humor.

"Roman?" Of course, he felt it first. If he hadn't, I'm sure the bastard would've found a way to go back in time.

She winced, her nose scrunching slightly. "Nope. He may or may not have gone on a rampage."

"Then who?"

"Luca."

One name. Two syllables. That was all it took for my pulse to rise steadily.

My skin became hot, the faint sensation of lightheadedness nearing as I recalled the way our bodies had molded together only days ago.

The brute talked, touched and invaded my space as if he had the right to. As if he was so sure he'd have me.

I didn't care what sort of adrenaline spiked through my veins with his mere presence. The hollowness inside my chest could rot for all I cared.

Stay in this position and I might adhere to your request.

Shallow breaths escaped me, sensing the weight of him on me as if he were still there.

No. No. No.

I dug my nails into my palms, ridding myself of those thoughts.

If I had known he was there, I would've never gone. The only reason I went was to keep up with my physical activities and Roman had given me a pass to the Underground Club.

"Are you okay?" Aurora shook me, her face coming into focus, green eyes assessing me in confusion.

I unclenched my fists, feeling the sting of where my nails dug into the skin.

"Yeah, sorry." My voice sounded hoarse, and I cleared my throat before pinching out a smile. "Just nervous about asking you something."

It wasn't the whole truth, but it was a save on my part. I couldn't tell Aurora that Luca indeed had tried pursuing me more than once and now I was. . . what exactly was I doing? Fantasizing about him? The brute wished I would.

"About?"

I leaned against the desk, crossing my arms. "Would it be okay if I stayed until the birth of the little one?"

She stared at me for a moment, her teeth worrying her bottom lip. "Has something happened?"

"What?" My throat constricted. "Nothing has happened, Aurora. I just wanted to be here for the birth." *And have enough time to bring Nicolai home.*

"You know you can tell me whatever is troubling you." It was the finality of which she said that. Not a question or reassurance, but a statement.

"What is troubling you, Irina?"

Our heads turned in unison toward the voice. Roman stood by the door, leaning against the frame as he regarded us with a blank expression.

"You can never stay away from your wife, can you?" I swear the man was never far in distance and had to see her every hour.

A sly smirk touched his lips as he walked toward her. "How do you think she got pregnant?"

"Roman!" Aurora scolded, her face heating from his boldness. "That mouth of yours needs disinfectant."

And if there was anyone who could get Roman to laugh, it was his wife. The sound was raw and hearty.

"Is this where I apologize?"

"Not to me." She stood from her chair, her mouth twitching in feigned seriousness. "To Irina, for being crude. Do it while I use the bathroom. This baby pushes against my bladder like it's their job."

"As you wish, *anima mia.*" He kissed her head before she walked out of the room.

Roman rounded the desk and sat in Aurora's chair, his elbows resting on the arms of it.

"I'm waiting for my apology." I joked, quirking an eyebrow at him.

"You wish."

I shrugged. "Worth a try."

"Is it a what or a who?"

"Excuse me?"

"The thing that's troubling you. Is it a what or a who?" he repeated.

His question caught me off guard. He had no reason to be concerned with my personal life and I hated that he was showing me a side of himself that I knew many people didn't see. It only made the reason for my stay harder.

I shook my head, a smile lilting my face even though dread warred in my chest. "Aurora misunderstood. There's nothing wrong with me."

"That's not what I asked, Irina."

The silence was near suffocating as I stared at him, feeling the blood drain from my face. "It's the same answer, Roman. I'm fine."

"If you're not, you can tell me." He leaned forward, his face hardening. "You're Aurora's family, which means you're my family too."

This was the moment our dynamic changed. He had become more than my best friend's husband. More than a *Don.* He'd become a. . . friend.

The click of the door sounded before Aurora walked back in. "I brought refreshments!"

There was beauty in the darkness.

As I sat in the gazebo, gazing up at the starry night, I savored the stillness that came with it.

My mind had always been a racing, raging mess, constantly overthinking and sent me reeling.

It never made sense to me, but sometimes I needed my old friend—that stillness, that soundless nothing to focus on my thoughts.

If I was alone, then no one could see the turmoil unfolding.

"The winters here are probably nothing compared to the winters in Russia."

Nicolai walked toward me, holding two mugs.

I cocked my head to the side at his sudden presence.

"You looked lonely." He handed me the mug and sat down on the chair next to me, the warmth of his gray coat radiating toward me. "Thought you might want some company."

"That sounds. . . sad." I huffed out a light chuckle.

My brother smiled at me, the dimple on his cheek appearing. "That's because it is."

My own smile crept across my face. He was quick-witted and knew how to lighten a conversation without being callous.

"Are you lonely too?"

He pushed his glasses up with the tip of his middle finger and peered up at the dark sky.

I basked in the silence as I waited for his answer. He had interrupted my quiet, but it didn't feel unwelcome as I expected. It felt almost normal, as if my body knew he was a part of me.

"I think loneliness is subjective." He took a sip of his drink. "To answer your question, no, I'm not lonely anymore."

My heart squeezed, pulling at the strings that were barely hanging together from this interaction.

"Anymore?" I whispered.

He pursed his lips before staring at me, his blond hair pale stark in the night.

I knew I was prying. I knew I probably came off as strange. I knew I shouldn't be emotionally invested when he had no idea who I was, but I couldn't help it.

I might've not known of his past, but I saw pain swimming in his brown eyes, dimming the spark they held moments ago.

Goosebumps arose on my skin. It almost felt like I was staring at my reflection.

"I'm being invasive." I shook my head. "You don't need to answer."

His eyes roamed over my face, a frown appearing on his sharp features. "Roman saved me when I was on the edge of losing myself." He broke eye contact, his elbows resting on his knees as he stared ahead. "He took me in and gave my life purpose." Then, in a tone barely above a whisper, he said, "He was the father I'd always wanted."

A bitter taste settled on my tongue as I digested his words.

Nicolai had gone through something terrible, *so* terrible that he'd almost lost himself in the process.

That hollowness inside my chest ached, eating all the emotions racing through me when all I wanted to do was scream.

It was clear that my brother was content with Roman and his crew, but I was selfish. It was wrong of me to try to take that away from him. I knew that. Yet, I was still here.

“Thank you for sharing that with me.” It was all I could say. Anything else would’ve sent me spiraling.

Nico shook his head as he chuckled. “I’m usually not an expressive person.” He caught my eyes, understanding passing through his own. “I guess misery loves company.”

My heart thudded, cold sweat breaking down my spine. “Did Roman teach you that?”

“Teach me what?”

“How to read people?”

The corner of his lips twitched. “Why? Was I correct?”

“No.” I stood from my seat, handing him my mug. “I’m not miserable.”

He nodded. “Goodnight, Irina.”

“Goodnight, Nicolai.”

CHAPTER 7
IRINA

My father always told me I was an organ donor.

He'd said riding motor bikes would inevitably lead to my death. He wasn't wrong. My fondness for bikes had a lot to do with the rush it brought me—that fine line between life and death.

But I was an adrenaline junkie, not suicidal.

The narrow streets of Italy were perfect to pass through. I'd borrowed one of Roman's bikes this morning and left the manor.

I'd lied to Aurora about wanting to explore on my own when I was actually meeting my cousin.

Viktor's surprise visit irritated me. I knew it was my father who asked him to come and watch over me, but I didn't care. I didn't need his protection, and I didn't want him here. He could blow my cover unintentionally.

I slowly rode down the back alley to where he told me to meet him. It was sketchy, but I knew he was staying on the down low.

A whistle came from behind me. I shifted the bike and braked, turning my head.

Viktor was leaning against the brick building, staring at me blankly.

I narrowed my eyes at him before getting off the bike and walking toward him. "Go home, Viktor."

"No can do." His callous demeanor had always ground on my nerves as if he was to be held in high regards by every living creature.

"You can and you will. I don't need a babysitter."

He stepped forward, glaring down at me. "I don't care, *Irina*. You focus on your mission, and I'll focus on making sure you don't waste my time."

"Your time?" I scoffed. "I don't even *want* you here."

"But your father does," he drawled humorously. "Already met one of them today."

Viktor was fifteen years older than me and had always made it his duty to rank up in the Bratva. When his father —who was my uncle and the previous *Pakhan*—died, Viktor assumed his position when he came of age. But instead his father gave that title to his brother—my father.

"One of them?"

"The Italians you've surrounded yourself with."

My heart thumped against my ribcage. "What did you do?"

"Luca, I think it was." He gazed to the side in thought, then shrugged. "Have you met him yet?"

Yes. "No."

"Hm." He stared at me, searching for something, but I had no idea what. "Anyway, I wanted to see with my own eyes who we're dealing with—what they're capable of."

"*We* are not dealing with anyone." *Shit.* He'd met Luca. This was bad, really bad. "Do whatever you want. Just stay out of my way."

Annoyance toward my father bloomed. I would've appreciated it if he had told me about this.

He clenched his jaw, his eyes homing in on me harshly. "Get it done, Irina," he gritted out.

"I'll tell Nicolai when he's ready." I crossed my arms, giving him the same pompous attitude he was giving me. "No sooner, no later."

"He's not a child!"

I stepped forward. "No, but he is my *brother*." And because he irked the shit out of me, I added, "Your future *Pakhan*."

I knew it grated on his nerves that he wouldn't be the leader of the Bratva and frankly, I couldn't care less what he wanted.

"Watch your fucking mouth."

My hands itched to wrap them around his slender neck and choke the life out of him, but I refrained. If he wasn't my cousin or an important part of the Bratva, I would've already wiped him off the face of the earth.

It was useless arguing with him. He was a narcissistic asshole who took his negative energy and suffocated others with it.

I walked backward toward my bike and lifted both my middle fingers at him. I didn't care how childish it was. I'd wasted my breath on him enough.

Nothing I could say would make him leave.

The last thing I wanted to do on a Saturday night was watch some gangsters shed blood as they fought each other like they were wild animals.

Yet, Aurora had dragged me, claiming that it was a tad bit amusing despite the deadly environment. Plus, Roman had to make an appearance to hold up his reputation.

Apparently, the fights were designated for exclusive members of the Club who dripped wealth and power.

I pulled on Aurora's shirt, grabbing her attention. "You really got over your fear of blood, huh?"

She smiled at me sheepishly and pointed a thumb in her husband's direction. He noticed—as he did with everything regarding my best friend—and kissed the side of her head.

I shook my head in amusement. *Shocker.*

The crowd's cheers became louder as Roman and Ricardo led us down to the basement.

My heart had begun to pick up speed at the rowdiness. The noise, the hectic surrounding, and the high of knowing danger was on the horizon were all too familiar.

The space was large, dark enough to conceal the sins of onlookers. The walls were brick stones, the ceiling high with lights faintly shining down on us.

We walked toward the stage until we reached the front, the crowd booming with excitement.

The ring was centered, closed off by thick ropes—although if someone wanted to, they could easily slide in and out.

And on stage I could see the back of a shirtless man, his skin stretching against pure muscle as he took his stance and moved to circle his opponent.

Time slowed, the blaring crowd becoming white noise as his opponent appeared in my line of sight. *Luca.*

My mouth parted as I took a step forward, the rage on his face unlike anything I'd ever seen before.

This wasn't the mischievous brute I'd come to know. In the ring, he was a different person. His mouth was a vicious slash, his eyes deadly as he stared at the man opposite him with pure savagery.

It was his whole physique that screamed beastly. With only shorts on, he appeared bigger and taller than when he had clothes on. Muscles rippled along his tatted body; every inch of his skin marked with intricate designs. Not only tattoos but *scars,* marred along his back and torso.

I knew I should've been frightened to know I'd caught his attention, but all I could think of was how the chaos inside my mind stopped for a brief second as I took in his raw form.

He had depth, but why did that make me curious to know what lurked underneath?

Luca's eyes flicked toward me and for a moment, he let me see what hid behind those caramel eyes. Then he smiled and swung his arm before it crashed into his opponent's face.

"Hey!" Aurora called out, pulling on my arm and bringing me back toward her. "It can get crazy in here. Don't go closer."

Too late. For the first time ever, a man piqued my interest—but I'd never tell her or *him* that.

He was out for blood, moving fluidly, *predatorily*. If I hadn't been paying close attention, I'd think he was dragging on the fight for longer than necessary.

He was putting on a show. One that had the audience cheering for him, women throwing their lingerie at him and men betting on him.

It was clearly not his first time in the ring, aiming hits back-to-back, enough to make the other man lose balance, but not enough to have him tap out.

"What's a doll like you doing in a place like this all alone?"

If it wasn't for the body pressed against my back disgustingly, I wouldn't have thought the stranger was talking to me.

I stepped away and casually looked around me. *What the hell?*

Aurora and Roman were nowhere to be seen and if it was crowded before, the audience had doubled in size now.

"How about some company then?"

I turned and narrowed my eyes at the well-dressed man. He smirked, licking his lips as if I was a prize he couldn't wait to take home.

I'd interacted with men like him before and I hated that previously, I'd needed to seduce them to retract information for the Bratva.

Not this time, though. I wasn't on a mission.

I smiled at him, my blood boiling over men who thought a pretty face meant docile and compliant. "If I wanted company, I wouldn't be here alone. If your miniature sized brain doesn't understand what that means, let me simplify it further. Go fuck yourself, preferably somewhere far away from me."

I faced the stage again, my breath catching in my throat. Luca had the man pinned to the floor as he mercilessly rammed his fists into his face, causing blood to splatter across his own. That wasn't what had cold sweat streaming down my spine—it was that the brute had his gaze set on me as he nearly plummeted the man to death. Or maybe he was already dead.

"I can't wait to break you into submission, doll." Hot breath fanned my face, the stench of alcohol strong.

"Back off before you regret it."

"Feisty," he drawled, his hand snaking around my waist. "I like that."

I nodded to myself. Looks like he'd regret it.

Grabbing his hand, I pushed back his fingers till I felt them crunch beneath mine.

"Ah!" He groaned, clutching his injury.

He took a step toward me, and I braced myself for his attack, but then he stopped. His eyes bulged as he gazed past me, terror evident on his face.

The audience's screams became deafening as I turned around and saw Luca walking toward. . . me?

Shock pulsed in my veins at the sight, my heart fluttering against my chest almost painfully, unaware of what was about to happen.

He looked barbaric, blood and sweat dripping down his face and torso. This was worse than when he was in the ring, the craze in his eyes adding to how untamed he appeared.

Adrenaline seeped into my bloodstream, injecting me with the high I craved.

Luca reached me in a few strides, but it seemed I wasn't his target. He grabbed the well-dressed man by the collar and shoved him to the floor as if he weighed nothing.

All I could do was stare as his fists drove into the man's face repeatedly, his face becoming distorted and unrecognizable.

I knew I should've tried stopping it, but I couldn't move. The hollowness inside my chest was numb, desensitizing me to the brutal scene in front of me.

Shouting and cheering echoed through the basement, the onlookers fueling Luca's unhinged behavior with their commentary.

Suddenly, my body jolted, pulling me away from my fixation. Roman came into view, assessing me as if he were checking for any injuries before he went to Luca, trying to tug him off the unconscious man.

"Irina," Aurora said from beside me. "Are you okay?"

Luca hadn't budged. And it was near alarming when Ricardo stepped in to help Roman.

What kind of strength did this Italian brute possess?

"I'm fine," I replied hoarsely. "Why isn't security stepping in?"

"That's not how it works here. Come on." She clutched my arm and pulled me behind her, away from the mayhem.

The aftermath of the rush still lingered beneath my skin, reminding me of earlier tonight.

Tossing and turning, I huffed in frustration. I didn't know how long I laid awake before the smell of musk hit me and I realized I wasn't alone.

Musk.

Before I could grab the knife hidden beneath my pillow, a hard body covered mine, thick thighs straddling me.

My heart sank down to my stomach when Luca's eyes caught mine. The streak of moonlight coming from the window lit the harsh planes of his face, shadowing the intensity of his gaze.

His palm landed on my stomach, the warmth of his skin seeping into me.

I should've been scared, knowing what he was capable of. Yet the only thing I feared was his touch. I loathed it and it had everything to do with the sensations it invoked in me.

That rush came back full force and my body buzzed to life, hungry for more of it, *needing* it.

But why did it have to be him to eradicate that hollowness inside my chest? I didn't even know the man, let alone want him. . .

"Luca," I whispered in warning, but my voice came out all wrong.

A deep sound came from the back of his throat as he slid his hand farther up my torso before he paused between my breasts.

I could feel the beat of my heart against his palm. *Thump. Thump. Thump.*

There were so many questions racing through my head. *How did he get in here? What did he want? What was he doing to me?*

He put a stop to them as he leaned down, his hand drifting further up until he'd wrapped it around my throat.

I melted into the mattress, trapped beneath him as I searched his eyes. They were manic and possessive. . .

Our noses were nearly touching, our breaths dancing in the space between us.

"Mine," he rasped, and his lips came down on mine, stealing my breath away.

Kissing Luca was explosive, a drug I never knew I needed. Injected into my veins so deeply I didn't think I'd ever come down from the high.

He squeezed my throat, opening my mouth for him so he could slide his tongue inside. Goosebumps sparked on my skin, my head swimming from every lash.

This was wrong. I shouldn't want this man. Not only was he a member of the Italian Mafia, but he was Roman's best friend. And I doubt he'd take it lightly if he knew what was happening under his roof.

Besides, men were tedious creatures, and I had no intention of getting involved with Luca, aside from the sensations his mouth was evoking in me.

I grabbed onto his shoulders and urged him to move on his back.

Without breaking contact, I straddled his waist and dug my fingers into his tee shirt, deepening the kiss.

He was utterly insane. Sneaking into my room in the middle of the night to claim me as his own. It enraged me beyond belief, but I couldn't ignore the way my insides fluttered from needing more of this insanity. *His* insanity.

There was something deeply wrong with me.

His hands settled on my waist, pushing me further down onto him, the sensation sending a shiver up my spine.

The kiss was harsh, as if we were starved for one another. He tasted of sin and smoke, the concoction of a psychopath.

I took it.

I wanted it.

I needed it.

My soul was being fed. That black hole inside my chest ceased to exist in a way it hadn't before.

If this was a onetime occurrence—and it was—I wanted my fill.

It wasn't only me who was selfish. Luca nipped, sucked and stroked my lips like he couldn't get enough of me. I felt his need to mark me in any way deep into my bones.

But I wouldn't allow it. I belonged to no one.

Catching his bottom lip between my teeth, I pulled on it slowly before releasing, "Get out of my room, Luca." I shifted to move away from him, but before I could, he squeezed my waist and flipped me onto my back.

His pupils were dilated, his lips parted and bruised, the look of pure madness.

I held my breath as he slid a finger down my cheek until he reached below my chin and nudged it.

That gesture meant something. It wasn't the first time he'd done it, and I had a suspicion it wouldn't be the last. It was almost as if he was telling me that he'd leave, but only for now.

Luca pushed himself off the bed and stood to his full height. He stared at me with his head tilted, eyeing the length of me before walking toward the door.

Then he stopped, his hand on the knob and his back to me when he spoke. "Any man who touches you will meet the same fate as the one who did it tonight." His head turned to the side slightly. "Death."

CHAPTER 8
IRINA

"You know we don't leave for another hour, right?" Nicolai joined me in the foyer, wearing a pressed gray suit.

"I don't like being late. What's your excuse?"

He pushed his glasses up with the tip of his middle finger and grinned. "I'm not fond of being late either."

I pressed my lips together in amusement. My brother and I were alike, and it pained me that he didn't know.

"Do you always dress so. . . pristine?" I gestured at him with the wave of my hand.

Every time I'd seen him, he was in formal wear, even if it was in casual settings.

He stared at me, but his eyes appeared drawn as if he weren't focusing.

"Nicolai. . . "

"Hm?" It was a reactive response, and I realized he wasn't with me. His mind had drifted to something that left him jarred.

I hesitantly put my hand on his shoulder. "Nicolai," I whispered.

Moving out of his line of sight, he continued to stare straight ahead, void of his surroundings.

His eyes had gone completely blank, a black abyss into nothingness.

My heart battered against my chest, unsure of how to approach him when I was a mere stranger.

But I couldn't leave him in this state.

"Nico. . . " I soothed, bringing my fingers to his cheek, hoping to drag him back from wherever he wandered off to. "It's alright."

His face was cold, and I hoped the warmth of my fingers broke through the wall that he'd put up.

After a long moment, he blinked, and I continued my movements until he did it again, the brown in his eyes appearing brighter.

"Nicolai?"

He finally came to, pushing away from my touch as if it seared him. "Don't *touch* me," he snapped.

I dropped the hand I'd caressed him with, unsure of how to respond to his sudden reaction.

He swallowed almost in difficulty before shaking his head. "I'm sorry. I don't know what that was."

A lie.

"Was it something I said?"

His eyes darted between mine and whatever he saw in my expression had him nodding subtly and, in this moment, he looked so defeated, my heart squeezed in anguish.

I wanted to know what haunted him. I wanted him to

know I was his sister, and I would slaughter his demons if he so much as asked me to.

"We don't have to talk about it." I smiled at him reassuringly before stepping away.

He opened his mouth and then shut it, raking a hand through his hair.

I waited until he spoke. "I haven't had an episode like that in a very long time. I. . . I," he paused, taking me aback. It was the first time he'd been lost for words.

"We don't. . . " I shook my head to indicate that he didn't need to justify his actions.

"I dress this way because there was a time when I didn't have clothes on my back." He sighed, his face a mixture of sadness and anger. "I promised myself I'd never be like that again."

The pounding of my heart reached my ears, quieting everything aside from my chaotic thoughts. This was worse than I could ever imagine. Had Nicolai been poor? Was it because of our father? What happened to his mother?

"Is that when Roman saved you?"

"Yes. I owe him my life."

"No, you don't." Roman's voice came from our far right and we both turned to see him walking toward us. "Nico, it's not polite to burden guests with your personal life." His words were directed at my brother, but his eyes were set on me.

It was evident on his hardened face that he was sensitive—as one could be when it came to a man like him—about Nicolai.

"He's not burdening me." Frankly, Roman didn't scare me, but I understood his protectiveness.

"Nico, go tell Ric to pull the car around."

He stood there, staring between Roman and me before shaking his head and leaving through the main door.

"Do you boss him around like that all the time?"

"I didn't know how I treated my crew was any of your business."

"He's not just your crew, Roman, and you know it." I stared at him as intensely as he was. "You have a soft spot for Nicolai."

His jaw clenched. "*Everyone* has a soft spot for Nico."

"Maybe, but it's different with you." I was pushing it, but maybe he'd give me a further glimpse of who my brother was. "What did he need saving from?"

Roman contemplated his answer, the furrow between his brows deepening. "He lost his mother at a young age and that might've been the worst thing that happened to him."

"Why?"

"Because everything that came afterward destroyed him."

"And his father?" I whispered.

"Dead."

My chest caved, that black hole widening and swallowing down the emotions I wanted to express openly.

It suddenly became hard to breathe, the thick strain in my throat ceasing me from speaking.

Should I tell Roman about his episode? Nicolai said he hadn't had one in a while, but it almost seemed intrusive to share that information.

"Is this you warning me away from him?"

"No," he said without hesitation. "You were right about it being different for me. He's my youngest and I'm wary of others when it comes to him."

"I. . . I don't understand."

"Irina, he has never shared anything personal with a stranger as fast as he has with you."

Stranger. How could I forget? I was a stranger to Nicolai in every sense of that word. It didn't matter if we were blood related. I didn't know him, and he didn't know me.

"You'll be gone in a few months, and I don't need him getting attached to you." He regarded me sternly, his eyes darkening into an opaque obsidian. "Nico isn't like the others."

I'd figured that out already. My brother was different from the people in his life. A fierce layer of protectiveness settled over me to take him away from it all.

And Roman was wrong. I would be in Nicolai's life, sooner rather than later. They just didn't know it yet.

When I was told we'd be going out for dinner, I hadn't expected it to be at Luca's house.

I gritted my teeth as Roman entered something in the keypad before he opened the door.

And yes, I did file the pin in my mind.

Luca lived on a huge piece of land, far away from the city and its civilians. It was a large cabin, luxurious but rugged.

It didn't surprise me. He probably murdered and hid his victims here. Psychotic brute.

Had he really killed that man like he said he did for touching me at the fight?

The interior of the cabin was rich in woodland colors, emitting a cozy ambiance. It was spacious but not overly so.

As we filtered through the corridor, the smell of spices wafted in the air and my mouth instantly salivated. I'd never been a good cook, and I rarely ever did it myself back home.

There was a main living area and a sunroom on the opposite side. It was all earthy tones and warm but the feature that had my mouth parting in awe was the transparent glass ceiling.

The night sky shone above, and with the dim lights inside, I could appreciate the starry view.

After admiring it all for far too long, I realized everyone had moved along, leaving me alone.

Why did it feel intimate all of a sudden?

I entered through another doorway, this one leading to the kitchen. The dining room was off to the far side of the room, a wall nearly hiding it from view, but I could see a glimpse of the crew seated.

My heart nearly fell at my feet when a large hand grabbed my jaw and planted their soft lips against mine.

And I knew who it was from just one taste.

I pressed my palms to Luca's hard chest and shoved him until he pulled back, the warmth of his body still radiating toward me.

I frantically looked around the room in case anyone

saw before he grasped my jaw again, turning it and claiming my lips once more.

He didn't waste time, plunging his tongue inside of my mouth, devouring me as if he were starving the past few days.

For a moment, I savored it, that adrenaline racing through my bloodstream for the mere thought of being caught in this psychopath's embrace.

It wasn't only that, his whole presence induced a crazed energy I wanted to inject into my veins.

His grip on my jaw was near painful but it only made me swirl my tongue against his in harsh strokes. Sin and smoke. It shouldn't have felt this good.

What was I doing? Letting a man strip me of my control and giving him the power to make me feel this way.

I shoved against Luca harder this time until he completely let go of me.

My breathing was harsh, rage bubbling inside me. "What was that for?" I seethed, deliberately wiping my mouth with the back of my hand.

His eyes narrowed at that before he caught my own. "I missed you."

Was this brute mental?

"You can't miss someone you don't know."

The side of his mouth tipped up. "But I do." His tone roughened. "I know the taste of your lips; the curve of your waist and it won't be long before I know the recesses of your mind."

"You're a *psychopath.*"

"One you like kissing."

Luca walked away, leaving me fuming and irritated. I'd rather roll over and die than admit he was right.

This was the last time I'd go anywhere without knowing the full details.

Dinner went by slow. Nicolai, Roman, Aurora, and Enzo were here but no sign of Sofia as I expected.

I sat beside Nicolai, observing the small talk happening around the table. The air was thick with tension as Luca sat to my left, the weight of his gaze heavy and lingering.

Today had been a tsunami of emotions that I needed to release before I went spiraling.

First it was a glimpse into my brother's past that had unfolded a new set of questions. It was far deeper than our father having left his mother, I knew it was.

Then it was the unexpected occurrences with Luca and hating it. He tipped me off balance and calmed that raging beast inside my chest without even trying.

My breathing shallowed, and I suddenly felt those same invisible hands around my neck.

Not here, not right now.

The clanking of forks against plates became too loud, the voices louder and the thrumming of my pulse the loudest.

A heavy hand settled on my upper thigh. Nerves pricked at my skin when I looked down to find tatted fingers.

It was all too much. I couldn't *breathe.*

A sharp pain radiated from my palm up my arm. I bit my bottom lip as I let go of the sharp end of my knife.

Drops of blood painted my plate and the whole room went silent, watching me.

Aurora stood from her seat; face scrunched in worry. "Irina. . . "

"I'm okay." I pushed my chair and stood. "It was an accident."

I had no idea where the bathroom was as I wandered down the hall, opening doors until I'd reached it at the end.

When I shut it behind me, I finally let out a choked gasp. The throbbing of my hand continued as blood profusely welled up in my palm.

I didn't know how deep I'd cut myself but it hurt like hell.

The worst was yet to come, but I needed to get it over with. I turned on the tap with my free hand before putting my injured one underneath the water.

It's not that I wasn't acclimated to pain, but it didn't lessen the aching, almost numbing sting of it.

I'd cleaned my own wounds before and once I assessed the cut, I could figure out if I needed stitches,

I peered around the bathroom, the furnishing a mix of dark hues of black.

There was a sleek cabinet by the sink mirror, and I was sure that a first aid kit would be in there.

I reached over and opened it. With the water still running over my hand, the angle of my body made it difficult to see the top shelf. And before I could grab anything, a shadow loomed over me and grabbed the kit from the shelf.

I moved away, glaring at the intruder.

"Ever heard of knocking?" I went to snatch the first aid from him when he lifted his arm, putting it out of reach.

His eyes turned to pools of dark caramel; his face unreadable. "Let me see your hand."

The bathroom wasn't small by any means, but it felt crowded with the intoxicating scent of musk and smoke.

I faced the sink. "I can do it myself."

"Congratulations," he said humorlessly. I looked in the mirror to find him standing behind me, invading my space more than he already had. "Now, show me your hand, Irina."

He was deadly serious. There wasn't an ounce of playfulness present as he stared at my reflection, the muscle in his jaw working.

I didn't move, the sound of running water echoing in the charged space. "No."

One second, I was on my feet and the next, my ass was on the countertop, Luca spreading my legs to wedge himself between them.

He grabbed my wrist and brought it between us. I tried pulling away, but he tugged harder, piercing me with those daunting eyes.

I scowled at him before averting my attention. The sooner this was over with, the sooner I could leave.

As he set up the first aid kid, I watched him from the corner of my eye, and it was the underlying anger marring his face that had me frozen in place.

Was he mad?

Luca moved swiftly, cleaning and bandaging the cut but I was hardly paying attention to his movements. My eyes were glued to his face as he concentrated on my hand.

Yes, he was a parasite who'd latched himself onto me, but he had also come after me and demanded to see where I hurt.

Pressure in my throat simmered, and I blinked away the stupid emotion that wanted to be let out.

It wasn't about the cut; it was everything it symbolized.

I never knew how badly I'd been deprived of genuine touch; how much I yearned for someone to *see* me and carry the weight off my shoulders until this brute walked in here.

I was exhausted, pieces of my soul chipping away since I was a young girl.

Maybe the blame was my father's or my mother's, but I wasn't any better than them. There was blood on my hands and grime on my body that was embedded into my skin.

Luca looked up, and I didn't even care that he'd caught me gaping at him. His features slowly softened as his eyes trailed my face.

Something sparked in the air, an invisible tie pulling us closer.

He was also scarred. *Beautifully scarred.* And although his were evident on the surface of his body, he still saw mine. An understanding passed between us that only we knew.

"Do you want to talk about it?"

"Oh, cause we're friends now, are we?"

He rubbed over my bandaged palm with his thumb. "I don't want to be your friend, Irina."

"What do you want then?" I asked, not sure if I wanted to hear the answer.

We stared at each other, neither one of us willing to bend first. His caramel eyes flashed intensely as he pressed his body between my legs, the warmth emanating from him seeping into me.

His thumb caressed my hand. "To know what happened tonight."

"I told you already." My free hand clutched the side of the countertop. "It was an accident."

"Bullshit."

"Excuse me?"

The back and forth swipe of his thumb stopped before he stepped further into me, his hand reaching up to grip my jaw. "I watch you, Irina. So, the next time you get lost in that head of yours, just know that I'm there with you."

My pulse raced as he seared me with his gaze. He had no idea what he was talking about. Aside from tonight... my stomach dropped. Oh no. The Christmas party. Had he witnessed my episode that night before cornering me?

"I'll tell Roman you're in here."

I held my breath in anticipation when he leaned forward.

Kiss me, you brute. Kiss me until I can't feel the hollowness inside my chest.

His eyes flitted to my mouth, my own nearly fluttering shut from the intensity of his touch and attention.

"I dare you," he whispered against my mouth.

CHAPTER 9
LUCA

"Has Viktor left?"

"Nope." I flicked the lighter on. "He's specifically interested in how we maneuver our drug shipments."

The inside of Enzo's office was sleek, hard glass and colorless—fucking depressing.

Roman hummed, appearing calm and collected but his eyes had darkened into a bottomless pit of nothing. "You show him the art museum yet?"

"Fuck. No." I was the owner of the building and a popular attraction site for our citizens. But they had no idea it was run to transport cocaine using the art pieces they admiringly gawked at. "Ric pulled his file for me and there was nothing suspicious." It wasn't surprising. The same way we erased material that traced back to our names, the Russians did too. "But I could kill him if you want?" I suggested because it seemed that he wasn't fond of our new guest.

"No. I'm fully capable of doing that myself, if necessary."

"Bummer," I feigned disappointment. "I'm always more creative."

"That's because you're a sadist who gets off on inflicting pain," Enzo remarked sarcastically.

"If you're boring just say that, Enzo."

He muttered something under his breath in annoyance before the screen on my phone lit up, displaying the picture of a smiling Eva.

I stood from my seat and answered. "What's wrong?"

"Luca." Her soft voice came down the line in a whisper. "Can you come get me, please?"

Pinpricks of ice slithered in my veins at her tone. "Are you okay?"

"Y-yes."

"I'm on my way."

That's all I had to know. When my sister needed me, I'd always go running to her.

I hung up and gave Roman a look, knowing he'd understand my silent words.

The way to my father's house wasn't long and I might've driven like a maniac but at least I didn't kill anyone in the process.

Once I stepped foot inside the house, Eva came running toward me, her small frame crashing into mine.

"Hey," I soothed. "Hey, you're okay now, Evangeline."

"Please, don't leave me. *Please*."

My heart thudded against my tightening chest.

Did my father want to die? It was blatantly obvious that he was the reason for her distress.

And even though my sister had begged me to not leave her before, I knew this time was different.

She shook against my hold, clutching me as if she'd die if she let go.

"What happened?" I was trying to stay calm for both our sakes, but I could sense that rage bubbling inside of me, wanting to be released.

Eva sniffled; her voice muffled against my chest. "He made me. . . present myself."

"What does that mean, Eva?" My jaw ached from grinding my teeth.

She sobbed harder, stumbling through her words as she hiccuped. "Those men saw me naked."

Guilt punched me right in the chest at how naïve I'd been.

Had my sister been lying to me all this time about how she was treated in this house?

I gently pulled her back, and she looked up at me with streaks of mascara running down her face.

Now that I could take in her appearance, I could see what she was wearing—a scrap of fabric that could hardly be called clothes.

The pulse in my neck throbbed as I shrugged my leather jacket off and put it around her. "Stay right here."

Her face paled, her eyes widening with uncertainty. "Luca, don't do it. Please, let's just leave."

I cupped her face and leaned down, so I was eye level with her. "I won't do anything. Stay here, okay?"

Doubt flickered across her features, but she nodded her head and wrapped my jacket tighter around herself.

It didn't take long for me to barge into my father's

office, grab the baseball bat he always left lying around like a fucking idiot and swung it across his face.

The sound of bones crunching fueled yet eased that rage inside me.

"I thought I told you to leave my sister alone, old man." *Another swing.* "Did I not accept your offer?" *Another swing.* This time with more force causing him to lose consciousness but I didn't care, unaware of where I was even aiming. Blood splattered across his desk and floor as I took another swing.

When his eyes fluttered, I made sure he heard my next words. "I should kill you for all you've done," I seethed. "But that'd be too easy."

He was barely breathing, his face swelling and body limp.

I stood and threw the bat on the floor, the sound of metal echoing in the room.

"You wanted a monster?" I asked, chest heaving. "Here I fucking am."

My mind hadn't calmed down since earlier and I knew it was seeking a release that only pain could ease.

I'd exerted myself, punching the black bag in front of me over and over again until my muscles screamed at me.

The Underground Club was empty, but it usually was around four in the morning. I enjoyed the quiet—only for a short while—until my thoughts plagued me.

Grabbing a towel from the rack, I wrapped it around my neck and wiped the sweat off my face.

I needed to head home soon before Eva woke up. I didn't want her to stress about my whereabouts because I knew she didn't enjoy my methods of calming down.

At least this time, I didn't kill anyone.

Stripping my sweatpants off, I wrapped another towel around my waist and made my way down to the sauna.

It was dark in the large room, the hot air inviting, and easing the ache in my muscles.

I exhaled a breath of relief as the tension dissipated slowly.

My life wasn't a walk in the park by any means but lately it seemed that it was getting harder to quiet my mind.

Eva.

My father.

Being the leader of the Camorra

Irina.

A smile touched my lips. *Irina.* My little rebel.

This insensible fascination I held for her kept spreading throughout my bloodstream every day until I couldn't think of anything or anyone but her.

And when she cut herself that night at my house, I'd never wanted anything more.

Her blue eyes might be frosted over by a falseness that not even she understood but I could see past that. I saw raw pain in them.

I wanted to know why she did it. What thoughts roamed in her head when she drew distant in a moment like that.

Did she see the world like I did? How cruel and unfair it could be.

A flicker of movement to my left caught my attention, and I averted my eyes to see pale blonde hair.

Irina sat on the highest bench, her hair slicked against her face and her eyes widening a fraction.

A slow buzz slithered beneath my skin and whatever tension that had melted away came back, coiling tight around my muscles.

"This is the men's locker room." I trailed my gaze along her body, the robe she had on parted slightly in the front. Her pale flesh glistened with sweat, and I knew my little rebel was naked beneath that fabric. "What are you doing in the men's locker room, Irina?" I asked with an edge to my tone.

"I didn't realize you were someone I had to answer to, Luca."

The way she said my name. . . as if I was the most inconvenient thing in her life made me want to record and put it on replay.

"Maybe you should write it down somewhere, so you don't forget."

She could do whatever she wanted but anyone could've walked in here and seen her half naked. *Another man.*

What would it take for her to understand that she was mine and only mine? Maybe I should resort to less pleasant endeavors.

"Or maybe you should mind your own business."

I stared at her, noting the rise and fall of her chest, the spark in her blue eyes that made me wonder if she enjoyed this push and pull between us as much as I did.

The tension was taut, stretching so thin it was close to snapping.

I removed my attention from her and closed my eyes. This game was far from done and I planned on savoring the chase.

Irina didn't make a sound; she didn't leave either as I expected her to.

She'd come here on her own and I wanted to know why. I knew she was physically active when she had kicked my ass the last time we were at the Underground Club but where did she learn that? *Why* did she learn it?

"How did you get your scars?" Her voice came out in a hushed tone.

I opened my eyes and caught hers, the color in them deepening into a midnight blue.

"What do I get in return?"

"You won't be getting my pity."

Adorable.

"Wouldn't dream of it." I chuckled before smoothing my features. "If I tell you, I want to know about yours."

Her throat bobbed as she swallowed. "I don't have any."

Like calls to like and if hers weren't apparent on her body, I knew they ran deep inside her soul.

There was nothing that I'd keep from this woman. I wanted her. And I *wanted* her to know the darkest parts of me, to understand that once she did, I'd never let her go.

And with Irina, I knew she'd walk me like a damn dog for me to have her.

"My mother was killed in front of me when I was only a young boy," I said, recalling that day so vividly as if it was yesterday. "My father was the one who pulled the trigger."

Her body went still as a statue. "Why did he kill her?"

"Wrong place, wrong time."

My mother was innocent and had fallen into a situation where her life was taken to prove loyalty. She'd overheard something that she wasn't supposed to.

"My scars are my father's creations. After that day, he saw to it that I learned what a true heir to the Mafia meant. He said it would make me stronger." I laughed humorlessly. "More ruthless and unforgiving but it only made me resent him."

"Did it stop?" she asked with a strain in her voice.

I searched her eyes, a flicker of anger swarming within them.

"At the age of fifteen, when I overpowered him and broke his hand."

We stared at each other, the air past boiling. Something shifted between us. It was evident in the way Irina's gaze lingered on my chest as if she was understanding the meaning behind my tattoos.

I didn't know if I was relieved or if it made me hate her for it a little.

She stood and my hands clenched at my sides thinking she was going to leave but then she stepped in my direction.

My breaths came out quicker when she reached me. It was hard to read her expression.

"You won't be getting my pity," she confirmed before surprising me by sitting on my lap, her knees on either side of me. The robe bunched around her hips, and I gripped her waist to keep her from changing her mind.

I didn't know what was happening or what kind of game she was playing at, but I didn't care either. Her body felt so fucking right against mine that I didn't care.

"I want to feel you." Her gaze was fixated on my chest, where my heart resided and ready to stop beating at any moment.

She raised her hand but before she could touch me, I caught her wrist.

No one had ever wanted to touch my scars, let alone stare at them for longer than a few seconds because of how distorted they appeared. That's why I had gotten the tattoos to cover them, not because of others' opinions but to stop being reminded of them.

And who takes care of you, Luca?

Eva's words replayed in my head, and it might've been for all the wrongs reasons, but I guided Irina's hand down on my chest, her fingers splaying to feel more.

I swallowed harshly, a knot in the pit of my stomach forming from her smooth fingers gently caressing me as if my skin were something delicate and to be treasured.

Her hands were wandering but my attention was focused on her face. She went over every groove, every ragged bump and crevice deliberately, up until she reached my shoulders, and her hands explored my back—the scars there longer and harsher.

Her jaw clenched as she gazed at me with ferocity.

Time ceased to exist in this space of uncertainty. Her warm hands burned hotter on my skin, sending bolts of electricity in every nook of my being.

"Let me ease your pain."

My fingers curled, pulling her closer to me. Was this her way of thanking me for tending to her cut? If so, I didn't want it. I'd done that for my own selfish reasons. To carve it into her mind that she'd never escape me—*that she'd never be alone.*

"I'm not in pain, *piccola ribelle.*"

"Then ease mine," she whispered, leaning down, and kissing me.

The second our lips touched; I was a goner. I had no idea how she could have this indescribable hold on me, but she did.

Her presence calmed that depraved part of me, and I never wanted it to end. I wanted her entwined with me.

I felt her hands between us, and I leaned back to see her untying her robe.

She pulled the fabric open and let it drop, her body completely naked and bewitching.

"You're killing me," I hissed through clenched teeth, tilting my head up and staring at her with hooded eyes.

"The thought of you dying at my hands brings me more pleasure than you think."

A low chuckle vibrated in my chest as I rubbed my jaw in amusement.

This woman was an oxymoron that was for damn sure.

"Kill me later. For now, let me worship you."

A light shade of pink flushed along her freckled skin, her breaths quickening as she bit her lip and held my gaze. "Say please."

Was she doing this on purpose? I was nearly ready to

have a stroke from one touch but now? Her words might be my undoing.

I was at the complete mercy of this woman and the dominance she exuded was sexy as fuck. It only made me want to feed into it. . . something I'd never done before.

"*Please.*"

A satisfied smirk curved along her mouth as she hummed in approval.

And then I worshipped her.

I was gasping for breath, lost in the surge of a high when Irina got up abruptly, grabbed her robe and left the room.

When I rinsed myself quickly in the shower, I changed and left the locker room, hoping she was still here.

She might've left but something told me she hadn't yet.

I waited outside, the sun slowly rising, an orange glow shading the horizon and pulled out a cigarette.

Inhaling a puff of smoke, I let it ground me, the adrenaline still coursing through my veins.

The doors swung open before Irina walked out, her feet coming to a stop when she saw me.

I inhaled another drag and walked toward her. "I'm taking you home."

"No, you're not." Her blonde hair swayed in the wind, and I could tell it was still wet.

My jaw ticked from her lack of proper attire.

I removed my leather jacket and put it around her,

pulling the hood over her head. A smile touched my lips at how it swallowed her whole.

"You don't need to drop me home and you definitely don't need to give me your jacket," she snapped. "Just because we got each other off doesn't mean I like you." I would've let her outburst slide but then she had to continue her obscene rant. "I could've found someone else and done the same thing."

My hand shot out and gripped her jaw, pulling her face close to mine.

Despite her pulse quickening, she stared at me with a narrowing of her eyes, her lips set in a firm line.

"I think I've given you too much leeway, *piccola ribelle.*" I brushed my lips across hers. "Would you like to find out what happens when you abuse my patience?"

"Do your worst." Straight white teeth as she smiled at me. The odd part was it appeared genuine. "I might be into it."

Her tongue would truly get her in trouble.

She jerked from my hold, and I watched as she walked toward a motorcycle parked at the corner.

No fucking way.

Irina pulled a helmet from the back compartment and put it on before swinging her leg over the bike.

The engine roared to life, and she drove out of the lot.

She was fast but not fast enough.

Once she was home safe, I'd leave.

I hopped on my own bike and tracked her. I was thoroughly convinced now, that this woman was made for me. And she looked damn good in my leather jacket as she sped through the empty roads.

She was aware of me following her, checking her rearview mirror consistently and speeding up further.

Irina could run from me, but she had to know that I'd chase her right? Until she screamed, cried, and begged for me to let her go. Even then, I wouldn't.

I kept my distance, if only to amuse her delusions that she could outrun me.

Roman's house appeared after a few miles, and we entered through the arched gates before Irina parked her bike and got off.

She removed her helmet and faced me, breathing harshly as the sun slowly peaked in the sky,

I leaned against my bike, my feet planted on either side.

The silence was a calm that settled deep into my bones. We stared at each other for long moments, an unspoken conversation with only our eyes. Irina's were an ocean blue, ready to drown me into its waters.

Neither of us said a word, afraid that it would ruin something that didn't make sense in the first place.

Then she stepped forward and paused for a second.

I tilted my head at her. *I dare you.*

Her hands balled into fists before turning away from me with a viciousness slashing across her face that made me grip the handles of my bike tighter.

She disappeared inside the house, the harsh click of the door breaking the trance.

I gazed up at the bright sky with a smile stretching across my face.

She kept my jacket.

CHAPTER 10
IRINA

I closed the door harder than needed before leaning against it.

The all-consuming feeling of being near Luca was like an electric wave, going up the tide and embracing me in its shock.

What was wrong with me?

Every man was the same so what made him different?

The urge to look out of the window and see if he was still there nerved me. I dug my nails into my palms to refrain myself.

I'd crossed the line tonight, a lapse of judgment on my part. *A mistake.*

I didn't expect to see Luca tonight, let alone touch him the way I did—the way he touched *me.*

I bit my lip, remembering the way his skilled fingers elicited my desires in a way it never had before.

And yes, it was my fault for being in the men's locker room, but the women's was under renovation and the

Club was empty. How was I supposed to know that he'd be there at that time?

And when he opened up about his past. . .

My fingertips buzzed from where I'd touched his jagged scars. I nearly recoiled when he'd told me how he'd gotten them. He'd only been a boy and had endured such obscene pain.

I shouldn't have let the spur of the moment get to my head. I had already been treading water since I got to Italy and it didn't help that Luca was always there, attempting to strip me bare and pull out my demons.

I want to know about yours.

His words replayed in my head. There was a sick sort of irony about us. At fifteen, he'd put an end to his abuse. At fifteen, I'd killed the first man who laid their hands on me.

Defeat sunk deep into my stomach. Dammit, he *was* different. Everything about him was different. Yes, he was insufferable and arrogant, but for some reason, he was the first person capable of seeing past the deceit.

I knew it the moment he'd stepped into that bathroom to clean my hand. He *saw* me.

My chest caved, pushing down the ruckus of emotions. I couldn't allow myself to empathize with him no matter how desperately I wanted to give in.

Luca could never be mine. Not in this lifetime or the next. He was the leader of the Camorra and part of Roman's crew. The same crew who took in my brother.

Luca would be over his fixation for me once I left and this game would be forgotten. Short-lived like everything else in my life.

My father would be ashamed of me if he knew what I'd done.

I swallowed the bitter taste in my mouth and walked toward the kitchen.

It was early in the morning, the silence comforting, and I lavished in it, knowing that the world was asleep.

I stopped short when I saw Nicolai sitting on the stool, his elbows perched on the kitchen island with his head bowed.

"Nicolai?"

He slowly turned and stared at me. The sight of him nearly causing me to stumble back.

This was the first time he appeared disheveled. Blond hair sticking out in all directions, eyes bloodshot and black rings around them.

"I didn't think anyone was up."

I walked toward him, taking the empty seat beside him. "I never slept."

He didn't say anything for a long while, gazing blankly at the bay windows from across the room.

The room felt smaller with each passing second and I couldn't sit here until it closed in on me, knowing there was something wrong.

"Are you okay?"

He cleared his throat, his brown eyes settling on me as his lips lifted in a tight smile. "Do I look that terrible?"

I nodded my head, trailing my gaze along his tortured features.

"To be truthful, I get these nightmares. . . and it's *suffocating*." He closed his eyes, his throat moving as he swallowed. "It feels like a noose around my neck, and I try to claw it away, but it never does."

A piece of my heart cracked, blood oozing out from his anguish. I understood that feeling all too well.

"What are they about?" I asked hoarsely.

"My past."

My eyes stung, and I had to grit my teeth to stop the unshed tears from welling up.

If I didn't ask now, then I didn't know if I'd get the opportunity again, not when Roman warned me not to get close to him.

"Did something happen to you, Nicolai?"

His face drained of color and the moment his mouth went slack, I knew he was slipping into that void that he'd been to last time.

Remembering what happened the last time I touched him, I refrained from doing it again.

"Nicolai," I said a bit harshly, pulling him back to the present before he slipped away completely.

He visibly shuddered before inhaling sharply, running a hand over his face. "You're a good friend, Irina, but I can't talk about my past with you when I can't even seem to come to terms with it myself."

I tried to clear the lodge of despair from my throat. Although it stung that he couldn't talk to me which was understandable considering all things, he saw me as a friend and that was what I'd hold on to.

"I get nightmares too," I whispered as if I was unsure whether to share this with him. "Sometimes I feel like it's better to stay in it than wake up and realize nothing has changed. You're still haunted by them until it happens again."

Nicolai's head snapped to me, and his eyes flashed with what appeared to be shock.

"You eventually learn to cope with it in your own way, but I can't promise you false words that it gets better."

His lips pursed as he nodded. It might've not been what he wanted to hear, but I hoped by telling him about myself reassured a part of him that he was seen and understood.

The sound of footsteps emerged, and we turned in unison to see Gianna—Roman's head housemaid—walk into the kitchen, stopping when she saw us.

"Early risers?" she asked in a motherly tone, a smile brightening her face.

"Something like that," I replied, glancing at Nicolai.

Aurora rummaged around the ballroom of the Underground Club, directing the workers on their tasks for her gender reveal.

She was a commanding woman, and I had no doubt it was her husband's influence.

I laughed, walking toward her as she huffed and rubbed her belly.

"You could've hired an event planner."

"No, I want to be involved in everything regarding my baby." She smirked and looked down at the swell of her belly. "I can't believe I'm going to be a mom," she choked.

"You deserve it more than anyone, Rora." I hugged her

from the back, my face resting on her shoulder. "And I'll be the best aunt."

Her head tilted back as she laughed. "I've no doubt about that. You'll drive us both insane."

A sadness overtook me as I kissed her cheek.

Please, don't hate me.

"It's all coming together nicely."

Workers moved around the open space, setting up blue and pink décor. It was extravagant and the grandest gender reveal I'd ever attended—not that I'd been to one before.

"It is," Aurora replied, her green eyes glossing over. "I can't believe how fast it's all happening."

"Our little girl can't come fast enough."

"You want the baby to be a girl?" she asked in amusement, turning to face me.

"Of course, I do. Who else will replace you as my best friend?" I smirked as she shoved me lightheartedly.

"Keep that same attitude when I have you changing diapers."

CHAPTER II
LUCA

It's easy to take control when it's right in the palms of our hands.

I stood, staring at my father on his bed, an oxygen mask covering his mouth.

"When will he be awake?" I asked Dr. Aldo.

He cleared his throat as he pushed back his gray hair. "It's too early to tell, but it could take a while. His injuries were peculiar, especially on his head."

I glanced at him, noting the scrunch of his nose. Dr. Aldo was a trusted employee, and he understood our line of business. I had no doubt that he knew exactly how my father received his injuries. Luckily, he never probed, and it was either because he didn't care, or he wanted to leave as quickly as possible.

"Keep an eye on him and let me know when he's conscious." I turned and walked toward the door. "Don't let him leave this room. I don't care what *methods* you have to use."

My father would die a slow death and I'd make sure he endured true pain before he rotted in hell.

Memories from the last time I was at the Club pulsed at the back of my mind as I walked into the ballroom.

I couldn't help but scan the area for a certain blonde, my blood running hot when my gaze landed on her.

Tight leather pants hugged her lean legs like second skin and a lace red top accentuated her waist. *Dammit.* I needed my hands on her again.

I walked in her direction and used the excuse of Aurora being with her to my advantage.

"Luca!" Aurora greeted me with a hug and, like the devil himself, Roman appeared, pulling her off me.

"Worried I'll take the mother of your children, brother?"

Roman's eyes blazed, jaw tensing. "You're a walking STD. You *attempting* to take my wife is the least of my worries."

A sound came from beside me and I turned to see Irina rolling her eyes, blonde hair swaying as she avoided my gaze.

I bit the inside of my cheek. Was she jealous? It could be from disgust, but I'd assume the former.

"Always the dramatic one," I tsked. "Hopefully, the baby doesn't follow in your footsteps."

My words were directed toward Roman, but my gaze was set on Irina because she wouldn't look at me.

"So, uh, what do you think the gender is?" Aurora

asked, pulling my attention away from her best friend, and I knew why. She worried her lip as she glanced at her husband and back at me before staring at Irina—who couldn't be bothered to interact.

I was close to snapping and putting her ass over my shoulder to take her in a dark corner. It seemed she only enjoyed my company when we were alone or when I was pleasuring her.

Roman glared at me disapprovingly and he could continue doing so.

The fact of the matter was, I'd already been bitten by my vicious viper, and I was a masochist for more. He couldn't scare me off. No one could.

"A girl."

Aurora clapped her hands giddily. "Irina said the same!"

My lips twitched in amusement, and I couldn't help but peer at her. She was staring off to the side, but I knew she felt my eyes on her.

Look at me, sweetheart.

Irina turned her head further, hiding her majestic face from my view and it grated on my nerves.

She wanted to play? Let's fucking play.

"I need a drink." I stalked off and irritation built at the base of my spine when Irina finally engaged with my two friends as I wandered farther away from them.

I signaled to the bartender, and a shot appeared before me. I downed it and slammed it on the counter, staring at Irina and hoping she could sense the heat of it.

She could deny me herself, but all she was doing was prolonging the inevitable. Irina would lose this game, and in the end, she would surrender to me. God knew she had me wrapped around her finger already and I was ready to get on my knees if she so much as asked me to.

Guests mingled as the party droned on and my skin prickled with the need to claim Irina as my own in front of everyone.

She was a magnet and everyone in this forsaken place seemed to be drawn to her, talking, dancing and eyeing her as if she was theirs.

She was mine.

And I knew my jealously was irrational when Gianna —who was Roman's head housemaid—danced with her.

"You're glaring."

Aurora's voice reached me, but I couldn't be bothered to face her. My attention was solely focused on Irina's hand on Nico's shoulder. That little shit.

"Am I?" I gritted my teeth.

"Yes, you are. So, wipe that expression off your face before Roman notices."

I knew Aurora wouldn't say anything to her husband about my gawking. She wasn't the type to create drama.

"With all due respect, Rora," I started, turning to see her looking at me curiously. "I couldn't give less of a fuck what Roman says."

"Then give one for what I have to say." She smiled, but it didn't reach her green eyes. "You've never disrespected me since I've known you and I love you like a brother." I could feel the *but* coming to that sentence. "But don't pursue my best friend when you know it'll complicate things."

She was letting me down easily, sugar coating what she really wanted to say.

It was true that I'd never cared to be in a relationship with most of the women I'd been with, but this was different. I knew it was when the mere thought of Irina breathed life into me.

Obsession, craze, delusion, or compulsion. It didn't matter what the reason was. My whole essence craved her, and it felt like I'd die if I couldn't have her—brand her right into my soul.

"You're right." I lied. "I'll move onto my next victim."

Her name started with an *I* and ended with an *A*.

She chuckled, shaking her head at me. "One day, you're going to meet a girl who will put a stop to your. . . ways."

The thing was, I already had. And she didn't even want me. Or she thought she didn't, but that would change very quickly.

"But before you do that, let's find out the gender of my little one."

Aurora went to join Roman at the center of the room. He immediately kissed the side of her head, causing her to giggle in his embrace. If it weren't for the affection he displayed toward his wife, it would've appeared he'd rather be anywhere else.

I couldn't help myself. My eyes seeking and falling on Irina—who stood on the other side of the room—her face lit up with awe.

All sound ceased to exist. My heart thrummed against my chest as her face split into a smile that could bring a man to his knees.

It wasn't until she jumped up and down with laughter that I realized the reveal happened, and I'd been too enamored by her existence to notice.

Blue confetti fell over the crowd as my ears rang from cheers and shouts of congratulations.

A boy. My mouth lifted into a smile. A little Roman would soon be running around here and I already knew my nephew would be mischievous, just like his uncle.

I crossed the room and embraced Aurora in a hug, smirking at Roman because we both knew his threats were empty and his wife loved me.

"If you ever need a babysitter, let me know, Rora."

"Not happening," Roman replied. "And don't call her *Rora*."

Aurora leaned toward me. "My beautiful bastard is possessive," she whispered.

"I heard that, *anima mia*."

"Well, congratulations, you two." I clapped my hands, walking backward. "I'll be sure he follows in my footsteps." I winked at Roman and slipped away before he shot me in the head.

He was an easy person to rile up, especially when it came to the ones he loved—which was a limited number.

The opening I'd been waiting for all night happened when my favorite Russian walked out of the ballroom.

I glanced at my surroundings to make sure no one saw before following her.

Irina walked down the corridor and up the grand staircase, the party sounding farther away.

My little rebel had no idea she led herself into my trap.

As she walked confidently down the hall, I picked up speed before I closed in on her.

With one hand at the base of her neck and the other wrapped around her mouth, I pushed her back against the wall.

She grunted from the impact; her breath warm against my palm.

"Running off somewhere, sweetheart?"

Her blue eyes narrowed in response as she looked to the side, unwilling to my meet my gaze.

"Why are you avoiding me?"

Her teeth clamped down on my finger and I hummed in satisfaction at her malevolence. It fed my tainted soul.

"Is that what you're into?" I let go of her mouth and trailed my hand down her delicate throat, gripping it. "You like it rough, Irina?"

Her pulse thumped against the pad of my thumb in a fast and rhythmic pace. I grinned, relishing in the effect I had on her.

"Get over yourself," she spat out. "You'd have to be someone of importance to have that type of control over me."

I rubbed my thumb up and down her skin, feeling it warm up. "Then give me your eyes, Irina. *Look* at me."

She continued staring to the side, so hellbent on disobeying me. I knew if I wanted to, I could force her, but where would be the fun in that?

"Let me see you. . . unless you're scared."

Her head whipped fast at that, her eyes burning into me with intensity. "There." She leaned in. "Happy?"

I pulled her to me by the throat. "Not one bit."

She searched my eyes, the tension closing in on us, stretching so thin, it would inevitably snap.

"How unfortunate for you that I don't care."

"A viperous tongue I long to taste even in my dreams," I rasped. "I will have you, Irina. One way or another."

"Leave me alone, Luca," she whispered, a strain in her voice.

"I can't."

"Can't or won't? I *don't* want you."

"You'll learn to want me."

"You're a psychopath."

"Yes." The tension snapped as I crushed my mouth to hers because not kissing her was as painful as her convincing herself she didn't want me.

She kissed me as if she wanted to punish me. For what? I had no idea, but I feasted on her lips, allowing her essence to seep into me.

Even with my hand around her throat and the other on her waist, I couldn't seem to bring her close enough. An animalistic need for her had come over me and it drove me insane, trying to figure out ways to brand her permanently on me—in me.

I pulled back, peering down at her swollen lips before holding her gaze. "You have no idea of the sheer power you hold over me, Irina," I breathed. "Put me out of my misery."

She clutched the front of my shirt and for a moment, I could see the internal war she was having inside those alluring eyes. Her hand shook against me, and I didn't know if she wanted to pull me closer or push me away.

With a guttural sound, she spread her palm and pushed against my chest, slipping out of my hold.

"Don't corner me again," she said, turning and nearly running back the way she came.

My entire body vibrated with anger. These stolen seconds weren't enough to extinguish this fire tearing at my insides.

One way or another, Irina.

CHAPTER 12

IRINA

"You're running out of time, princess."

Viktor leaned against the brick wall of the alleyway, his hands inside his pockets as he stared at me with distaste.

The feeling was mutual.

"These unwanted meetups are useless. I already told you I'm doing this on my terms."

"Is that why you've been avoiding your father's calls?"

I narrowed my eyes at him and his stupid, patronizing tone. "What else did he tell you?"

"That he doesn't mind coming here and resolving the issue in his *own* way."

"He'd be a fool to start a war with the Italians."

He hummed, nodding his head. "War is on the horizon, cousin, so I suggest you hurry the fuck up."

My skin had become cold, and it had nothing to do with the winter breeze. Viktor knew how to push my buttons, always acting as if he was more knowledgeable and superior to others.

"Then I'll speak to my father. And you definitely don't need to be an instigator." I knew he was constantly in my father's ear, pushing him to stir the pot where it wasn't needed. "Go home, Viktor. When the mission is done, you'll know."

His head tilted at me, eyes icing over, and I knew that expression all too well. He used it to instill fear in his victims as he interrogated them.

I stood my ground, my hands curling into fists as his gaze lingered over me in assessment.

"No ty yeshche bol'shiy durak." But you are an even bigger fool.

"What is *that* supposed to mean?"

"Your jacket."

Two words and my heart had begun to race uncomfortably in my chest, sweat gathering at the base of my neck.

Shit.

"I thought you didn't know Luca Canaveri, Irina?"

My skin pricked at *his* name. I swallowed through the thick restraint in my throat. "I don't."

"I never predicted you as a liar." He strode toward me and before I could step back, he pulled me to him by the collar. "Not only is this disgusting jacket too big on you, but I recall these same initials when I'd met him."

A heavy weight settled over me and I breathed through my nose to calm myself down. I hadn't been thinking when I'd grabbed it this morning.

"Are you screwing him?"

"No!"

"Isn't that all you're good for, anyway? Spreading yourself like a whore to serve the Bratva."

My fist slammed against his face, a sharp pain shooting from my knuckles and up my arm from the force of it.

"If I whored myself out, so did you," I seethed, bubbling rage burning inside me. "Yet, you're still at the fucking bottom like you've always been."

Viktor would never retaliate and hit me. He knew if my father found out, his death would be on display for the others to see—to understand the consequences of disrespecting his daughter.

He sneered, wiping the blood from his nose. "By all means, princess, do what you have to do in order to complete your mission." Then he laughed sardonically. "We all know how you use that pretty face of yours to your advantage, anyway."

His words sliced through me, coiling deep in my stomach, and it couldn't have hurt worse than if he'd actually hit me.

He was wrong.

I glared at him, my jaw aching from clenching my teeth. It was useless arguing with him because at the end of the day, we both knew he was right, and I hated it. *I hated myself.*

As I walked away from him, I let that hollowness inside my chest cave, allowing my emotions to be swallowed by the putrid hole there.

Nightfall had come, and I had been walking the streets of Italy aimlessly, pondering over every single nuisance in my life.

Viktor's visit had been my breaking point, and my mind wouldn't shut down.

I needed to breathe, the noose around my neck becoming tighter with every passing minute.

I needed a high to ease the discomfort of being in my own skin.

A nearby pub came into view and I didn't hesitate as I walked inside the small tavern. This was going to end badly, but I needed a release in the only way I knew how.

Taking a seat on a stool, I signaled to the bartender.

I didn't count how many shots I let burn down my throat, but I drank until my thoughts were a jumbled mess, worse than they were before, but at least a simmering numbness coated me thoroughly.

A pretty face. A pretty body. All you're good for.

I shook my head, my vision blurring and mind hazy.

Nicolai will never accept you.

You're a liar.

Aurora will hate you.

Roman will hate you.

Luca is playing with you.

Luca.

My heart squeezed from the onslaught of agonizing thoughts, and I gasped from the pain.

I'd been feeding into Luca's delusions. He only wanted me because he couldn't have me. I was a game to him, the first woman who hadn't fallen for his charms.

And he knew which pieces to move until I was right where he wanted me.

The sting of tears pricked the back of my eyes, but I refused to shed them. I'd gone this long without expressing these emotions that would only hurt me if they were let out. So, I did what I knew best: I shoved them deep into the crevices of my soul, burying them.

It was easier this way.

I took another shot, the bitter taste of alcohol settling on my tongue.

A scalding tear slipped from the corner of my eye, making a path down my cheek and I quickly wiped it away, inhaling deeply, not allowing the rest to follow.

I felt pathetic. The universe had never been on my side since I'd been a child, so why did I expect it to be different now?

The bar grew rowdy, my head pounding and pulse racing from the rush of adrenaline.

I stumbled as I stood from my seat and staggered out of the pub.

My vision was unfocused, and I couldn't remember where I was, or which way was home.

Home. Where was home? I belonged nowhere. Wandering aimlessly through the tragedy of my life and never being stagnant.

Black spots appeared in my line of sight as I unsteadily walked down the pathway of the bar, holding myself against the brick wall.

I was usually good at holding my liquor, but I must've overdone it with how heavy I was breathing. My legs weakened until I tripped and braced myself for the fall.

But I never did.

A solid hand wrapped around my torso, pulling me up until I came face to face with the root of all my problems.

Luca was furious as he loomed over me, his jaw set tight, eyes a raging storm against the starless night.

I pouted at him, mimicking his expression before a laugh bubbled out of me and I'd have fallen over again if it weren't for his harsh grip.

He didn't find any of it amusing as he suddenly lifted me into his arms, the rush making my head spin.

As I rested my head against his shoulder, I couldn't help but stare up at him. Even at this angle, he was beautiful. Smooth golden skin, prominent cheekbones stark under the moonlight, the angle of his nose sharp above his full lips. God, he was so beautiful it made my heart race at an abnormal pace.

Luca gazed down at me with those intense caramel eyes, and it sped faster.

Had I said that aloud?

"Is this where I say thank you?"

Oh. No.

CHAPTER 13
LUCA

Irina slept soundlessly as I watched her.

When I locked up the museum tonight, I hadn't expected to see her on the narrow streets of Italy, drunk no less.

Anger stroked along the base of my neck from her stupidity. Anyone could've taken advantage of her.

I expected Aurora to be with her at all times, which made me curious as to why she had been out alone getting drunk.

There was depth to Irina, and she might be able to deceive the world by hiding herself in a shell, but not me. I saw right through those cracks in every snide remark.

As she slept, I remembered her unexpected comment before she passed out in my arms.

She thought I was beautiful.

I didn't think I'd ever been described that way before.

My lips lifted into a smile, recalling the way her face fell when she realized I'd heard her.

Okay, maybe I didn't mind drunk Irina if only to hear her unfiltered thoughts aloud.

At least then I would actually know what she truly thought of me.

I stared at her, the rise and fall of her chest steady. Her hair fell like a halo cascading around her angelic face.

If she thought I was beautiful, I wondered how she perceived herself.

My fingertips vibrated with an urgency to feel her skin against mine.

Whatever power she held over me consumed me entirely. Every nerve ending in my body came to life when she was near, and I was addicted.

Light sniffles drew me from my thoughts, causing me to stand and move toward Irina.

Her face was pinched in anguish, her body thrashing beneath the covers as if she were trying to free herself from something.

I put one knee on the bed and leaned over her, placing my hand against her chest, her heart beating wildly against my palm. "Irina."

A broken whimper slipped from her lips as she continued trembling.

Damnit. "*Irina*!"

The more she fell into the abyss of her nightmare, the harder it was to reach her.

Wrapping my hand around her throat, I squeezed, hoping to reach her.

Every second that passed, my blood ran colder, and I felt helpless.

That same helplessness I experienced when I saw my mother die.

"Irina, wake up, sweetheart." I shook her, urgency running through my veins. "Wake up!"

A loud gasp escaped her as her eyes shot open, wide with panic.

"Fuck." I slumped forward, finally being able to breathe.

"Luca?"

I wrapped my hands around her, bringing her up until I crushed her to my chest as if I needed more reassurance that she was with me.

What are you doing to me, piccola ribelle?

Her hands rested against my back, hesitant. "What are you doing here?"

"You don't remember?"

"I remember you carrying me. . . "

I pulled back, searching her face. "You passed out, and I brought you home."

"And you didn't leave," she whispered, a furrow creasing her forehead.

The air became charged with thick tension as her words hung in the silent air.

"Do you want me to leave?"

Her blue eyes shone with trepidation as she searched my own, seeking answers to unsaid questions.

"No."

That one word took root in my chest, the beginning and end of me.

I lifted the covers and laid beside her, our hands

inches apart and resting in the middle as we faced each other.

Time halted as I traced the outlines of her features as intently as she was tracing mine, her blue eyes warming my skin with every touch.

Neither one of us said a word, comfortable in the stillness.

Eventually, her eyes became heavy, but before she dozed off to sleep, her hand inched closer to mine.

Hands reaching but never touching.

The tense push and pull between us that had always been there.

Only now, it was different.

The night melted into the first rays of morning when I snuck out of her room.

I hadn't slept at all, exhaustion heavy on my muscles, but how could I when it was insignificant compared to spending hours memorizing Irina?

I could've stared at her for another few hours and it wouldn't have been enough.

When I got the call that my father was awake a week later, I came to see him.

The door clicked shut when Dr. Aldo stepped out of my father's room.

"He's stable," he said, holding his notepad to his chest. "You can see him if you'd like."

I nodded my head and put my hand out in front of me.

He eyed me nervously before dropping the two vials

in my palm hesitantly. "Do you know how a syringe works?"

I smirked at his dubious expression. "I'll manage. Stay out here and I'll call you when I'm ready."

He nodded before walking away with a hunched back. Old man refused to retire.

I entered the room and leaned against the wall with my ankles crossed, letting the glass tubes clash in my hand back and forth.

My father's eyes flicked toward me; his body completely immobile.

"Looks like I won't be needing this one." I raised the first bottle so he could see and walked toward his bed to set it down on the table nearby.

If what the doctor said was true, he still had sensation in his body.

To test this theory, I grabbed his index finger and pushed it back until I felt the bone crunch beneath my skin.

His face became red and sweaty, a tear streaking down his face as he stared at me in horror.

I couldn't help but laugh aloud, my blood heating from excitement. "This is going to be an afternoon well spent."

There was no ounce of sympathy or pity present as I broke each of my father's fingers until he'd passed out. I couldn't imagine being motionless and voiceless while experiencing excruciating pain, but I also wasn't a horrid man like him.

I stepped back from my work in satisfaction as I admired his hands, his fingers crooked and bent in odd directions. In a disturbing way, it was sort of artistic.

My phone vibrated in my pocket, and I dropped the syringe on the bed before reaching for it.

My trainer's name flashed across the screen, and I cursed before answering it on the third ring.

"Where are you?" His voice came down the line, a bit muffled by the background noise.

"Cleaning up a mess."

"Clean it later and get your ass to the Club," he said in agitation. "You already missed your session this morning, so I hope to hell your heads screwed right for tonight."

A fight was exactly what I needed after this visit. "I'm on my way."

I stole a glance at my unconscious father, staring at his blanching face. I'd visit him again soon and break another part of him.

Leaving the room, I handed Dr. Aldo the supplies. "Give him the morphine and wrap up his injuries."

"You didn't know how to use the syringe after all." He gave me a sly smile, enjoying himself at my supposed ignorance.

"Something like that."

The crowd roared to life when I stepped onto the stage, heightening the adrenaline pumping through my veins.

Overhead lights shifted over the audience, my name a chant on their tongues.

It would never get old how my mere presence could invoke such thick energy permeating the air. It fueled my need to wreak havoc on the poor fucker across from me.

Fighting was an outlet for me, a way to relieve the anger residing in the dark parts of my soul.

The whistle rang, igniting a surge of manic power slicing through me.

My opponent tonight was a burly man with a snarl attached to his sweaty face, glaring at me as if I was his worst enemy.

I took my stance, a smirk stretching my face before I gestured for him with two curled fingers.

It ticked him off—exactly as I expected—and he lunged forward with a growl, swinging his fist toward me.

I ducked, steering away from his weak aim until I stood behind him, my heart rate accelerating when he turned and came at me again.

This time, I leaned back, avoiding his fist before head-butting him with a vicious strike.

He stumbled back, blood oozing from his nose and the sight itched at the crazed sensation pricking my skin.

There were no rules to the fights that happened at the Underground Club except for one. Every fight was to the death. Whoever took the life of the other would be titled the winner.

And I'd never lost.

I had to admit, though, a sick part of me enjoyed letting them get in a hit or two before bathing in their blood. It kept the crowd entertained and my high fresh.

The man came at me full force and I laughed as his weight crushed me to the floor, the piercing screams of the audience deafening.

He threw a punch against my jaw, the taste of iron

bursting on my tongue, causing me to turn my head and spit it out.

One.

The moment my eyes locked with Irina's in the crowd, standing right behind the roped border, my smile widened.

Her expression was pure shock as she stared at me wide eyed with her mouth parted. She flicked her gaze to the man pinning me to the floor before it shifted back to me, her brows furrowed. If I didn't know better, I'd think she was nervous.

I winked at her as another punch landed on my cheek, the skin tearing.

"That your lady out there? She's real pretty." Hot breath fanned my face. "Bet she'd look even prettier underneath me."

Two.

Black spots appeared in my vision, and I felt the last of my control slip from my fingers. With a hard upward thrust of my body, I swung my leg until I had him caged between my thighs.

All my senses enhanced into a frenzy of fury as I clutched him by the hair and made him acquainted with my fist, the satisfying crunch of bone beneath my knuckles.

Blood sprayed across my torso as I pummeled into his face, every grunt escaping him more ragged with each hit.

I paused, breathing harshly as a raging heat encompassed my sweat covered body.

Gripping his head with both hands, I made him look at

me, terror coating his eyes before I covered them with my thumbs and pressed down.

A horrible scream tore from him as I ruptured his eyes, crimson leaking down his face.

"That's for staring at what's mine." My tone was as lethal as my hands.

His annoying wailing grated on my nerves, but it was the perfect opening to stick my hand inside his throat and grip his tongue. With a sharp tug, I ripped it out, his body writhing beneath me until it stopped.

"And that's for speaking of her," I said to his unconscious—most likely dead body.

When the ringing in my ears dissipated, the blaring noises of my surroundings rushed in, making me overly aware of where I was.

I pushed up off my hands as they announced my win and scanned the roaring crowd.

My chest rose and fell fast, muscles stretching taut as my gaze caught Irina's blue eyes.

I didn't know what I expected to find, but it definitely wasn't the raw hunger sparking in them.

A hand landed against my back, bringing my attention to my trainer. "Go on and clean up," Alessio said, his face tense. "You brought in a lot of money tonight with that stunt."

I'm sure it did, but that *stunt* might've just jeopardized fighting in the near future. I doubted anyone would want their organs ripped from their body while conscious.

Wiping the sweat off my brow, I nodded my head at him before leaving the ring.

The crowds' applause increased in volume, following me all the way to the back where the locker rooms were.

I closed the door behind me and looked up to find a random woman sitting on one of the benches. She leaned back on her hands, legs stretched in front of her as she eyed me with a mischievous glint.

"Are you lost?" I asked blankly.

I'd been in this exact situation more times than not, and each time, it became less amusing.

"Yes." Her voice dripped with seduction, red lips pouting. "Glad you found me." She moved her hands toward the knot on her trench coat, fingers tracing them slowly.

I swung the door open and walked toward my locker, irritation pulsing at the back of my head. "Leave through the door and take a right. Exit should be there."

Nails dragged across my skin lightly. "How about we play first?"

I turned around and caught her wrists to refrain her from touching me further.

Her eyes glossed over in desire as she bit her bottom lip. "I'll let you do whatever you want to me."

Oh for fuck's sake.

I didn't have a chance to tell her off because one second, she was standing there in anticipation and the next, her face fell as she dropped to the floor, blood pooling around her head.

My gaze flicked toward the door, heart racing as it landed on *my* woman.

Irina stood there, blue eyes a storming hue as she kept her gun aimed in my direction, setting me on fire with one vicious look.

CHAPTER 14
IRINA

My gun was aimed straight ahead, even after the woman had fallen to the floor, bleeding out.

The adrenaline pumping through my veins was erratic and addictive.

I should've felt some sort of guilt for what I'd done, but that emotion never came as I stared at Luca, his head tilted in amusement.

"Are you going to shoot me next, Irina?"

"Depends on your answer to my question," I replied, my fingers circling the trigger. "Who was she?"

Jealousy. A sick and vile feeling I'd never experienced before until now. It slithered its way into my bloodstream, blinding me with rage when I saw her with him. I hated it.

It was irrational when it was plainly obvious women swooned over him constantly. For what reason? I had no idea, but it definitely couldn't be for his skill in ripping tongues out.

Okay. So maybe it was exactly that.

He was a completely different person in the ring. A possessed beast with one purpose: to kill.

"It hardly matters anymore when she's dead." With lazy strides, he closed the space between us. "Don't you think?"

I stared him down, his piercing whiskey eyes full of mischief, his torso slick with sweat, and thick thighs stretching his shorts.

"*I think.*" I pressed the end of the gun to his chest. "You should answer the question."

The air was heavy, suffocating me with its warmth as the seconds ticked by.

He bit his lip, gazing down at me with heavy lids when he stepped further into me, ignoring the weapon between us. "Are you jealous, *piccola ribelle?*"

"Of a dead woman?" I narrowed my eyes at him. "Get over yourself."

He flicked his gaze between the gun and my face before wrapping his hand over mine, forcing it down with a strength no human should possess.

With his other hand, he gripped my throat, his expression lethal as he pushed me against the wall. "Dead because of *you.* Don't stand here and lie to my face."

I lifted my chin in defiance, the pulse in my ears a thunderous rhythm. "Or what?"

The smirk plastered on his face was manic as he leveled his face to mine. "You couldn't handle it."

My breathing slowed as the gleam in his caramel eyes darkened to a dangerous shade.

This brute was mental, spearing through my hard exterior and invading my senses with his presence.

"And if it wasn't already obvious." The gun fell to the floor as he covered my body with his own. "*You* are the source of all my desires."

The charged air intensified, prickling along my skin.

We were treading on a thin line, stealing moments filled with insufferable tension while others were oblivious.

That knowledge shouldn't have given me a rush, but it did and I couldn't help but feed into it.

"Let another woman touch you again. . . " I swept my tongue across his bottom lip. "And it'll be your blood on the floor next."

With a shove against his solid chest, I walked out of the room, the door slamming shut behind me.

I was so far over my head that I allowed myself to be reckless when I'd never acted irrationally before.

That's what it felt like where Luca was concerned. He made me impulsive and lose control of my senses until all I could focus on was *him*.

It infuriated me that he affected me at all, let alone invoke any sort of feelings from me.

I paced my room, wishing I could rewind time and not have given into this dangerous game. I was evidently losing and as the days went on, it was harder to end it.

Pulling my phone out of my pocket, I clicked on my father's name.

After one long ring, he answered, "*Printsessa.*"

"*Papa.*"

"I've been waiting for your call."

My heart thumped against my chest; his tone suggestive but to what? I didn't know.

"I would've called sooner." I walked to the window and sat down on the bench to peer at the night sky. "But things are different than I expected."

He cleared his throat. "How so?"

"Nicolai. He's. . . " Warmth spread through my chest when I thought of my brother. "He's so kind and intelligent."

"And?"

I leaned my head against the glass, the coldness seeping into my skin and calming me. "And he deserves better."

The line was silent, and I wished I could have had this conversation in person to gauge his reactions.

A part of me wanted to tell him more about his son but a bigger part of me was selfish.

"Tell me you haven't lost sight of the reason for your visit?" he asked, sounding almost disappointed I would even think otherwise.

"No," I whispered. "I haven't." How could I forget when it loomed over me like a gray cloud?

"There's *nothing* I should worry about then, right?"

"Is there something you'd like to say?" I asked, annoyed at his patronizing tone.

"Viktor informed me about your recent meeting." A nauseating sensation crawled up my spine, my blood running cold. "Said you were wearing Luca Canaveri's jacket."

My ears rung as I steadied my breathing. "It didn't

mean anything." *Lie.*

"And I believe you, *Printsessa.* You'd never stoop so low as to get involved with one of *them,*" he said confidently, my stomach churning at the surety of his statement.

I was already involved because of Aurora but he already knew that. What he really meant was, I'd never get involved romantically in any way shape or form unless it was to serve his agenda.

"No, *Papa.*" It sat bitterly on my tongue.

"Remember what I taught you, Irina. Beauty is deceptive and yours can be used as a weapon."

"What if I didn't have it?" The words slipped off my tongue faster than I had time to think about it.

I waited tensely for his answer, the clock on the wall ticking away, expanding the silence.

"That would never happen."

I slumped back, my palms clammy. Not a 'You'd still be my daughter' or a 'You're more than your appearance' but a useless reply that didn't hold any value to it.

My chest ached with the energy it took not to break down.

I loved my father, I did. But he never *saw* me. Even within those four walls of our family manor, he never saw me—understood me.

"When you complete your mission, you'll be home in Russia where you belong, and we can be a true family again." My heart splintered, the pain spreading throughout my body. "Doesn't that sound nice?"

"Yes," I breathed when all I felt was the weight of his words curling around my neck in a suffocating grip.

CHAPTER 15

IRINA

I'd exerted all my energy into the punching bag, rage drifting off me with every hit.

It was late in the night when I had decided to come to the Underground Club and get in a workout.

Was I disappointed that I didn't run into a large brute? Only slightly.

Every time I was at the Club, it reminded of that night in the sauna. It was the first slip in my demeanor, and I'd let Luca touch me in all the ways I didn't want him to. Physically. Mentally. Emotionally.

I passed by the front desk, nodding my head at Giuseppe who hosted the night shift. I'd gotten used to seeing his face more than the other workers and I'd like to think he made exceptions for me when I'd come at odd hours of the night, considering there was usually no one else around.

"Goodnight, Miss Irina," he said before I slipped out of the building.

I had my head down, searching in my bag for the keys to my bike when my skin pricked at the sensation of being watched.

With my jaw clenched tight, I looked up to find Luca leaning on his bike—where it was parked next to mine. His stance was casual, a cigarette hanging from his mouth as smoke billowed out, but his caramel eyes were set on me, narrowed intently.

"Are you following me now?" I asked, trying to avoid the way my heart somersaulted in my chest from having him near me.

His low chuckle slithered along my spine, my stomach fluttering from the deep sound.

He took another drag, watching me as smoke wafted in the air. "How else would I reach you?"

"You don't." He didn't have my number or access to me at all times and I intended on keeping it that way.

"Are we back to this again then?" He tilted his head to the side. "Pretending that we aren't—"

"Aren't what?" I asked sharply, the vein in my neck throbbing.

My annoyance wasn't only directed at him; it was at myself too. For not being able to stay away from him no matter how many times I reminded myself of all the reasons I should.

Thick tension coiled around us as we stared at one another, waiting for the other to break.

He threw the bud on the ground and crushed it beneath his boot. "I want to take you somewhere," he said, diverting the conversation.

"And why would I go anywhere with you?"

"Because you're curious, *piccola ribelle.*" He killed the distance between us, staring down at me with a heady expression. "You can waste time and fail to convince me otherwise or you can sit your pretty little ass on your bike and follow me."

I'd rather bite down on concrete than admit that he was right.

I hoped the glare I shot his way would set him on fire until he turned into ash for being right.

"Brute," I mumbled, ready to turn away from him but he caught my chin, pulling me back to face him.

My breath hitched as he pinned me in place with a sheen of possessiveness coating his eyes. He split me open with the scrutiny of his gaze as if he were trying to dissect the very essence of my soul.

Heat flared inside my chest, obliterating any notion that this would ever end. Whether it'd be happily or tragically, I knew if what we had ever ended, we'd perish with it.

After a moment, he nudged under my chin and returned to his bike before revving the engine to life.

I stood conflicted, trying to force my thoughts into some semblance of order. I'd never been at war with myself like I was right now, and it had everything to do with the beating organ inside my chest.

In the end, I'd submitted to what I really wanted.

Luca turned his head toward me and even with his helmet on, I could feel his eyes tracing every inch of me as I straddled my bike.

He pulled out of the parking lot, and I followed him, my heart racing from adrenaline.

One more time, I told myself. One more time, I'd play this game and then I'd be done.

The streets were empty as we sped through the night. Riding became a different type of high when Luca was with me. It was nothing like the first time when he followed me home.

This was pure ecstasy coursing through my veins, an addictive sensation settling deep into my bones.

I leaned forward, gripping the handles as I rushed past him, chasing it further. I had no idea where I was going, but I couldn't stop myself.

Luca flashed his lights at me, catching up to me with little effort before he flicked his gaze toward me at the same time I did.

My mouth split into a smile and it was exhilarating knowing he couldn't see it. Hidden just like the confusing feelings I had for him.

He nudged his head to the left before steering that way and I slowed down to follow him.

After a few minutes, we pulled up to a familiar white building, the area scarce from passerby's.

I removed my helmet and stared up at the art museum I'd met Luca at for the first time.

My heart pounded behind my rib cage as I peered over at him. "What are we doing here?"

"You said your first impression of me wasn't memorable, so I'm. . . redeeming myself."

I did but only to spite him. "I thought you already did that when you smeared your blood across my lips?" I asked sarcastically, crossing my arms over my chest.

He lowered his head but not before I caught a glimpse

of his grin. "I did, didn't I?" He almost sounded pleased by what he'd done.

"Yes, you did, and I'd rather not repeat it."

"Pity." He walked toward me until our feet were touching. "A date then."

I quirked a brow at him as butterflies swarmed in my stomach. "You don't seem like the type who goes on dates."

His eyes bore into me, deep enough to leave a scar on my soul. "That's because I'm not." He pulled a set of keys out of his leather jacket and nudged his head to the side. "After you."

"Oh, cause you're such a gentleman," I hissed under my breath before striding toward the stairs.

The warmth of his chest pressed against my back as he leaned into my ear. "Only for you, *piccola ribelle.*" He placed a kiss beneath my ear, and I felt my resolve crumble right before my eyes.

He gave me affection so casually as if it were a normal occurrence for us. As if he'd given it to me a thousand times before.

When he unlocked the main door, I followed him inside, the automatic lights casting dimly in the foyer.

We walked down the hall until we reached the main display room. It appeared exactly the same as I remembered it except this time the art pieces weren't erotic.

My eyes widened, captivated by the focus of these designs. Each piece was an intricate display of colorful chaos, harsh strokes and edges blurring along the canvas.

It was extraordinary and unlike anything I'd ever seen before.

I moved along the room, appreciating the uniqueness of them all until one had me pausing before it.

My chest caved as I stared at the peculiar creation. It was a black and white shading of a figure caged in an hourglass. The upper half of its body was intact, hands reaching toward the confined space of its entrapment and the bottom half was spilling down to the bowl where time ceased.

"What do you see?" Luca's voice broke the silence, reminding me he'd always been there.

I didn't understand why he'd brought me here or what his intentions were but there was something about the irony of this situation that had me sharing a glimpse of myself.

"Moments are short-lived." I could feel the heat of his gaze against the side of my face as I stared at the artwork that resonated with me far beyond any verbal interpretation of what I felt. "And time doesn't wait for anyone."

My voice echoed around the room, cementing my fear against the crafted walls and I wanted to hide.

Luca didn't say anything, but I could feel him watching me, stripping me under his scurrility and it became unbearable to be near him when his presence was all-consuming.

With a shaky breath, I turned my head and caught his eyes, the emotion flickering in them weakening me down to the bone. Every second that passed, I could sense myself succumbing to this tragedy.

He lifted his hand, a lone finger tracing a path from my cheekbone down to my chin. "I never stood a chance," he whispered as his gaze lingered to my mouth.

I didn't know the meaning behind his words but the expression on his face was enough to make me understand. It was the softness around his fervid eyes, the scrunch between his brows and the downcast of his smile that pulled me deeper into him.

"Why did you bring me here, Luca?" My voice sounded hoarse to my own ears, wavering slightly. "This art. . . "

"I watch you, Irina. So, the next time you get lost in that head of yours, just know that I'm there with you."

His words slammed into me with such force, I took a step back. He'd said this to me once before but the gravity of them weighed differently now. He wasn't only telling me; he was *showing* me.

My pulse raced beneath my skin, my breathing turning shallow as the pressure in my ears intensified.

Anyone but him. Please. Don't let it be him.

He nudged under my chin, breaching through my unnerving thoughts and crossed the room, pausing at the exit for me to join him.

I aimlessly followed him into another area of the museum, too busy sorting through my turmoil of emotions to take notice of the glass ceiling above us until Luca turned the lights off.

It was a replica of the one in Luca's house, only this time, the stars shined so brightly, I tilted my head in awe for a better view.

"Do you like it?" he asked, standing beside me.

"I. . . " When I looked at him, a knowing gleam sparked in his eyes causing my heart to thud against my chest. "You knew."

He shrugged, a playful smile crossing his mouth lazily. "You were in my house."

He said it so casually as if it was the only reasonable justification.

How long had he been watching me that day, lurking in the shadows like a psychopath when I was too enamored by the view in his home?

"You're truly something else," I whispered. "You know that?"

He tilted his head in amusement. "Is this your way of flirting with me?"

"You wish, Luca Canaveri." I felt my own lips twitch into a small grin.

If there was a moment in time that I could freeze between us, it'd be this. The mind-numbing trance of free falling into the pleasurable unknown and all it took was one enchanting stare from him with the silence of the starry night above us to make me feel this way. I didn't want it short-lived, I wanted it over and over again.

He clapped his hands once as he walked backward toward the center of the room where there was a pile of pillows and blankets on the floor. "The view is better from down here," he said, a light energy radiating from him.

It was hard to believe he'd never been on a date before when he'd set up one so perfectly, it left me jarred.

"I hope you're hungry." He continued speaking to me, opening containers but it sounded far away as if I was drowning, a suffocating pressure crushing me.

It became hard to breathe, the familiar sensation of a harsh grip around my neck, clawing at me and pulling me under.

I stumbled back, clutching my shirt as my body trembled in anxiousness.

The moment Luca looked up at me from what he was doing, I couldn't take it anymore. Pretending that this was normal and allowing myself to be oblivious in this false fantasy where he and I could ever be.

I backed away in the direction of the archway as he took a step toward me, his hand reaching out to me as confusion dawned on his face.

With my heart in my throat, I ran out of the museum, hearing Luca's footsteps close behind.

Adrenaline coursed through my veins, blood heating and pulsing beneath my skin as I stumbled out of the museum doors and climbed on my bike.

"Irina!"

I pushed the kickstand up with my foot and drove away as he reached for me, his fingers ghosting over my shoulder.

The air whipped across my face, my eyes glossing over, and I couldn't tell if it was from the wind or unshed tears.

I wanted to get away. Not only from Luca but from everything that made me who I am.

Lights flickered in my direction, a blaring horn following it.

I didn't have to turn to know who it was. I leaned forward with a frustrated exhale and accelerating until I couldn't see or hear anything but the harsh beat of my heart pounding in my ears.

I didn't want to feel the hollow ache in my chest anymore, where it deepened the longer my emotions festered.

I didn't want to feel at all.

A cold relief slithered down my spine as I sped up, the empty road ahead a dark canvas.

The looming presence of danger and catastrophe dissipated, leaving behind acceptance in its place.

It only took a split second. A shift in balance and I lost control.

I couldn't stop the inevitable as I fell off the bike, my body hitting the ground hard and knocking the breath out of me.

It must've been the adrenaline that blocked the pain as I skidded across the cement because I didn't hurt anymore.

My father always told me riding would lead to my death, and the thought made me smile. If only he could see me now.

I blinked up at the sky, feeling the darkness sink down on me and I sighed, closing my eyes.

"*Fuck.*" Suddenly, I was jolted up, strong arms holding me. "Irina." A firm tap on my cheek had me staring at the one person who never let me go.

One touch from Luca and the pain burst along my body in an unbearable pang.

I whimpered as he picked me up, gazing down at me with a profound desperation etched across his sharp features.

"You're going to be okay, I promise," he whispered, and his words sank right into the cracked parts of my heart.

CHAPTER 16
LUCA

Muffled noises slipped from Irina before she whispered, "It. . . it hurts."

"I know, sweetheart." I held her close as I took the steps two at a time. She felt right in my arms, as if this was exactly where she belonged. "I'm going to take care of you," I said, staring down at her.

Her eyelids fluttered before she set her gaze on me, brows scrunching in vulnerability. "I know."

Emotion surged in my bloodstream from the softness of her tone, and it was a complete contrast to how she usually acted toward me.

Rain pattered against the arched window of my room as I laid her down onto my bed and turned on the side lamp.

I clenched and unclenched my fists to rein in my anger before I completely lost it. She'd been reckless tonight and could've gotten herself killed.

She swallowed, eyes roaming my face. "You're angry."

I lifted her gently by the waist and used my free hand to remove her jacket—my jacket.

"I am."

She was so close I could hear every harsh intake of her breath when I touched her.

I reached for the hem of her wet shirt and attempted to lift it when she held my wrist.

Our eyes locked, and I stilled my movements. "But that doesn't mean I'm going to hurt you," I assured her, feeling my pulse pound in my ears from having her here with me.

She let go with a sigh and I removed her top, ignoring her nakedness. Her jeans were next—where I found the dagger she once held at my throat—until she was only in her bra and underwear.

"Give me a minute." I headed into the bathroom, grabbing the supplies I needed to clean her injuries.

I didn't know what the hell got into her tonight, but it left me even more confused on where we stood. One second, she was staring at me with imploring eyes, as if she didn't hate me, and the next she was running out of the museum in fear—an expression I'd never seen on her before.

Irina was staring out the window when I reentered and I stopped in my tracks, watching the shadows of rain droplets dance across her skin.

She appeared so unlike herself in this moment that a fierce longing rooted deep inside me, and I knew that I'd protect this woman even if it meant I had to die in the process.

"I'm not supposed to be here," she said, still gazing at the rainfall.

I walked toward the bed and kneeled in front of her. "I think. . . you're exactly where you need to be."

Opening the first aid kit, I grabbed a cotton swab and soaked it with water before bringing it toward her cut lip.

I could feel the heat of her stare as I cleaned the blood there before grabbing another and doing the same to her cheek and the gashes across her arms and legs.

I finished applying the ointment to her cuts before wrapping them. "They should heal fast with no scarring."

"Take this." She was quiet as I handed her a pill with a glass of water. "It'll help with the body aches."

I set everything on the side table before grabbing a shirt from the drawer.

I cautiously put it over her head and helped her arms through it. She was compliant, and it was off-putting to see her be this docile.

I went down on my haunches, resting my elbows on my knees. "Don't you ever scare me like that again, Irina."

Her silence flared my temper as her eyes turned a deep shade of blue, emotion glossing over them.

"What the fuck were you thinking?" My tone was harsher than intended, but this push and pull between us was maddening.

When I thought she wouldn't answer me, she surprised me by lifting her hand in the space between us.

I stilled, tracking her movement before catching her gaze. Her face was drawn, trepidation flickering across her features. Then she reached toward me hesitantly, caressing my cheek with the tip of her fingers.

"That I wanted to be selfish."

I cupped her hand, flattening her palm against my skin, savoring the gentleness of her touch. "Then *be* selfish."

Her thumb swiped back and forth, soothing the dark depths of my soul.

Thick tension spiked in the air surrounding us as we stayed like this, our eyes locked with intensity.

It was the worst type of torture wanting something you couldn't have.

Her hand slipped from mine, breaking the trance. "I'm not like you."

"What is that supposed to mean?"

"I don't chase dead ends!" Her face hardened as she glowered at me. Long gone was the warmth I saw in her moments ago. "I don't want you, okay? So just *stop*. Stop cornering me. Stop this fixation you have for me. Stop pretending you care. Just stop. It's. . . it's embarrassing."

I narrowed my eyes at her, noticing the slight trembling of her chin, and I couldn't help but laugh humorlessly. "Are you finished?"

If she thought her ill intended words were enough to get me to leave her alone, she was in for a surprise.

Grabbing the covers, I put it over her, confusion washing over her features. She opened her mouth, and I could feel the impending vice of her viperous tongue.

"Don't continue giving me more of your empty words, Irina," I warned. "Shut up and go to sleep."

"You know I can't stay here. If Roman finds out-"

"If he finds out *what*? Weren't you the one who threatened to tell him about us?" I hovered above her, my hands resting on either side of her head. "What happened, *piccola ribelle*? Are you all bark and no bite?"

"There's no *us*."

I wrapped my hand around her throat. "No one can stop me from having you, Irina. Not even you."

Her pulse beat beneath my thumb as I leaned down until we were mere inches apart. "Not even you," I whispered before placing a kiss at the corner of her mouth—right where the cut was—and pulled back, watching the blue in her eyes darken.

Unsaid words danced in every breath she took, and I intended to steal each one until we were interlinked. Until she couldn't erase me from herself.

I stood up and walked to the other side of the bed before sitting down, my back to her.

The silence settled heavily around us, and I knew she was wary of sleeping in unknown territory. It was evident that she was always on edge with how she carried a knife everywhere she went.

"You're safe with me."

I waited for movement or a retort but when I turned my head, Irina's eyes were closed, exhaustion lining her face.

My lips twitched at the sight of her snoozing form.

She could lie to herself, lie to *me*, but her body betrayed her. She trusted me.

I didn't know how much time had passed as I watched her sleep before the first incoherent sound slipped from her lips.

Leaning up, I moved forward, her face twisting as if she were in pain.

She thrashed against the bed; her head tipped up as she whimpered.

I kneeled beside her and touched her face, her skin ice cold.

"*Irina.*"

Her body convulsed; her mouth shut as her face slowly turned into a sickening blue.

Fuck. She was choking.

I grasped her jaw, forcing it open and pushing two fingers to the back of her throat. "Come on, sweetheart. *Breathe*."

Her throat was tight, and she kept sputtering, choking on nothing.

That same helpless panic arose in me, my body tense as her lips lost color.

With my free hand, I squeezed her throat and stuck my fingers further down her throat. "Come on, Irina."

It felt like a damned eternity before her eyes shot open and she gasped.

Relief flooded my system instantly, and I picked her up, wrapping my arms around her.

She coughed against me, clutching my back as if anchoring herself. "Luca?"

"I'm here." I rubbed her back. "I'm here."

She buried her face in the crook of my neck, inhaling deeply as her body trembled.

"How often does this happen?"

She pressed further into me, the beat of her heart clashing against my own.

"Do you want to talk about it?"

Her head shook, and I clenched my teeth.

"I'm holding onto scraps here, Irina."

She leaned back and faced me, her eyes searching mine in dread. "I'm tired, Luca." Her voice wavered. "Can you. . . can you just hold me? Only for tonight. *Please.*"

A disturbing feeling settled in the pit of my stomach.

There was a rawness to her words that put me on high alert. And as I held her in my arms, my mind raced with the possibility that her nightmare wasn't a figment of her imagination, but her reality.

I recalled the night she'd shot that woman in front of me. It had left me curious more than anything how she was capable of killing someone in cold blood. Not that I was any different but with Irina, it only made questions arise.

And I knew there wasn't an ounce of good conscience in me because I should've told Roman that his wife's best friend might be a psychopath, but I kept my mouth shut.

For some fucked up reason, I wanted to unravel Irina's secrets and keep them for myself.

Pieces started to come together, yet the puzzle was distorted and the only way I could figure it out was if Irina fully trusted me.

I nudged under her chin lazily as I said, "You never have to say please, *piccola ribelle.*"

Grabbing her by the waist, I laid us down on the bed. Her amber scent calmed my staggered thoughts as I enveloped her in my embrace.

She clung to me; our bodies entwined beneath the covers, and I could feel warmth seep into her skin again.

"Thank you," she said against my chest, her breathing evening out before she dozed off to sleep.

This time, there was no nightmare.

CHAPTER 17
IRINA

I'd been awake for an hour, wrapped in Luca's warmth.

I watched him sleep, admiring the lines and crevices of his rugged face.

His body was covered in tattoos, starting from his neck, and each design was intricate, weaving around his muscles—a work of art.

An unfamiliar sensation bubbled in the pit of my stomach and, for some unknown reason, I wanted to stay in his embrace.

Was it so wrong for me to want that?

He'd seen me at my worst multiple times and didn't loathe me for it.

And I was selfish when it came to him because I knew he'd break my fall. He'd shown me once that I didn't have to be alone in my pain. And he continued to show me.

A sharp sensation drifted to my chest at the realization that I'd never stood a chance of avoiding him.

I could admit that I'd been malicious toward him, and it came from the wretched parts of my soul where it was hard for me to see the good in others.

I could also admit that he calmed a part of me that I never thought would rest. Every time I was with him, it felt as though the hollowness inside my chest was being stitched anew.

Luca had managed to breach that barrier and take a piece of me for himself.

He was unlike anyone I'd ever met before. As infuriating and maddening as he was, he managed to dig himself into my life without weighing the consequences.

A smile touched my face as I traced his aristocratic nose with my finger. The brute was a heavy sleeper, oblivious to the turmoil happening inside me.

I'd come to figure out that this wasn't a game to him. That I wasn't another object on his board.

Not when he'd cleaned my wounds for the second time.

Not when he accepted my silence for answers.

Not when he brought me back from my nightmares and held me as if he wanted to take my pain away. As if my feelings were valid.

The sting of unshed tears burned the back of my throat as I moved my finger down to his full lips. "The truth is, I do want you, Luca. I know that now," I whispered, knowing he wasn't conscious to hear my words.

I palmed his face, stroking the light stubble underneath. If only I could see those whiskey eyes of his.

Leaning in, I pressed my lips to his, a tear rolling down my cheek. "But you and I can never be."

We're on different sides of the same coin.

Whatever was happening between us had already exceeded to depths I shouldn't have allowed, and I needed to put an end to it.

My father was waiting for me to complete my mission and I'd extended my stay in Italy longer than necessary. I needed to tell Nicolai who he was and leave.

It was better this way, less messy, and the last thing I needed was to be involved in something as complicated as this.

I rose from the bed carefully, reaching for my clothes from last night and hesitated, staring at his leather jacket before grabbing it.

He could get another one.

I took one last look at him and, because I was a masochist, I peered around his room in hopes of understanding him a little better.

His bedroom matched the rest of the house, earthy tones with darker shadings. It was simplistic, unlike himself.

I glanced back at Luca, stretched out across the bed. Life had carved his body into something haunting. Old scars and new covered by shades and lines of ink. Proof of his experience in depravity in some form.

Maybe in the next life, I'd have that time to trace them all.

My throat felt tight as I moved toward the door.

Until we meet again.

It was harder than I thought, sneaking back into Roman's house, but I'd made it into my room without being noticed.

Immediately, I headed into the bathroom, stripped out of my clothes and stood beneath the shower head, rinsing the layer of filth I could never seem to get rid of.

The click of the door sounded, and I didn't need to turn to know it was Aurora. No one else ever came into my room uninvited—except for that one time with Luca.

I touched my lips with my fingertips, remembering the devastating way he kissed me for the first time that night.

"Where have you been?" My best friend's concerned voice echoed in the space.

"What do you mean?" I asked, washing my hair in hopes of avoiding further conversation.

"You didn't come home last night, and Gianna saw you come in this morning."

Shit.

"Didn't know Gianna was a gossiper," I muttered.

"Are you being serious?"

I shrugged. The conversation was taking a turn for the worse, but I couldn't seem to stop myself from instigating it.

What did it matter, anyway? Aurora would hate me after what I'd plan on doing.

I shut the water off and wrapped a towel around myself before stepping out to stand in front of her.

Her eyes widened as concern swept across her features. "What the hell, Rina? Your face!"

My heart dropped; I'd completely forgotten about the cuts.

"What happened?"

"I fell off my bike."

Aurora's eyes turned a deep shade of green as she narrowed them at me. "Really?"

"Yes, *really*." The harder she stared at me; the stronger fury slithered its way up my spine. "What's with the tone?"

"You were out all night. . . " She paused, her head tilting in suspicion. "Why are you being so defensive?"

The air grew tense, and anger brimmed to the surface as we stared at each other with irritation. It was too much. With leaving Luca and Aurora's questioning, I couldn't take it.

"You're overbearing!" I waved my hand in exasperation. "You come in here while I'm naked—might I add—and interrogate me?"

Hurt flashed across her face. "Is that what you think?"

The gaping hole in my chest leaked with pain. My silence was enough of an answer.

"Sorry I give a shit about your whereabouts in a foreign country," she spat out.

"Save the motherly concern for your child."

She stumbled back, her mouth parting as her brows pinched in shock.

I'd gone too far. I regretted the words as soon as they fell from my mouth. "Wait, Aurora, I didn't mean that." I grabbed her wrist when she attempted to leave.

Her face flashed with hurt, eyes full of love, and it killed me. "I worry about you."

"I know, I'm sorry." Leaning down, I placed a kiss on

her baby bump, emotion surging up my throat. "You don't need to worry about me. I promise I'm okay."

I didn't know how to fix something that was meant to be broken, anyway.

CHAPTER 18
LUCA

The inhale of smoke was welcoming as it eased down my throat.

Viktor stared at me with a bored expression, eyeing me as if I was an imbecile.

"I'm heading back to Russia."

"So soon?" I asked, tone laced with sarcasm. The pompous fucker had abused his welcome with no significant work done on his part.

My men reported back to me daily on Viktor's contribution. All they'd gathered was him overlooking the shipments and products, which shouldn't have elicited a long stay. It was odd.

"I've seen what I needed to."

I narrowed my eyes at him, swiping the cigarette along my lips. "Which was?"

His calculated gaze settled on me with an iciness that would've had an ordinary person clawing at their skin. "When I meet with the *Pakhan*, you'll hear from me."

"I look forward to it." I threw the stick on the ground and crushed it beneath my boot. "We wouldn't want to complicate matters, now would we?"

Viktor approached me, removing the glove from his right hand. "Not at all." He extended his arm, a callous smirk ghosting across his mouth. "Pleasure doing business with you, Luca Canaveri."

I clasped his hand and shook it, catching sight of the tattoo on his wrist. "Is that a Bratva thing?" I stared at the intricate triangle design on his wrist. It was unlike anything I'd ever seen before.

Viktor snatched his hand away. "Thing?" he asked venomously. "Those of us who are in respectable positions receive these." He shook his head in what appeared to be annoyance before stalking off toward his car.

Not only was he an asshole, but a sensitive one at that. I'd rather swallow shards of glass than work with him.

Good fucking riddance.

I typed against the keyboard harder than necessary, staring at the multiple monitors in front of me.

I delved into work, trying to fight the urge to go to Irina and choke the fuck out of her for making me feel this way.

It was wishful thinking that I'd wake up this morning to find her nestled in my arms, but this was Irina. She ran away every *single* time.

The start of a raging headache burst at the back of my head from the difficulty it was in figuring her out. Every time I thought I was close to doing so; I was left even more confused.

I sighed, feeling a pang in my chest because I missed her, anyway. I missed her when she was gone, and I missed her when she was with me.

It was fucking absurd.

And so was taking out her gun from my desk—the one she'd dropped that day in the locker room—and caressing it as if it was her.

I leaned back in my chair, a grin plastered on my face recalling how she shot the random woman who tried seducing me.

And my little rebel said she wasn't jealous. If I was a psychopath, as she liked to call me, then she was equally delusional.

I traced the lines of the barrel, feeling the grooves beneath my fingertips.

Irina was athletic from what I had seen and sure it wasn't odd that she knew how to use a gun either, but killing someone without hesitation? That was something else entirely.

There was more to her than being an attorney from New York, and I wondered if she was only fooling me or everyone around her.

The Irina I saw when she was with me wasn't the same Irina I saw when she was with the others. And a gut feeling told me it wasn't her dislike for me. . . no, we were way past that.

As I threw the gun on the desk, it hit the edge and fell to the floor, the bullets sprawling everywhere.

I leaned down and picked one up, my brows furrowing as I brought the solid piece of copper closer.

There was a tiny symbol engraved on it and-

What the actual fuck.

An unsettling sensation took root in the pit of my stomach as I stared at the intricate triangle carved on the side.

The same mark I saw on Viktor's wrist.

My blood ran cold as the pieces finally came together until the full picture flashed before my eyes.

A tsunami of emotions raged inside my chest as I sat back, the steady beat of my heart becoming erratic.

What have you done, Irina?

CHAPTER 19
TRINA

I couldn't prolong the inevitable.

It was midday when I walked down the pathway of the backyard and toward Nico's.

I'd learned that he didn't live in the house like I expected but in the shed out back.

The cold air didn't do anything to dull the nauseous heat spreading from my chest.

I was going into this conversation blindly, but instinct told me that my brother would hear me out. He wasn't hot headed and irrational like most men in our world. I could trust him.

I knocked on the wooden door twice before stepping back, fidgeting in place. It was unusual for me to be this nervous. I'd been in situations less comfortable, yet *this* had me more tense.

But the difference was my heart was on the line.

This was the first time I'd let someone see how damaged it was.

Lies. Luca saw it and you ran.

My throat tightened as my subconscious screamed at me to turn around.

I was torn, the weight of my responsibility crushing me beneath gravity.

It was then that the door creaked open, pulling me from my thoughts as a composed Nicolai appeared on the other side.

His smile lasted all of a second before it dropped. "Why do you appear frightened?"

I blinked in uncertainty, anxiety rippling off me in waves.

"Can I come in?"

He nodded and opened the door wider.

I walked into the small space, the shed a replica of the main house. It was tidy and didn't feel as warm.

I took a seat on the black leather couch, linking my fingers together.

"Are you hurt?" My brother asked, seating himself beside me.

"No."

"Are you here to accompany your misery again?" The side of his mouth lifted in a grin.

I choked out a laugh because that couldn't be closer to the truth. "Something like that."

He waited for me to continue, pushing his glasses up with the tip of his finger.

Nerves wound tight around me as I tried breathing through my next words. "I need to tell you something."

"What is it?"

"I don't even know how to say it," I admitted.

If my father knew I geared off track and exposed myself to Nicolai this way, he'd see it as a betrayal.

And maybe I was naïve and blind for believing that I was doing the right thing, but I was *tired.*

For once in my life, I wanted something for myself.

"You can trust me, Irina." His brown eyes were warm as he gazed at me with care.

"It's. . . it's about your father." The stillness after I uttered those words created a pressure in my ears until all I could hear was the thump of my heart.

"My father?" A darkness shrouded him, his face icing over in swiftness.

"Roman told me he's dead." I shook my head, my heart ready to come up my throat. "But that's not true."

"I don't have a father," his voice roughed.

"Nicolai. . ."

"You don't know what you're talking about." He stood abruptly, his hand raising toward me in defensiveness. "How would you even know that?"

I stood along with him, my body slightly trembling as I grabbed my chest in hopes of stopping the constant pain residing there.

Time ceased as we stared at one another.

His face appeared agonized, turning a pale color, while mine fell in sadness, eyes watering.

"Look at me," I whispered, as if that answered his question. "I know you see the resemblance."

He shook his head, eyes pinched shut, and I knew he was fighting internally. "No."

"Nicolai. . ."

"No."

"I'm your sister."

As if my words gutted him, he stumbled back, gazing at me in bewilderment.

"No!" I took a step toward him before his hand shot up again, stopping me from coming closer. "Don't."

"Nicolai, *please*," I whispered, his rejection stinging. "Let me explain."

"Explain what?" he spat out. "This sick joke?"

"I would *never* do that to you."

"How would I know?" he raged on, his eyes rounding in a viciousness I'd never seen on him before. "You're a fucking stranger to me!"

The scabbed wound inside my chest split open, blood rushing out and threatening to consume me—drown me in its misery.

It was hard to swallow that pill and put myself in his shoes. I understood his reaction, but I didn't think it'd be like this. He was cruel and nothing like the man I'd come to know.

"I don't want to be strangers anymore." My eyes darted between his brown ones. "Hear me out, and if you want me to leave afterward, I will."

The lies piled up, and it sickened me. If Nicolai didn't accept to come with me willingly, I had to resort to less pleasant methods and I really didn't want to do that.

His silence was my cue to continue, even though that was the worst thing he could've done.

He'd told me I could trust him, but now I wasn't sure if I could. Problematic outcomes whirled through my mind as I collected my thoughts.

But I was *exhausted*. I didn't want to continue

pretending and lying when this was the one chance I had at convincing him I only wanted to make up for our lost time.

I wanted a family.

"I know I'm in no position of asking this of you, but I need you to promise me that this stays between us."

"I can't d-."

"Promise me," I enunciated, my face stiffening with urgency.

Nicolai must've seen the desperation written on my face because he sighed and sat down again with his elbows resting on his knees.

The fabric had become thin and worn. There was no use in prolonging the tear.

"You're heir to the Bratva. The next *Pakha*n."

Tension rose in the cold room as his face hardened.

I stilled, expecting a flicker of his surprise, but he was stoic, his eyes glazed over in wrath.

My mouth parted as shock coursed through me. "You knew."

The muscle in his jaw pulsed as he scathed me with his gaze. "How come no one knows that the *Pakhan* has a daughter?"

I pulled the side of my jeans down slightly and showed him the triangle tattoo on my hip. "It was safer to keep me hidden."

"Safer for who?"

I remained silent. He was tearing me apart with his words, and I couldn't do anything but take it.

"So, you're one of them."

One of them.

I looked ahead, unwilling to meet his eyes. His tone of voice had a tinge of judgment in it, and I couldn't handle it if I saw that crossing his face. Not from him. "Yes."

"Does Roman know? Does *Aurora* know?"

I swallowed the bile threatening to rise at the mention of my best friend's name. "No."

"Wow," Nicolai scoffed. "You truly have everyone fooled."

The ache in my chest bloomed with fury as I flicked my attention to him, a burning sensation ripping my flesh. "Don't judge me when you don't know a *single* thing about the sacrifices I've made. The moment I found out about you. . . " I paused, my lips trembling. "I felt hope. A spark of something I hadn't experienced in a very long time." I blinked away the unshed tears, continuing to bare myself. I couldn't contain the torture anymore. "I was determined to meet you. A brother I'd lost enough time with."

"Irina. . . "

"No, let me finish. I know this is hard for you. I do," I choked, my eyes glossing over further. "But would it be so bad to accept me as your sister? To get to know me? We all have flaws, but I would love you for yours."

Nicolai watched me, his expression softening back into what I'd come to know. But I could see the speck of hesitancy swirling in his chocolate brown eyes as he regarded me.

"No, it wouldn't," he said in sadness. "But I can't. You're our father's daughter and he's not someone I wish to know."

If my heart wasn't broken already, it would've happened in this moment.

"What are you saying, then?"

"What do you want from me, Irina?" he asked exasperatedly. "Do you expect me to pick up my life and move to Russia to become the next *Pakhan*? To carry *his* name when he couldn't have been bothered to find me after all these years. To have saved me from what I endured as a child!"

His voice grew louder with each word, each one a whip on my skin from how tormented he appeared.

One day, I'd know his story—his past. I only hoped he would give us that time.

The word yes was on the tip of my tongue, if only to serve my own selfishness. If he went, I'd go with him. I wouldn't leave him alone.

The small chance of succeeding in persuading him to come with me had become nonexistent.

In a final attempt, I made a decision.

"I can't change the past, Nicolai or our fathers' actions and for that, I am sorry."

He removed his glasses and raked a hand across his face, causing his blond hair to become unruly.

"But I'm leaving Italy in two days. If you decide to seek answers about who you are, come with me."

"I thought you were staying until Aurora's birth?"

"I can't."

A quietness settled over us and if I stayed in this suffocating space of unsaid words, it'd consume me.

"You'll always be my brother. . . Nico."

I was nearly out the door when his soft voice reached me.

"Thank you for finding me."

I sat in Aurora's study with her and Roman, sipping on tea as I broke the news to them that I was leaving tomorrow.

"You know you aren't a burden to us," Aurora reassured me.

I smiled at her warmly, squeezing her hand. "I know. But it's time for me to figure out my life."

"Well, we'll be waiting for you when our little one is born," Roman chimed in, his gaze flicking to me in what could only be described as affinity. "I'm sure he'd love to meet his aunt."

These two had become the closest thing to a real family for me and here I was tarnishing it.

"I'd really love to meet him too," I whispered, emotion thick in my throat. But the chances of that were slim to none when I'd have to force Nicolai in coming to Russia.

I hadn't told my father that this mission had failed, but I knew once I did, he'd be more ruthless in getting him back.

War was on the horizon, just like Viktor had said.

"I think we should throw a farewell dinner and invite everyone." Aurora became giddy, and I laughed at her sudden appreciation for extravagant parties. She loved spending her husband's money, and he loved showering her with it.

"That's not necessary."

I didn't want to face Luca, even though a part of me was disappointed that he hadn't sought me out after that night he held me as if I was the most important thing to him.

"It is," Aurora sang, reaching over and hugging me, her cinnamon scent reminding me of home. "When it's for my favorite friend."

"Oh?" I drawled. "Who are these other friends you have?"

"I'd like to know too," Roman said, a spark of mischievousness roaming in his obsidian eyes as he stared at his wife. "Might give them a personal visit to become acquainted with my gun."

"Roman!" Her tone was stern, but her lips twitched in amusement. "You are becoming a father soon."

"And?"

"And I won't have you talking like a madman."

"One can only hope our son takes after me."

"God save whatever poor soul ends up with him if that happens," I mused.

"I mean, you're his aunt so I can agree with that statement," Roman shot back and continued the bickering between the three of us.

My chest ached from the affection pouring into the room and it *hurt*.

"Touché." I stood from the leather chair and smoothed my sweaty palms over my jeans. "Uh, I better go pack."

They both nodded and continued their conversation as I slipped out of the study.

Instead of going to my room, I walked out the back and made my way down to the gazebo.

The air was warmer tonight, the perfect weather to wind down and collect my thoughts. My life had always been a constant chaos, and it felt as if the air I was breathing was toxic, slowly killing me. For once, I just wanted to breathe a lungful of air that made me want to live again.

Time passed as I sat in the same position on one of the wicker chairs. The sun set until it was pitch black, the only light source coming from the one above me.

A flicker of movement in the darkness stole my attention and I surged up.

"That's it then? You were going to leave without telling me?" Luca's voice reached me before he did, and I nearly lost balance from the sheer power of his tone.

He came inside the gazebo and set his daunting caramel eyes on me. The energy he exuded was downright terrifying, and it didn't help that I was already on edge.

"We don't owe each other anything," I muttered, holding my ground.

He chuckled, shaking his head but the sound raked across my skin as if to tell me he didn't believe my lie.

I watched as he reached for the ropes around the gazebo's curtains and untied it, letting it drape around one side.

"I'm curious. How many people know about you?"

His question left me confused and his motive to this conversation even more confused.

"Your skill set in lying is quite impressive, and it took me a while to figure you out." He chuckled again, undoing the second set of ropes as my heart pounded in my chest.

"And what did you figure out?" I asked hoarsely.

He undid the third set.

"That you serve the Bratva."

My knees nearly buckled at that while my heart skipped a beat or two.

Had Nicolai told him? No, that couldn't be right. Not only did he promise me, Roman would've already raised hell on me.

Luca was a resourceful man and whatever information he'd gathered to come to this conclusion had led him to the right one.

"I have to admit, sulking over your gun because it reminded me of you was quite pathetic of me." His hands caressed the final curtains aimlessly as if he was in deep thought. "But it did lead me to this." He threw something my way, and I caught it midair.

I opened my palm and found a small bullet. My confusion grew until I peered closer and my stomach dropped.

It had the Bratva's mark. Those of us in higher positions had access to them and they were used to make a bold statement or send a message to the opposition. I was not only stupid enough to have used it in a fit of rage but dropped my gun in the process. Right into Luca's hands.

There was no point in lying when the proof was staring at me in the face. It only made me wonder why Luca came to me instead of informing the others.

"What are you going to do about it?"

Luca turned and caught my eyes, the look on his face feral. "What I should've done months ago."

He undid the final set of ropes, the curtains hiding us from the outside world.

I swallowed the lump that had suddenly formed in my throat. Without thought, I took a step back, shaking my head at him slowly.

It wasn't hard to figure out what the dangerous gleam in his eyes meant.

He tracked my movements, leisurely sweeping his gaze over me before chuckling darkly, rubbing his jaw with a tatted hand.

My heart raced, the anticipation of his next move leaving me panting.

Like a predator he walked toward me, causing me to take another step back until I was pressed against the gazebo's border, sweat forming at the base of my neck.

"What happened, *piccola ribelle*? Not so brazen anymore?"

The push and pull between us had become potent. Each step he took in my direction increased the intensity of my unwarranted desire.

"Come closer and I'll rectify that."

"Are you going to hurt me, Irina?" His bottom lip curled between his teeth and the darkness in his eyes rooted me in place. "Although, I never minded mixing pain with pleasure."

I'd been too lost in his heated trance that I hadn't even noticed him invade my space, swiping my blade from the leather jacket I stole from him.

"The question is, do you?" he rasped out, swinging the knife between his fingers, admiring the weapon like a psychopath. "Guess, we'll find out."

His intention was clear as he flicked his gaze to me again before he curled a fist around my shirt.

"Wait—"

He was skilled, words dying in my throat as he cut my

shirt down the middle rapidly, the sound tearing along with my sanity.

The night breeze hit my exposed chest, eliciting goosebumps along my body.

Luca hummed in satisfaction as he used the blade to part one side of the fabric, baring me to his gaze. He ran the sharp end of it against my skin, the sensation causing me to hiss.

The brute smirked, his presence overwhelming me.

I feared that if I gave into this, I'd never recover. It was bad enough I'd already lost this game between us and fell for his charm. I actually *liked* the man.

But I wasn't really putting up a fight to escape him, was I?

Rolling my shoulders back, I let the jacket fall from my body, my intent clear.

His gaze snapped to mine, his nose flaring from contained wantonness. I could see it written on his face, that control he was trying to keep intact, but I wanted him raw and untamed.

"Not so brazen anymore?" I teased, arching a brow in challenge.

His tongue slid against his bottom lip as he shook his head, his eyes piercing into me. If it weren't for my attentive gaze to his every move, I would've missed it.

"How will you have me then, Irina?" he asked, his voice a deep caress to my every nerve.

With a shaky exhale, I whispered, "Naked."

When Luca reached for the back of his shirt with one hand and pulled it off, I nearly fell to my knees at his physique. I'd seen him shirtless before, but it didn't take away from how breathtaking he was. There was beauty in his every scar.

I slipped of my own torn shirt, letting it fall at my feet along with his.

My chest heaved at the electric current running up my spine. He stared at me as if he wanted to devour me whole until there was nothing left.

With his eyes locked on mine, he undid his belt, the clanking sound of it heightening every sensation spiraling through me.

As his pants hung open, he tilted his head, waiting for me to remove my next piece of clothing.

But he was cheating. And we both knew it.

Narrowing my eyes at him, I hooked my thumbs in both my underwear and pants before sliding them off.

His sharp intake of breath was all the confirmation I needed to know I played this game better than he did.

But his patience ran thin as he muttered, "Fuck it." And lunged for me faster than I could blink.

His chest collided against me as his lips fell upon mine. It wasn't harsh or rushed as I had expected.

He took his time kissing me, as if I was the air that he needed to breathe. Every flick of his tongue against mine was in desperation, his grip on my lower back tightening my stomach into knots.

With my hand against his hard chest, I let it slide down his torso, feeling his warm skin burn me from the inside.

He continued to tease my flesh, nipping, sucking and biting until my head felt heavy from the taste of him.

It was too much. He was everywhere, seeping deep into my bones and igniting an inferno of emotions.

I moved my hand further down, his muscles flexing with every brush.

There was something about the way he reacted to me that drove me insane. It was addicting, my entire being needing more of it.

A squeal ripped from my throat when he lifted me and laid me flat on the marble table. My heart thumped against my chest as I propped myself on my elbows.

Luca stood back, running his gaze down my body possessively, his eyes blazing with pure and wild hunger.

It was torture, this slow ripple of suspense that made my skin spark.

"*Luca,*" I breathed, my voice dripping with a longing I didn't know it was capable of.

A sick part of me loved his dominance. He made me crave his attention and instead of being ashamed to submit to it, I felt empowered.

"I'm going to make you forget about every man that has ever known what you've felt like."

And he did.

We stayed in the gazebo until a sliver of energy came back to our limbs.

His hand caressed my hip, his thumb digging against my tattoo—the same mark on the bullet. "You must be held in high regard," he murmured against the crevice of my neck.

"What?"

He pulled away from me before grabbing his shirt. "Your tattoo. Viktor told me the meaning."

My heart dropped to my stomach at the mention of his name. How could I have forgotten that they'd met, putting me in a dangerous position.

Luca handed me my clothes, eyeing me curiously. "You know him? He's got the same tattoo on his hand."

I recalled the past conversations I'd had with my cousin before answering him. "He's our exporter," I lied. "How do you know him?"

He had no right to question me, but I had to tread carefully to avoid giving an unwarranted reaction or it'd make me sound defensive.

"You're telling me that you didn't know he was in Italy?" He worked on buckling his belt as he tracked my movements. "He was here for business."

"No, I didn't." Another lie. "We all have our own tasks to focus on."

"And what does that entail for you?"

My chest tightened as I put my shirt on slowly, giving myself time to think.

"Data."

He hummed and leaned against the table as he crossed his arms and set his attention on me.

Shoving my legs through my jeans, I briskly added. "I need you to keep this to yourself."

"Why?"

"Aurora doesn't know and I'm not ready to tell her."

"I doubt it'd hinder your friendship."

If only you knew the truth, you'd think otherwise.

I stepped toward him; his face leveled to mine now that he was perched on the table, making it easier for him to see how serious I was when I said, "This stays between us."

He tilted his head, reaching for me. "Is that why you've been pushing me away?"

My hands settled on his shoulders and the intensity of his expression had me leaning further into his embrace, inhaling his familiar scent of musk and smoke.

I couldn't answer him without falling apart. Lie after lie yet the answer to that question would always be yes. It didn't matter if he didn't know the reason.

He gripped my chin between his fingers. "What did I tell you before." His voice carried a dark edge to it, sinking deep into my soul. "No one can stop me from having you, Irina. Not even you."

CHAPTER 20
LUCA

Aurora's name lit up my phone which meant one of two things: she was going to yell at me for who knows what or it was Roman trying to reach me.

"Where are you?" she asked when I answered, and I could picture her green eyes narrowing in agitation.

"And here I thought you were the nice one," I mused, staring at my father's limp body. I'd come to *visit* him again and the sight of his bloodied face brought me pure joy. Courtesy of your one and only.

"Maybe if you weren't late for dinner, I'd still be *the nice one.*"

Right, the goodbye dinner for Irina. A farewell I had no intention being a part of because she wasn't leaving. I wouldn't let her.

"I'm on my way." I sighed before hanging up.

I set the bottle of wine on the kitchen island in front of Aurora as she feigned annoyance.

"A peace offering for being late." I smiled at her, knowing she could never stay mad at me. Honestly, I think she's always been one for dramatics, so I play the part to keep her happy.

Ever since she came into our lives, she's been a light, more so because of her ability to tame the beast, as in her husband.

"You're lucky it's white and not red." She snatched the bottle and put it in the fridge to chill.

"You traumatized me the last time I brought red."

The sound of her chuckling came out playful as she peered at me. "You were scared, huh?"

"*Terrified,*" I joked, bulging my eyes for theatrics.

"Well, take your terror into the dining room. Everyone is already seated."

"Will Enzo be here tonight? I haven't seen him around lately."

Her smile faded as she planted her hands on the kitchen island. "He's not doing well with Sofia being in rehab."

I nodded my head in understanding. It wasn't a secret that Sofia was unwell—had been for a while now. And that Enzo had become a shell of a ghost because of it.

We only hoped that whatever it was, they'd get through it.

"I'll check up on him when I can."

"Thanks, Luca." The green in her eyes dampened into a forest hue. "He'll be happy to see you."

After a few minutes of helping her around in the kitchen, we joined the others.

Irina was to my left, her presence so beautiful, I couldn't help but rest my hand on her thigh. Touching her was never enough, I'd always craved more and *more.*

Her face turned a light shade of pink as I moved my hand further up her thigh, my fingers resting in between.

Memories of last night resurfaced, and I had no doubt that she was doing the same.

Roman stood abruptly, his chair scratching against the floor and catching our attention.

"A toast to Irina," he said, holding his glass up, a dark aura radiating from him. As he walked around the table, I tracked his movements with suspicion until he stood behind her. In swift motion, he held a gun to the back of her head. "For being a fucking liar."

The room stilled, the air thickening with tension as all sounds ceased.

It was on instinct—a reflex as I stood and pulled out my own gun and held it to Roman's head. "Put your gun down, brother."

A flicker of dismay and surprise crossed his features before it hardened into anger. "She means nothing to you."

And that was all it took for my composure to shatter. "She means *everything* to me." I breathed hard as adrenaline coursed through my veins. "She *is* everything."

We stared at each other as understanding dawned on him. He didn't have to say it for me to feel the void of my betrayal.

"I invited you into my home and accepted you as family." He removed his attention from me, speaking directly to Irina as she stayed seated. "Only for you to manipulate us like the snake you turned out to be."

"Roman," I warned. He was my best friend, but I wouldn't allow him to speak to Irina with that tone.

"Shut up, Luca," he seethed, his body rigid. "This is none of your business."

"Put your guns down," Aurora demanded in distress, rounding the table to where we stood. "*Please*."

Nicolai surprised me by standing from his seat and inserting himself between Irina and Roman. "Not here. . . " Pain marred his features as he looked at him almost pleadingly.

Irina tilted her head to the side—uncaring of being held at gunpoint—and peered at our youngest member. "You broke our promise?" And the hurt in her voice was enough for me to feel a fiery rage settle in my bones.

Nico didn't meet her gaze, and I was at a loss for what had conspired between them and this *promise*.

"Someone tell me what the hell is going on." Aurora's voice came out strained. "Right now!"

"Don't do this." Irina peered at Aurora, but her words were directed at Roman. "She's *pregnant*."

The tension in the room was scathing, and it was stretching thin, on the verge of snapping.

"Tell her." Two words from Roman, carrying underlying steel as he pressed the end of his gun further into her scalp.

Irina's face portrayed an internal war as her gaze flicked to me and I didn't think she realized that her eyes were searching mine for comfort.

As if she knew the predicament we found ourselves in, she shook her head in defeat and my heart pinched tightly.

"I'm the daughter of Ivan Morozov," she whispered, averting her eyes from me. "The *Pakhan's* daughter."

My blood ran cold in disbelief as I stumbled back. That was impossible.

"And Nicolai is my brother."

There was a ringing noise blaring in my ears as we all stood stunned by her words.

Irina being the daughter of the Bratva's leader was one thing but Nicolai being her brother. . . that was catastrophic.

It suddenly made sense why Roman appeared to be a second away from pulling the trigger.

She wasn't in Italy to visit her best friend; she was here to take Nicolai away.

Everything she told me was a lie, and I fell for it.

"Tell me one good reason why I shouldn't spill your disgusting blood across my table." Roman asked.

I pulled the safety off my gun, the sound powerful. "You do that and yours will follow."

I hated Irina in this moment because even though she played me like a fool, I would always carry this burning need to protect her.

"I told you to stay away from her, Luca." His eyes had turned a dark shade of midnight, a brutal current blazing in them. "And now you're defending a traitor."

"You don't order me around." I shook my head, fury rippling in my veins. "Not when it comes to her."

Aurora wrapped her hand around his biceps, urging

him to calm down. "There must be some sort of explanation to all of this."

Irina eye's glossed over in an ocean blue as she watched her best friend defend her even now when she'd hidden her true identity.

If I knew anything about this woman, it was her love for Aurora, and I knew it must've killed her keeping this secret from her.

"What explanation, *anima mia?* She's a fraud who tried and failed to take away my so-" He paused, closing his eyes as the muscle in his jaw worked. "Nicolai."

"Irina." Aurora gazed at her, tears streaming down her face as she shook her head in bewilderment. *"Why?"*

"I'm sorry for lying to you but I won't apologize for who I am," she stated before turning to face Roman, the end of his gun now pressing against her forehead. "This is your one and only chance to kill me."

I stared between the two of them, my skin buzzing from uncertainty. I swear if he pulled that trigger. . .

"If you don't, you're going to wish you had."

Aurora stepped back as if she'd been slapped in the face. I could see the perplexed look in her features as she saw a side of Irina she hadn't seen before.

This was Irina Morozov, daughter of the *Pakhan*.

Nico was the one who interjected and held a firm grip on the gun, pushing it away from her head. "She's my sister. Please, Roman."

The air became dense as the minutes ticked by before Roman spoke again. "Get her off my property."

Irina didn't waste a second before she stalked out of the dining room and disappeared.

If she thought this was how we'd part ways, she was fucking delusional.

I took a few steps in the direction she left in before Roman's voice boomed in the air. "If you follow her, we're no longer brothers."

His words hung in the air between us, our impending downfall.

There was a calm that had settled within me, and I knew there was no turning back from this.

It was pouring when I stepped outside, the rain seeping through my clothes in seconds.

I spotted Irina shutting the trunk of her car before making her way to the driver's side.

As she reached for the handle of the door, I slapped my palm against it to stop her from opening it.

"What about us?" I asked, my voice nearly drowned out by the rain pattering against the pavement.

She stilled; her blonde hair plastered against her back.

"I don't care about any of it. Whose daughter you are or what you've done. None of it matters to me," I pushed, willing her to meet my gaze. "I'd raise hell for you if it meant you were mine."

My chest hurt from how hard it was pounding. If she left, I had a feeling she'd take my heart with her.

"You've completely and utterly ruined me, Irina."

Her sharp intake of breath was emphasized by the first strike of thunder.

I stepped around, my own breathing growing erratic as I cupped her delicate face in between my hands and rested my forehead against hers. "*I* am yours."

The storm continued to pick up speed, cooling the heat radiating off me.

Her face was distraught, piercing blue eyes darting between mine in helplessness. She curled her fingers around my wrists and squeezed. "But *I* am not yours, Luca."

My heart skidded to a stop as I nodded my head. "You are."

"Do you hear yourself?" She laughed cruelly, pulling back but still holding onto me. "You sound crazy."

"You've made me crazy!" I blazed at her, tilting her head up to cement that into her brain. "You drive me insane with your denial and your *fucking* lies."

"Then what would you like me to say?" She squinted against the unforgiving rain. "We fucked once, and it meant nothing. *We* are nothing."

"You're deflecting. It was more than that and you know it."

She'd been vulnerable with me and trusted me with her pain. And even though she was lying again, the bite of her words sank deep into my skin.

"Am I? Or are you too dense to not know when someone doesn't want you." Her mouth pursed as if contemplating her next words.

She completely stepped away from my embrace, her eyes frosting over in malice as she regarded me, and it felt as if a part of me disintegrated.

"Your own father didn't want you, littering your body with scars to prove it."

Thunder reverberated in the distance as a tender pang

struck me. I stumbled back, my face slacking as her words pierced me.

I'd never taken any of her viciousness to heart, but this? This was *cruel*. I'd opened up to her about my past and she used it against me, plunging a knife so deep into my chest, I felt it mold into every crevice.

There weren't any words left in me to give her, none that would change her mind and make her understand that it didn't have to be this way.

With one last glance in her direction, I walked away. I was done chasing after her when all she did was string me along.

If she ached for me as intensely as I did for her, she would come to me.

This time I wouldn't be the one to pursue her.

CHAPTER 21
IRINA

The cold rain intensified the hollowness inside my chest.

Watching Luca walk away from me had felt like a million shards of glass cutting me open, my blood pouring onto the pavement of where he once stood.

It didn't matter how badly I wanted the outcome to be different. It was meant to be this way. I was only stupid enough to grasp onto a string of hope that was never strong enough to hold us both.

With everything that I had experienced in my life, this was the first time I regretted being associated with the Morozov last name.

My chest ached with grief, but it was different this time. This ache was rough as sandpaper, grating against my heart until I thought I might wither away from agony.

Clutching my shirt to ease the crippling pain, I dragged myself inside the car.

The rush of emotion brimmed to the surface until the dam broke.

Why did it have to be *him* who *saw* me? No one had ever taken the time to see beyond the superficial parts of me. And Luca might've not understood the reasons of why I was this way, but he never made me feel less than because of it.

He didn't know the effect he had on me when he held me, healing wounds I thought would never be sealed.

I'd always looked after myself but with him. . . when he was near me, it felt as if I didn't need to hold myself together because deep down, I knew he'd catch my fall.

His presence brought me comfort, I realized, and I'd single-handedly ruined that.

Tears spilled down my cheeks as I reversed the car and drove away.

Luca and I never had a fair chance. He was the first man I wanted, but he'd never be mine.

He'd been hurt in ways I couldn't imagine, shared that with me when I'd given him no reason to, and I'd used it against him.

I knew it was the only way to push him away from me, but I'd cut myself open in the process.

Another piercing cry fell from my lips as I remembered the way he looked at me after. As if he truly hadn't expected me to say those words. As if every menacing thing I'd ever said to him wasn't an indication that I would.

He had given up on me, exactly what I wanted. But if that was true, why did the hollowness inside my chest expand with a throbbing dullness I couldn't get rid of since he walked away.

I was a terrible person. The kind who tainted everything around them because deep down I knew it was easier to be alone than to let someone see how damaged I truly was.

I'd already accepted my fate and giving myself up to Luca would disrupt that. This was bigger than the both of us, and I'd been burned too many times to fight against it.

I was Irina Morozov.

Daughter of the *Pakhan*.

Trapped.

A raw scream tore from my throat as I continued sobbing in the confined space, suffocating in my own rot.

This *thing* inside of me was poisonous, my impending death on the horizon if I allowed it to swallow me whole.

I pounded my fist against the steering wheel as tears streaked down my face, my vision blurring.

The rain pattered harshly against the front window, making it harder to see, but I soaked it in, wishing I could've blurred the image of Luca walking away from me instead.

I felt his presence all around me; in the air I breathed, the skin he touched, the mark he unknowingly left on my broken heart.

He was everywhere.

The sound of my phone rung in the air, causing me to jerk my head toward the dashboard where Viktor's name flashed.

I swallowed the hurt from my voice and answered. "I'm coming to Russia. Alone."

"Long overdue. I'll tell your father you've failed." The lift in his voice was evident, and I knew he was satisfied with this turn of events. "I told you war was on the horizon."

My throat burned with the need to wreak havoc on him, but words caught in my throat as a car came straight at me, the lights blinding me as it sped closer.

All I could do was scream as I shifted the starring wheel, unable to see anything from the rain, tears, and lights.

It all happened so fast. One second, I was swerving to avoid the oncoming car and the next my body jolted forward from the unexpected impact.

All the blood in my body rushed to my head as I coughed, spots forming in my vision. Adrenaline pumped in my veins, my heart racing from the position I was in.

Breathing through my nose, I tried staying calm as I removed my seatbelt and laid my palms flat against the roof to push myself up. My efforts rendered useless. I was stuck.

With a frustrated grunt, I looked through the broken window in hopes of getting help.

All I could see were trees and rain fogging the gloomy air.

Anxiety gripped me in a vise, and I realized I wasn't ready to die yet. Regret sliced me in half with so much I wanted to say.

I punched the roof with my fists. "Help!"

After a few seconds, headlights flickered, catching my attention and I squinted until I'd made out a tall figure running toward me. It was hard to see their face when my car was flipped over but pale blond hair stuck out to me. My heart beat wildly against my chest.

"Nico!" I called out for him, tears spilling from my eyes as relief washed over me. *He'd come after me.*

"I'm com-" His sentence went unfinished as he stopped running, his body motionless for a moment before dropping to the ground.

A violent scream tore from my chest as I watched a masked man stand above my brother's fallen form, his hand swinging around a baseball bat.

Panic seized me, my skin vibrating with the need to escape when he lifted his head, watching me.

Confusion and fear twisted my insides as the man took slow strides toward me, as if he wanted to prolong whatever he had planned for me.

Sweat ran down my forehead as I thrashed carelessly, urging my body to free itself, but he'd already reached me, his boots the only thing visible outside the window.

I held my breath when he didn't move, my throat burning from the urge to scream, but I clamped my lips shut. I'd never give anyone the satisfaction, not even if death stared at me in the face.

Gravel crunched beneath his shoes as he went down on his haunches, his hands dangling between his legs.

Anticipation of his next move swirled thickly in the air. Slowly, he tilted his head down until I could see his covered face, his gaze cold as it landed on me.

When he reached for me, my arms went flying, anywhere I could hit him, but his intention wasn't clear until his free hand clamped over my mouth, soft fabric caressing my skin.

My eyes widened for a second as a distinct odor invaded my nose before I felt myself drift away.

The surrounding air was stiff as I gained consciousness. My head was heavy, pounding profusely, which made it harder to gain clarity.

With weighted limbs, I moved my body slowly, something biting into my skin from the action.

I blinked rapidly as everything came crashing down on me. *The fight. The crash. Nico.*

With suddenness, my eyes shot open, my senses heightening from renewed adrenaline as I peered around my surroundings.

There was nothing in the small room to indicate where I was. Only stained concrete and yellow walls.

Cold fear sank down in the pit of my stomach when I saw Nicolai across the room from me. His body was slack in a chair with his bloody head lolled to the side.

I pulled against the thick chains covering me. But with my wrists bound behind my back and my feet knit together, my movements were restricted.

"*Nicolai,*" I said sharply, hoping I could wake him. He'd been hit in the head, and I knew him being unconscious wouldn't be of use to either of us.

After a few minutes of calling his name, he finally stirred, his brown eyes unfocused before they set on me. It only took one glance in my direction before he leaped forward, as if he could somehow reach me despite being restrained.

It was then that I noticed the chairs we were held in were cemented onto the floor. *Shit.*

"Are you hurt?" my brother asked, looking over me with his brows furrowed.

I shook my head. "Your head. . . we need to get you help."

For the next minute, I watched as he exerted energy into trying to break free, but with a frustrated grunt, he looked up at the ceiling.

"Don't worry," he said. "I'm going to get us out of here."

"How?"

"Trust me."

I scoffed, anger surfacing within me. "I did once and look where it got me."

He caught my gaze from across the room, his hair disheveled across his worried forehead. "I didn't know. . . "

"Didn't know that Roman would hold a gun to my head?" I asked, venom laced in my tone. "Me either."

Silence fell upon us, and it would've been calming if it hadn't been for the eeriness of our situation.

"What would you have wanted me to do, Irina?" I could hear the bite in his words. "You think I don't *want* to know my own sister? I know what it's like to be without a family, but I couldn't get up and leave Roman. Not when he's been the only family I've known since I was twelve."

My throat tightened from all the emotions pulsing along my body, and I hated it.

I hated it because I knew I couldn't fault him for telling Roman. It hurt that he couldn't give me the same courtesy of trusting me, but Nicolai was young and tortured. We might share the same biological father but we both knew Roman would always be held to that status for him.

The click of a door cracked in the air, pulling our attention to the corner of the room.

The same man who brought us here walked inside, his identity still hidden by the black mask.

My throat became dry when I saw the flash of a knife in his hand. He ran his lean fingers across the sharp blade almost affectionately.

"Touch her and it'll be the last fucking thing you do."

My head snapped toward Nicolai at his rage. I'd never heard him sound so lethal.

I watched as the man continued caressing the weapon, ignoring him as if he hadn't spoken at all.

My blood pumped wildly in my veins, my ears ringing from the anticipation of the unknown.

With a hard swallow, I steadied my breathing. "Who are you?"

The man ignored me too, walking further into the dull room.

"What do you want?"

He sighed deeply, as if annoyed by my questioning, but I didn't care. If he wanted to hurt us, he would do it anyway.

Cold sweat ran down my spine as he approached me until he held the knife to my throat.

Nicolai's protests could be heard faintly as my senses dulled down to the end of the knife piercing my skin, but I stared at the man motionless, refusing to cower before him.

Whoever he was, whatever his motives were, he'd regret it as soon as I was free.

He dragged the blade down to my collarbone—not inflicting harm, but the threat hung between us like a ticking bomb.

The sound of my shirt ripping down the middle had me turning my head away from him.

Dread twisted my insides, and I waited for the familiar bile to rise, but it never did.

That knowledge sent despair through me with defeat lodging itself deep into my bones. At least, if I felt something—*anything*—I would know that I wasn't broken. That I had a chance to survive.

With my pulse roaring, I glanced between the knife and the man, noticing he had paused above my breast.

As if he was waiting for my attention, he dug the sharp end into my skin and dragged it until I buckled against the pain.

Nicolai screamed in rage, the chains on the floor rattling from his constant movement.

I curled my bottom lip between my teeth and bit down to stifle my cries.

I stared at the man as he took his time cutting me, drawing it out until my skin was burning, blood oozing and mixing with my sweat.

With uneven breaths, I panted harshly to ground myself against the torture as he moved onto my legs, slashing right through my pants until he hit flesh.

Tears streamed down my face, hot and heavy, but I clamped my mouth shut, tasting the tang of blood burst onto my tongue from biting so hard.

Nicolai said he'd get us out of here and I tried desperately to hold on to that with every piece of me that bled out, but I was losing myself.

A wave of dizziness passed over me and I couldn't breathe. The sting of each slash worse than the last until all I felt was the pulsing pain from head to toe.

The man never uttered a single word, solely focusing on his task of marring my body, scarring it.

My body. The one thing the Bratva used to their advantage. And now it was flawed.

What importance would I be to them now?

With my teeth chattering, I gasped out the word I hardly ever uttered, *"Please."*

He regarded me for a moment, his gaze trailing my body until the malicious gleam in his brown eyes intensified.

His fingers dug into my jaw until he had a firm grip on my face before he leaned in close, setting the blade above my brow.

My vision grew blurry, and I didn't know if it was from my tears or sweat running down my face. The tightness in my chest was unbearable, and I was *terrified*.

If he cut my face, I would become *nothing*. I would be useless without my beauty.

"Enough!" It was Nicolai's voice that finally stilled his movements, his voice hoarse. "What do you want? Whatever it is, I'll do it. Just. . . leave her alone." His pleas went down through deaf ears.

The man's breathing became erratic, as if my brother's words fueled his baseless anger and I knew that not only would I go scathed, but so would Nicolai.

The scream bubbled in my throat until it pierced the

air as the man slid his knife down the right side of my face. Every single sense homed in on the excruciating throb of my split flesh searing through me.

He pulled back, and I sobbed as the vision in my right eye became dark and red from the blood trickling into it.

I couldn't stop the violent tremors racking my battered body, every tremble adding to the ache. The pain was unbearable, and I didn't know where it began or ended as I inhaled shakily.

"Irina. . ."

"Irina!"

"Irina, look at me!"

Someone was calling my name, but it sounded distant, muffled, as if I was underwater.

"Open your eyes!"

I blinked rapidly, unaware of when I had dozed off and looked across the room where Nicolai was saying something, but the ringing in my ears made it hard to hear.

With a groan, I tried tilting my head, but it felt heavy, as if I was paralyzed. I tried the same with my body, but it was lax, as if gravity was pushing me down.

Panic settled over me as I searched around the room hastily with my eyes, but the man was gone, leaving me in a state of fear.

"Drugged. . ."

I peered back at Nicolai, evening out my breathing to get rid of the cloudy sensation overpowering me.

"You were drugged," he said almost calmly, though the pinched expression on his face told me he was anything but.

My tongue was stuck to the roof of my mouth, dry and bitter, causing me to make an incoherent sound.

"I don't know when he'll be back, but I need you to stay awake. I can't. . . " His voice cracked. "I won't know if you're okay if you fall asleep."

Fresh tears scorched my face, flaring the cut into a fiery blaze, reminding me of everything I lost.

"You have to stay awake, okay? Can you do that for me?" His voice rose with each word. When his gaze trailed along my body, emotion flashed across his troubled features. "I'm sorry."

Something broke inside of me. No one had ever apologized to me for anything. Yet, here was Nicolai, my brother, saying those two meaningless words when he'd never been the one at fault.

The cold air chilled my lifeless body, and I nearly recoiled at being on display like this. In a way, I was relieved I couldn't see the damage myself and the thought of having to, sent my mind spiraling.

My breaths grew ragged when the clicking sound of the door erupted again and the man entered the room.

I didn't think I could take any more of this agony, not when I was as still as a statue.

How much time had passed since the accident? How would we escape? Why did Nicolai give me false hope of getting us out of here?

I tracked the man's movements with my eyes as he walked toward my brother, and I grunted in panic as he reached for him.

He looked back at me, his eyes narrowing as I

continued making muddled noises, wishing I could speak. If I could save Nicolai from harm, then I'd do anything, even if it meant taking it myself.

My weak protests were useless because the man swung his arm back before his fist collided with Nicolai's face, blood splattering onto the dirty ground.

Tears beaded down my cheeks as I whimpered, my throat becoming raw as he continued pummeling his fists into Nicolai until he'd passed out, but he didn't stop there.

Reaching for the baseball bat resting against the wall, I knew his intentions.

I closed my eyes, the horrid sounds of bone crunching and snapping cementing itself into my memory.

Being immobile while my brother was beaten to a pulp made me want to *die.* I couldn't breathe, drowning in vulnerability and suffering.

With the little energy I had left, I blocked out my surroundings, trying to muster up a memory I could get lost in.

"Luca?"

"I'm here." His voice was like a balm to my wounds. He rubbed my back soothingly. "I'm here."

I buried my face in the crook of his neck, inhaling his scent to ground myself back to reality.

It was a nightmare. I'm not back there anymore.

"Do you get nightmares often?"

I ignored his question and the one after that. I wasn't ready to open up to anyone about my life. I knew what it was like to be vulnerable, and I hated it.

How do I explain to someone that I'd spent my entire

life feeling lost, a stranger in my own skin and I was too broken to let anyone see how broken I was?

I pulled away from him, searching his eyes. "I'm tired, Luca." My voice trembled. "Can you. . . can you just hold me? Only for tonight. Please."

He nudged under my chin lazily, as he always did. "You never have to say please, piccola ribelle."

A sharp sensation brought me out of the comforting memory, my eyes blinking open.

The man was standing over me, blood coating him with his cold eyes staring into me.

A piercing pressure fell onto my right arm, and I knew he was drugging me again. My heartbeat accelerated, unknowing of what it was this time.

It didn't take long for my consciousness to sway and become heady before he walked away, but I never passed out.

Minutes ticked by, and I stared at Nicolai from across the room. He was covered in so much blood that he appeared unrecognizable with his body slumped and his head thrown back.

Death appeared closer, and I wondered if this was how my story would end, cut open and still as I watched my brother take his last breaths.

It was hard grasping on to life when my eyes were fluttering in and out of sleep, unsure of what was real and what wasn't.

My body didn't feel like my own, as if I was in an upended state, my brain fogging up and creating figures, shapes and sounds that heightened my anxiety.

When darkness brimmed the edges of my vision, I swore I heard the sound of my own heart breaking at *his* voice.

"Not so pretty anymore, Irina," Luca said.

CHAPTER 22
LUCA

The blade slid along my father's arm smoothly, blood pouring out in a slow stream.

Irina leaving fucked me up in the head and I'd let out steam in the only way I knew how. Violence.

"I've gotten bored with your existence," I said, finding another patch of skin to cut through. "You suck the joy out of everything, even in death."

An incoherent mumble came from him, bringing my attention to his hollow face, sweat and blood dripping down his forehead.

"You've done enough talking." I lifted the blade between us, assessing it under the light above us, the crimson color vibrant. "Not that you're able to, anyway."

I spun the knife with my fingers before wrapping my hand around the hilt and jabbing it in his thigh.

A silent scream vibrated from him as he shuddered against the bed.

"It's *my* turn to talk now." I dragged the knife down until I'd ripped through muscle and flesh.

Was it normal to feel unaffected by my own father's pain?

"Isn't it ironic?" I chuckled, wrenching the blade out. "You always wanted me to be exactly like you and, in a way, you succeeded." I emphasized my words by digging it in his other thigh as resentment rose to the surface. "But there's one difference between us." I glanced up at him, fury thrumming in my veins. "You're going to die, and no one will mourn your loss." *Stab.* "Not me." *Stab.* "Not Evangeline." *Stab.* "No one."

Red drenched the mattress by the time I finished mangling his body, and yet a part of me wasn't satisfied. It hadn't been for weeks. I was done.

Leaning over him, I brought my face close to his, forcing him to see the coldness I felt on the inside. "You took my mother from me," I seethed, the memory engraved into my mind as if it had happened yesterday. "You took and took from me, but I'll never allow you to do the same to Evangeline." I brought the knife to his neck and dug it in, his eyes filling with fear. "And I'll be paying my thanks by taking everything from you." Slowly, I slid the knife across his throat, dragging out his death more than I already had. "Your legacy dies here."

Blood seeped from his mouth; his face stunned, before his eyes rolled back as he let out his last breath.

I stared at him for a few moments, wondering how I could bring him back to life to do it all over again.

Grabbing the towel from the bedside table, I wiped my hands clean as I walked out of the door.

Dr. Aldo stood patiently beside the door; his questioning eyes narrowing at me in suspicion.

"One less patient for you to worry about." I nudged my head at him. "Congrats."

I'd walked down the room when my phone buzzed in my pocket.

Roman's name flashed across the screen and instantly I knew something was wrong. After what happened last night, he wouldn't have called me if it wasn't urgent.

Was it Irina?

I said I'd let her come to me this time, but my patience only extended so far. If I had to drag her back to Italy kicking and screaming, I would.

"What's going on?" I answered, panic gripping me in a vice and what I felt last night didn't compare to the terrible sensation coursing through me now.

"Nico is gone."

"What do you mean '*gone*'? Did you check his location?"

After Nicolai was brought in by Roman and we learned of his background, my best friend inserted a GPS chip beneath his skin.

The trauma Nico had experienced made him compliant enough to undergo the quick procedure.

It had been a bit strange to us all how sympathetic Roman was toward him, but we quickly learned that their relationship was more of a father and a son than a *Don* and his crew member.

"I had to." He sighed. "He hasn't come yet."

"And?" It wasn't abnormal that our youngest member had a tendency to go out.

“I’m headed to his location.” He sounded too calm, and I knew it was worse when he did.

“Did you call Ric?” I asked as I signaled to my security team to go upstairs. My father could rot elsewhere.

“I did. He’s on his way there right now with the men to scope it out.” A loud horn echoed down the line before he cursed. “Hold on, I’m sending you Nico’s location.”

A second later, I zoomed in on the blinking red dot displayed on my screen, squinting my eyes to see where exactly he was.

It looked to be a small building, the area surrounding it deserted. The fuck?

And there it was. The confirmation to my suspicion. Something was wrong.

“Luca.” Roman didn’t wait for me to acknowledge him before he said, “If she had something to do with this, I’ll fucking kill her this time.”

I’d never driven my bike so recklessly in my life.

My heart was beating against my chest harshly, blocking out everything else except for blue eyes that cut me deep, denting and molding a place into my heart.

Irina might be malicious when she wanted to be, but I knew she would never harm Nicolai.

I’d caught up to Roman on the way as he rode his truck, speeding down the roads as fast as I was.

I turned my head at the same time he did, his expression disturbed before he held his phone up to me where Ricardo’s name was displayed.

My stomach twisted in knots as he stepped on the gas, and I almost wasn't ready to see what I'd find when we arrived at the location.

My thoughts were spiraling, and I held onto this idea that Nico was having a bad night and ended up getting shit faced fuck knows where. But even I knew he'd never been reckless in that regard.

Five minutes later, we were parked and running toward a gray building. It was old and abandoned, as if it had no purpose of being there.

Barging through the steel door, we moved around swiftly, scoping the area inside to find the space empty, a putrid smell emitting in the air.

"Ricardo!" Roman ran down the aged hall, opening doors to more vacant rooms.

"Over here, *Don!*"

We headed toward the sound of Ric's voice, my mouth turning dry with every step until I stood inside a stained room.

As if every cell in my body came to life when she was near, my gaze landed on Irina.

My breath caught in my throat as I nearly tripped over my feet getting to her.

She was lying on the floor with one of our men crouched over her, assessing her.

"What happened?" My voice sounded hoarse to my own ears as I dropped to my knees and grabbed her unconscious body, pulling her against me. "What the *fuck* happened?" I asked, louder, staring down at her.

Irina's face was bloody, a sharp cut across one side of

her face. With trembling hands, I pushed back her matted hair hesitantly. It was short. . . choppy.

My finger fell upon her pulse, evident but slow.

"We gotta go," Ricardo shouted. "Now!"

With my pulse racing, I wrapped my jacket around Irina, trying not to focus on the blood covering her body. I took deep breaths to calm myself down. She was my priority right now, but when I found out who did this to her, they'd be left for worse.

Cradling her body, I picked her up and finally peered around the room.

Roman was bent over Nicolai, his hands palming his face as he whispered something to him, almost like a chant.

But Nico was knocked out cold, battered and bruised, blood covering every surface of his body.

Nausea unfurled in my chest at the horrific scene in front of me.

When Ric set a hand on Roman's shoulder, he looked up and I could see the glistening streaks of tears on his face.

"We have to go, *Don*."

He nodded and together, they hauled our youngest member up.

I needed answers, and I needed them now. Whoever did this had a vendetta against Irina and Nicolai, marring and mangling their bodies until it was near unrecognizable.

The next hour went by in a blur, my head pounding from the unwanted adrenaline. I was on high alert, my body trembling in restrained rage.

When we arrived at the hospital, the doctors immediately admitted Nico and Irina to treat them. All it took was one look at their appearance and their faces had drained of color.

Threats were made and questions went unanswered. They knew better than to involve the feds.

I waited and waited, impatiently walking the halls of the clinically pristine walls for an update on their conditions.

Although my attention was solely on Irina, I was worried about Nicolai. He was hardly breathing when we brought him in, his once pale hair smeared with crimson.

Roman was worse than me, his eyes distant with fury swarming in them as he sat on a chair in the waiting room, his body tense and still.

This was bad, *really* fucking bad.

My mind tumbled until a fiery surge of emotion caught ahold of my chest, potent and persistent.

I clawed at my collar, feeling the air in my lungs cease.

If I hadn't let Irina go, this wouldn't have happened. She would've been angry, but safe. And so would have Nico.

If I hadn't let her walk away, she wouldn't have been tortured within an inch of her life.

If I had fought harder, she wouldn't have been stripped of her sanity.

The start of a panic attack burst to life, my vision darkening as claws sank deep into my bones, pulling me beneath the lethal surface. The feeling had been foreign for a long time, the last one happening when my mother passed away.

Please, let them be okay.

I had never known longing and desperation until Irina slipped from between my fingers. The mere thought of never molding my body against hers again, never breathing in her intoxicating scent again, and never getting lost in her presence again made me want to sacrifice my soul if it meant hers would be okay.

My back hit the wall as I gasped for air, losing this internal battle with myself. I needed more time. *We* needed more time.

Hands pressed into me, suffocating me further into oblivion. *No. No. No.*

"Luca. . ."

I squeezed my eyes shut as I covered my ears to rid of the distant voices entering my twisted thoughts.

My head throbbed viciously, senses overwhelming me with every tremor racking through my body.

"Luca!" The hands grabbed ahold of me, slowly anchoring me back to a place I could breathe in again.

"It's me," the voice said. "Roman."

Roman?

Breathing heavily through my nose, I urged my brain to stop tumbling into the abyss.

"You're okay, brother."

The sound of his rough voice came out clearer, his hands squeezing my shoulders in comfort.

With a shaky exhale, I blinked away the black spots dancing in my vision until his face appeared before me, concern slashing across his features.

The underlying panic was still present, but my best friend kept me rooted.

"I can't lose her," I choked out, shaking my head. "What I feel for her terrifies me and I haven't even come close to understanding it."

He stared at me, his obsidian eyes softening slightly as he sighed in resignation. "Trust me, I know that feeling all too well."

CHAPTER 23
IRINA

You know the feeling of falling in a dream while you're asleep?

Coming to my senses was sort of like that, more excruciating than I expected. For a moment, I'd been disoriented, the sound of beeping machines and the smell of antiseptic jarring me.

I knew I wasn't fully conscious, the dark memories of the last few hours rushing in, making it hard to come back from.

It felt like a fever dream, but the nauseating pain in my body proved that it was very much real.

The back of my head pulsed as my chest caved in until I was drowning in my thoughts. The sharp slashes of the knife, the humiliating feeling of being seen by my brother, watching him get beat nearly to death while I was numb to the bone and helpless.

"Ni-Nico. . . " I didn't know if I was calling for him in

real time or in my head. My tongue was stuck to the roof of my dry mouth, the words barely a whisper.

Panic set in as blackness drew in on me, threatening to keep me in that horrific place.

Chills ran up my body, trembling uncontrollably as my throat became tight, lodged with hurt and despair.

Before I faded completely into the void, rough hands warmed my skin, wandering everywhere in light touches.

"Sweetheart."

That voice. . .

Not so pretty anymore, Irina.

My heart thrashed against my ribcage as the voice registered with a sickening realization.

With energy I didn't have to spare, I peeled my eyes open—my eye, adjusting to the bright lights overhead.

As the blur in my vision diminished, the face of someone who brought me devastation and joy appeared.

Fear sliced through me, screams spilling from my mouth at the haunting voice of his last words to me.

He'd been there. He did this to me. He hurt me and Nicolai.

Luca's voice was muffled by my cries as I thrashed against his hold, my limbs burning from the effort to get away from him.

"Don't hurt me, please!"

The beeping sound of a machine quickened as my nerves slithered over me like a sick and twisted caress.

Other voices reached me before multiple sets of hands pinned me in place, a sharp sensation pricking my arm.

The last image I saw before I was pulled under the

harsh waves of my subconscious were caramel eyes, distraught and distressed.

"I should've never let you go."

"You have *no* idea what you mean to me, Irina."

"If only you knew the unexplainable hold you have over me."

"Don't hate me. I can't bear it."

I'd woken up to Luca's broken voice as he whispered to me, his hands clutching mine.

I hadn't let it be known to him that I was awake, savoring his gentle touches and words.

What kind of person was I to crave the touch of the same man who put me in the hospital?

Yet it didn't make sense. How could Luca possess this kind of tenderness for me when I was 'asleep'?

Confusion warred in me, and I wanted to cry. I wanted to let the tears fall freely, draining myself of this unbearable ache that would be the cause of my death.

My heart couldn't handle anymore suffering. It was torn and withered, reaching its limit.

It was hard to accept that he was the one behind what happened when my gut told me differently.

My fingers twitched as I opened my eye, finding his gaze easily.

"Why did you do it?" I murmured, exhaustion lining my tone.

My gaze soaked in his beauty. I couldn't deny myself of that when he was this close to me. It took everything in me to not reach out and trace the angular planes of his face. But I refrained.

His eyes were glossy and red, as if he'd been crying, which further proved my gut to be right. But I needed him to say that he would never hurt me in such a vile way.

"Do what?"

"I heard you. You. . . you." I choked on my words, suddenly aware of how I must look right now.

With a trembling hand, I touched the right side of my face, feeling the soft fabric of a bandage covering it.

"You did this to me."

Luca shook his head rapidly, bringing my hands to his mouth and peppering kisses across my knuckles. "I'd sooner cut my own hands than ever do that to you."

"But I heard your voice."

"The doctors said you were drugged." Luca might've appeared calm, but his tone of voice did nothing to hide his anger. "Believe me, whatever you heard, it wasn't me."

A whimper escaped my lips as hot tears scalded down my cheek before it turned into a full blown meltdown.

He didn't hesitate to climb into the bed beside me, gently wrapping me in his arms as he pressed kisses to my temple, healing my wounds with each one.

"You'll never be hurt again, Irina. I swear it."

That only made me cry harder.

His firm body was a safety net for me, and I let myself fall into his embrace again. But this time was entirely different. I willingly showed him this side of me, tears and all.

How could I believe that this was a mistake when it felt as if I was right where I was meant to be?

One day, I'd share the dark parts of me with Luca but for now, this was enough. . . for the both of us I hoped.

When my body stopped shaking and my cries turned into sniffles, I tilted my head to look at him. "How bad is it?"

We both knew I'd be left with scars that would never fade but I wasn't ready to see them littered across my body.

His tired eyes roamed my face; pupils dilating. "You're the epitome of perfection, sweetheart."

Perhaps to him, I was. To me, I'd lost my value. I'd been stripped away from the only thing that brought me security. I knew that made me shallow but when all my life I'd been praised for my beauty and then taught to use it as a weapon, it was hard to let go of that. Who I was before was all I knew, and to me, it solidified my relationship with my father. Now, I was the scraps of my identity.

"I suppose it doesn't matter now, anyway." I cast my gaze away from him. "What's done is done."

Luca's fingers made a path down my check, his touch rising goosebumps on my skin until he cupped my jaw, turning me toward him again. "Irina. . . "

With a trembling hand, I grabbed his wrist as I shook my head. I wasn't ready to continue that conversation.

"Is Nicolai here?" It should've been the first question I asked but if I was found, then I knew my brother got out with me. He had to have.

"He is."

I pulled back, his curt reply doing nothing to ease the tension radiating off my body. "And?"

"And we can talk about him when you're better."

I made a move to sit up when a shooting pain struck me, a hiss escaping me as I clasped my bandaged abdomen.

"Irina." Luca cursed, gently pushing me back down. "For once, don't fight me. *Please*."

"Just tell me he's okay," I whispered, my body fighting exhaustion long enough to hear his answer.

He sighed in defeat. "He's stable but hasn't woken up yet."

My heart thrummed rapidly, a layer of sweat coating my cold skin. Images of Nico's limp and bloody body flashed across my mind, and it hurt to know I might've been the cause of his condition.

He was a victim to being at the wrong place at the wrong time. I had no idea who did this to us and why, but he might've been left unscathed if he hadn't come after me.

"This is all my fault," I choked, pulling at my hair. He should've never been there.

My hair. . .

The sound of my blood pumping sounded harshly against my ears; my breathing labored as I ran my fingers through my hair. *No*.

"Wha-what. . . " I couldn't breathe, my vision darkening as I kept touching the uneven strands.

Hands circled my wrists, stopping my movements but I was too far gone in my own grief to see or hear anything else.

"Hey. . . hey. You're okay."

I thought I had no tears left in me but I did, my sobs echoing against the four walls of the room.

After some time, weak and tired, sleep overtook me as

soothing words and touches anchored me in place, away from unbearable nightmares.

The next time I woke up, the curtains were drawn closed, the room dimly lit.

I was pressed down by something heavy—someone. Luca had his arms wrapped tightly around me, and he was very much asleep as he cuddled me.

A large, tattooed man in a bed too small for him yet he slept so peacefully with our limbs intertwined. Even I couldn't help but crack a smile as a surge of warmth spread though me at the sight.

"I warned him to stay away from you, you know."

My head snapped toward the familiar voice.

Aurora sat beside the bed on a chair, her face dragging in clear tiredness with puffy eyes.

"Luca is the type of man who doesn't settle down and I was scared of the consequences of his actions if he pursued you."

I knew Roman warned off Luca but hearing Aurora confess to doing the same shocked me. She'd never interfered with my relationships, not that I'd ever settled down either. I guess Luca and I were the same in that sense, though I wasn't sure of his reasoning.

"But I was wrong." She looked between the two of us before holding my gaze. "I've never seen such suffering and torment on anyone as I have on Luca since you were admitted."

I inhaled a shaky breath, my heart thundering so fiercely, I thought I might pass out from the sheer force of it.

"I don't deserve his empathy." It was the truest words

I'd ever spoken. "I haven't done a single good thing for this man to earn his undivided attention."

"I know what love looks like Irina..."

"Don't," I cut her off. "That's not what this is." The backs of my eyes stung as I whispered, "You weren't there to hear what I'd said to him before I left."

The pain was still fresh from that moment in the rain, perhaps worse than the throbbing ache of my body now.

"I repulse myself, Aurora. Now, tell me, how can he love someone as unpleasant as me?"

Aurora's expression filled with pity, and I had to turn away from her or it would destroy me further.

"*I* love you," she said with raw emotion. "You're worthy of love, and I won't be convinced otherwise."

"Even though I lied to you?"

When she didn't respond, I built up the courage to stare back at her, feeling my chest cave in a little.

"Even though you lied to me."

My lips pursed as I tried my best to not break into a million more pieces.

"Why didn't you tell me that you were the *Pakhan's* daughter? You could've trusted me."

Rummaging through the many reasons I could give her; I knew none of them could sugarcoat the true reason I had never allowed myself to admit until now.

"Because you were the only pure thing in my life, and I'd rather have kept it all inside than corrupt you with my burdens. Because I had someone to call my own." My voice wavered with nerves. "I didn't want you to leave me."

The silence was comfortable and welcome as I submitted to the truth. The heaviness I carried for all these years eased up and I felt like I could breathe properly for the first time.

"I never meant for anyone to get hurt." The situation became messier than I intended it to, and I knew that it would be worse once I contacted my father. "I'm sorry."

My best friend reached over and grasped my hand, squeezing it in comfort. "I wish I'd been your person, the same way you were mine. Perhaps, one day you'll give me the chance to know you completely as you are." She shook her head in amusement, lightening the stifling air. "Flawed and all."

Laughter bubbled in my chest, and I peered over at the brute lying beside me to make sure I hadn't woken him up.

"If it's not love, then it must be something close to it," Aurora said as I stared at him. Butterflies took flight in my stomach at the thought of Luca carrying intense affection for me. "The question is, what do you feel?"

The words slipped from my lips with ease. "Something I've never felt before."

CHAPTER 24
LUCA

Something I've never felt before.

Irina's words were cemented into my brain since I heard them last night.

The dynamic between us was built on a thin line of denial and lies, and if she knew that I heard her admission, she would've done everything in her power to prove otherwise.

Because it was in Irina's nature to push others away, even if it meant they'd hate her. She had a seed full of misery in her and I was determined to rip it out.

Patience was never my thing, but I was in it for the long haul for this girl.

And now that I knew Irina had grown a liking to me, I'd make sure it became as fervent as the feelings I carried for her.

My lips twitched in amusement. I knew my little rebel would come around.

If it weren't for the circumstances we'd all found

ourselves in, I would've relished in it more but there were too many questions and not enough answers.

"We're taking him home today." Roman came to stand beside me, his attention resting on Nico's unconscious body.

I had already known that piece of information, only because I'd asked the nurse when Irina would be discharged.

"How long do they think he'll be in a coma for?"

The thought of the little shit never waking up again and berating us on our informal speech gutted me.

If he didn't wake up, it would wreck Irina, and I didn't think she'd recover from that.

Wake up, Nico. Just wake up.

"Doctor said only time will tell," Roman answered, his voice low and detached.

I faced him, assessing his disheveled appearance; overgrown beard, bloodshot eyes, and the same clothes he'd been in since the morning we'd brought them into the hospital.

That was three days ago.

"Have you slept yet?"

When he ignored me and proceeded to stare through the clear glass as if that would miraculously wake Nico up, I grabbed ahold of his shoulder.

"Roman, you need to sleep. You're no good for anyone like this. Not Aurora, not Nico and definitely not the little one who's coming any-day now."

When he tilted his head to hold my gaze, a flash of hurt but most of all betrayal lined his features. "You know who isn't good for *anyone*? The one who put us in this fucking predicament in the first place."

My chest burned, torn between my own predicaments. "She had nothing to do with what happened."

"Maybe not. But it doesn't take away from the fact that he's fighting for his life right now."

"He went after her on his own."

"Because he cares!" He pressed the heels of his palms against his eyes. "He always fucking cares too much."

This whole situation was fucked, and I didn't even know where to begin in fixing it. Roman thought I was disloyal, Nico was in a coma, and Irina's mental health was a black abyss.

"We all care," I said sternly. "*Irina* cares. Have you even seen her?" My blood ran cold every time the image of her lifeless body appeared in my mind—not that it ever left. "No, you haven't because if you did, you'd know she's suffering as much as her brother is."

"I'm not some heartless fucker, Luca," he snapped. "Irina should be so lucky I even agreed for Aurora to visit her."

I scoffed, shaking my head at his pettiness. "With all the power you have, you'd never be able to break those two apart. They're like sisters."

Roman opened the door to Nico's room. "And we were like brothers but look where that got us."

As he shut the door, I stood dumbfounded, staring at the empty space.

I knew Roman felt betrayed by me because I chose Irina but if he were in the same position as me, he would have chosen Aurora too, regardless of the repercussions.

He *had* chosen Aurora, and it was fucking hypocritical of him.

But the truth was that my brother was hurting, and it had nothing to do with me and everything to do with Nico. That was his son in every way, and no DNA test could ever change that.

With a heavy heart, I entered Irina's room.

She was awake, her gaze unfocused as she peered through the window.

"I want to see Nico. Has he woken up yet?"

I sat down on the bed beside her and shook my head.

Her throat worked as she swallowed, and it pained me to see her plagued by her own torturous thoughts.

Life had drained her these past few days, and it was evident in her hollow and sunken face. Bones protruding and haunting blue eyes.

I interlinked my hand with hers, noting the irony of her cut hand and my torn one. I'd be lying if I said I hadn't gone out for a quick killing spree to release the built-up anger and tension inside of me.

"You'll both be discharged today."

Subconsciously she reached for her patched eye before she curled her hand into a fist and put it down.

Her cheeks bloomed with color when she caught me staring at her, and it might've warmed my chest if it weren't for the displeasure crossing her face.

"Don't be embarrassed, Irina. Never with me."

"I'm not." Her defenses were up again as she let go of my hand, turning away from me.

I pulled her hand back, leaning into her. "Don't hide from me either."

Her eyes narrowed in distaste as she sneered at me. "Or what?"

"Or I'll find you in whatever hell you've imprisoned yourself to and drag you out."

I'd heard her full conversation with Aurora. I knew she believed she wasn't worthy of love. That she didn't deserve *my* love.

That word was underwhelming for what I felt for Irina.

What I felt for her was a compelling force that deprived me of my ability to breathe when she wasn't near. It was an unbearable ache in my chest when I couldn't endure her pain, so she didn't have to. A longing so potent that she'd taken my heart alongside her own and the day that hers stopped beating, mine would too.

A sorrow filled furrow formed between her brows. "You don't even know me."

"I know that you're sorry for what you said to me."

Her mouth parted in surprise as she searched my eyes, multiple emotions flashing in hers.

"You're damaged, Irina." I lifted her hand, keeping my gaze locked on hers as I placed a kiss on a cut marring her porcelain skin. "But so am I. It doesn't mean you're a bad person."

"I am," she whispered, her fingers flexing until she caressed my cheek with tenderness. "I *am* sorry."

Her touch was warm, power at the palms of her hands to tame me.

"Let's get you out of here, yeah?"

Her expression turned to uncertainty as she asked. "Can I have my phone first? The nurse said she'd bring in my belongings, but she hasn't."

When I didn't make a move to give her what she wanted, her face fell. "Luca?"

I stood away from her. "I can't do that, sweetheart."

"What do you mean you *can't?*"

"Exactly as I said." I held her phone up before placing it back into my pocket. "You won't be getting your phone back."

"Have you lost your mind?" She scrambled to get up and winced at the same time I stepped forward. *Fuck.* "If my father doesn't hear from me, he'll come here, and we'll have an even bigger problem. War!"

My jaw flexed watching her in discomfort. "Let him." I gritted out. "Nurse!"

Seconds later, multiple nurses rushed in and immediately held Irina down.

I'd suspected she'd be difficult and when status and money carried in your name, no one ever denied you.

"Get off me!" She writhed against the bed, eyes blazing as she stared at me with pure hatred. Long gone was the tenderness from earlier, replaced by betrayal.

"Sir." The nurse holding the syringe waited for my approval.

I knew by doing this I was jeopardizing the small amount of trust she'd put in me, but when I'd said I was never letting her go, I meant it.

"Put her down."

"Luca!" The strain in her voice chipped at my soul but it had to be this way. "I hate. . . hate you," she mumbled as her eyes blinked close.

As long as I had her, I didn't give a damn about a war.

CHAPTER 25
IRINA

The brute had put me down like I was some deranged animal.

Anger surged through me, hot and heavy as I laid in Luca's bed, the aftermath of being sedated wearing off quicker than I expected.

Did he think that I'd be some compliant doll and stay here with him? This wasn't some sick fairytale, and he surely wasn't my savior.

With energy I hardly had enough of, I slowly got up, the burn of my injuries sizzling across my flesh.

I really needed to talk to my father, not only to defuse the situation with Nicolai but figure out who the fuck did this to us.

Was it an enemy? What could have they possibly gained from this?

On shaky feet, I exhaled a breath as I walked toward the bedroom door. The last time I'd been in here, I'd said goodbye to Luca, and it felt like a lifetime ago, the heartache still lingering in the air.

I couldn't stay here.

When I reached for the knob, the door swung open, *his* larger-than-life presence entering the room.

"Going somewhere, *piccola ribelle*?" He approached me lazily, his caramel eyes drinking me in.

"What do you think?" My blood boiled at his casual demeanor, as if he hadn't drugged me to sleep. "I will not be your captive, you psychopath."

"I thought we'd already established that I was one." He towered over me, a mocking grin curling his lips. "Besides, I wouldn't call you a captive."

"You brought me here against my will." My teeth ached from clenching them. Why did I have to get involved with someone who was as delusional as they came? "If not captivity, then what?"

"Captors usually aren't driven to the brink of insanity by their captives." He leaned down until he was eye level with me. "Are they?"

His scent surrounded me, an immediate blockage to my sensibility and morality.

What the hell was happening to me?

"They usually aren't pained by the mere thought of their captive hurt." His tone became vicious, as if he was angry with me but mostly himself. "Are they?"

"Luca. . . "

He pressed his forehead against mine, his palm holding my jaw. "They usually aren't concerned for their captive's soul more than their own. Are they?"

Thick emotions whirled in my chest, adrenaline

spiking through my blood from his words. If only it were easy to give into him and forget about who and what I was, but I couldn't.

"We're only biding our time, Luca," I whispered, my voice cracking, and I didn't even care how weak it made me seem. "We both know how our story will end, and it'll never be a happy one."

In a flash, I felt his demeanor change. His fingertips had gone cold, his gaze even colder before he stepped away from me.

"Take off your clothes."

My stomach dropped at his abruptness. "Wh-what?"

"We need to clean you."

"We? You're not getting anywhere near me."

"Would you rather I resort to unpleasant methods?"

"You did it once. I wouldn't put it past you to do it again." He'd taken away my will like every other man I'd ever encountered, and it hurt because I knew he was nothing like them.

Luca stood there with pursed lips and arms crossed, not denying it.

I wanted to continue fighting him, but I was exhausted. It would get me nowhere and right now I wanted to be left alone.

He might be dealing the cards here, but I'd make sure I had the upper hand.

With firm movements, I let the hospital gown fall off my body in a heap at my feet.

My heart beat against my chest at a painful rhythm, aware of how exposed I was—how I looked but I bit the inside of my cheek to refrain myself from hiding.

I may not be ready to see the aftermath of what happened to me, but I wouldn't allow anyone to make me feel ashamed for something I couldn't change.

Yet, the way Luca unashamedly took his time trailing the length of my body, proved he wasn't just anyone.

The wild glint in his eyes made me shift on my legs from his attention.

He noticed, nose flaring as he caught my eyes, and I suddenly forgot why I was angry with him.

Tension simmered in the warm air between us, and my pulse thrummed rapidly at the possibility that he'd *mark* me here and now.

I held my breath as he took a slow step toward me, as if a pace faster than that would have me running off.

Then without a word, he diverted his darkening gaze away and crossed the few steps to the bathroom.

When the sound of running water resonated, I followed him inside just as he was peeling off his clothes.

With his back turned, I admired the sculpted planes of his body all over again. It was hard not to when he was this beautiful. Toned muscles wrapped tight with sharp scars and black ink that were more prominent in the bright light.

The realization hit me full force.

He wasn't here to spite me. He was here to ground me as my mind cluttered with grim thoughts.

My throat tightened, the sting of tears burning my eyes. I was a coward, afraid of accepting my reality when Luca unabashedly displayed the fucked up parts of himself so openly.

How could I perceive him as beautiful yet perceive myself the opposite?

With a swelling ache in my chest, I dragged my feet to where he stood before wrapping my arms around him from behind, burying my face in his back.

It was hard to hold on to my anger when he'd done this for me. He was always there to catch me when I fell, and it *hurt*. It hurt knowing he was the only one who was patient enough to peel back my layers and see what lurked beneath the surface.

"Thank you."

After what felt like minutes, he finally sighed, holding my arms with his calloused hands, the beat of his heart pounding erratically against my palm. If I didn't know better, I'd think he was nervous.

"I'm going to take off your bandages," he said, his grip on me strong.

The urge to pull away and plead with him to leave me alone pulsed heavy, but I held him tighter, the warmth of his skin melting the iciness coating my own. I wouldn't be afraid.

He turned around, an ominous shadow looming over his troubled face. "I'm not here to hurt you."

With my eyes locked on his, I saw the truth in his words, knowing he'd done more for me than I could ever repay.

I nodded my head, trusting him wholeheartedly.

My breathing turned shallow as he reached for me and peeled back the first covering, then the next and the next.

Cool air hit the newly exposed skin, a sense of lightness cascading over me.

I watched his focused expression as he gauged my reaction and the cautious way he continued removing them. His gentleness was such a contrast to his appearance, it almost made me laugh.

He held my hand, directing me inside the shower where the inviting water sprayed down on us.

With my back pressed to his chest, he anchored me, his presence a protective embrace to my jittery nerves.

"I'm going to touch you," Luca stated, his voice heavy —cautious. "Is that okay?"

I nodded as I leaned my head back against his shoulders, eyes closing.

"I need to hear you say it, Irina."

"Yes," I whispered, my heart somersaulting in my chest. "It's okay."

If it was anyone else, I didn't think I'd even have the courage to take the risk.

I expected the first brush of his touch to cause me distress but instead I was met with a comfortable ease.

It was difficult to understand my bodies reactions when I stopped caring about them long ago but as Luca continued his ministration, he unintentionally healed a lost part of me.

He took his time carefully washing me, his fingers caressing my body in light strokes and the tenderness of his touch let the unshed tears from earlier fall freely.

My heart felt full, ready to ignite and burst from receiving affection in a way that had been foreign to me for a long time.

When he moved onto my hair, I held my breath as he

massaged my scalp, the lack of length evident as he quickly rinsed it.

"Turn around, sweetheart."

He guided me to face him because apparently my mind was too messed up to understand what he was saying.

"Do you trust me?" he asked, his eyes blazing with intensity.

My mouth went dry as the water cascaded on us. Luca was pulling at my heartstrings, and I couldn't stop the way he made me feel. He'd pierced his way into my life and sank himself into a part of me so deeply that I couldn't place where he began, and I ended.

"Yes."

He brushed his knuckles against my cheek softly and I leaned into his touch, completely mesmerized by the way he was looking at me.

There had to be a name for this chaos whirling inside my chest. It couldn't be normal to have difficulty breathing because of someone, right?

Lost in my own thoughts, I hadn't realized what Luca did until it was too late, the cool air brushing my bare eye. My flawed eye.

My lips quivered as I tried holding back my tears. "Why?" For some reason, Luca seeing my face marred was worse than him seeing my body.

"I told you to not hide from me," he answered with zero hesitation. His fingers delicately traced my eye as if he wanted to engrave the crevices into his memory. "If only you could see yourself through my eyes, then perhaps you'd understand the level of desperation I feel for you. *Wanting* you. *Needing* you."

I should've been scared to hear such an admission from a man like him, but the emotion that strum through me wasn't fear.

It was acceptance.

Submission.

He was mine.

CHAPTER 26
IRINA

"I'm getting déjà vu by looking at you."

I pushed the blanket off my face to glare at my best friend. "Did you just make a joke out of your trauma?"

"It's called healing," she retorted, climbing on the bed to lie beside me. "Lighten up."

I couldn't *lighten up*. It seemed that it was always one step forward and three steps back with Luca.

He had locked me in this room for a week now, tending to me like my own nurse during the day and holding me in his arms like a lover at night—even when I'd pretend that I didn't want it.

Every day I'd ask him the same question of when he'd let me go. And every day he'd ignore me as if I'd never asked them in the first place.

I was angry. This constant push and pull between us drove me mad. I wanted him. I *had* him. But I couldn't ignore the circumstances.

It was futile warning him with the possibility of war between the Italian Mafia and the Russian Mafia, but he cared even less about that.

I hadn't spoken to my father or Viktor since the accident, and their silence also terrified me. They had the means to come for me, which meant they were playing in the grand scheme of things. It was only a matter of time before they made their move.

Pure terror gripped me at the position I'd found myself in. If I could just talk to my father and explain everything, then maybe I'd have a chance at stopping him.

Instead, I'd become a liability and being useless made it all worse.

"Aurora." I faced her, watching as the sun beamed across her face, brightening the specks of green in her eyes. "I need your help. Please."

Her gaze searched mine in defeat. "You know I can't."

"Do it for your son," I said, manipulating the situation like a jackass. "If I stay here, your lives will be at stake."

"And what will happen to yours?"

Her question caught me off guard, but I masked my surprise. "Nothing," I lied, the word sitting bitterly on my tongue. The truth was, I didn't know.

I'd pushed down my emotions into the darkness of my soul, avoiding my reality.

Not only did I fail my mission at bringing Nicolai to Russia but I'd lost my most valuable asset, my beauty. And what happens to assets that are of no use anymore? They're discarded.

Would my father see me as useless as I see myself?

Nausea twisted my stomach in knots. I'd never questioned the dynamic between my father and me before, but sitting with my thoughts in silence the past week had sent me spiraling.

I once felt his rejection when I was younger, trapped in the four walls of my childhood home, and I was terrified to feel it again.

"Irina. . . " Aurora's face was closer as she leaned over me, blurred by the sheen of tears coating my eyes. "Where'd you go?"

I felt my face crumble as I curled into a ball at her side, silently weeping for the little girl in me who was had lost pieces of herself and didn't know how to fix it.

I'd been desperate for affection, desperate for validation and acceptance that I didn't think twice about maintaining my loyalty to my father and the Bratva.

I choked on a sob, loathing myself for being the cause of my own hurt.

Aurora embraced me in a tight hold, her cinnamon scent cascading around me in a comforting hold. *Home.*

I tried steadying my breathing, each inhale painful from the heavy weight inside my chest.

If I continued on like this, spending my days in self-pity, it would be my demise. I had cried more in the last two weeks than I had in my whole life. It was uncomfortable and unlike me.

Wiping the excess tears from my eyes, I tilted my head back in time to catch Aurora's worried expression.

I was a terrible person for stressing a pregnant woman.

"Is this where you tell me what's going on in that blonde head of yours?" Her attempt at easing the tension was awkward but admirable.

The woman was harboring enough already, with her spiraling brother, her pregnancy, and Nicolai's recovery.

My brother had woken up two days ago and the thrumming urge to see him was intense, but I *wasn't allowed.*

Not that Luca would even give me the opportunity to escape. It didn't come as a shock to find out Roman was the one who refused to let me visit.

"Not today, but I do need you to do something for me."

"Anything."

Ten minutes later, we were standing in the bright bathroom.

Aurora brushed the wet strands of my hair gently. "I've never done this before, but I'll try my best."

"It can't be worse than what it is now," I laughed half-heartedly. Whether it turned out good or not, didn't matter anyway, considering I was still unable to look at myself in the mirror.

"I'm going to start cutting now."

My face heated with uncertainty. "Wait!"

I tried composing myself before Luca walked inside, his footsteps faltering as he glanced between Aurora and me.

With one look, he stripped me bare and my body ignited to life, every nerve ending yearning for him to come closer.

Aurora cleared her throat, fidgeting in place, but I was too lost in him to pay her any attention.

He stepped further into the room until he opened the drawer below the sink and pulled something out.

A buzzing sound filled the space, and my breathing turned shallow as I saw him shave his hair off with ease.

The erratic pounding of my heart spread through me like wildfire, burning me from the inside out.

I was held captive by every piece of hair that fell to the floor, along with it the heaviness in my chest.

Moments later, he shut the razor off and dropped it back inside the drawer.

Without a word, he crossed the room as he held my gaze, caramel eyes warming every inch of my body.

The second he was out of sight; I felt his absence like a dull pain that never went away.

"I was right. . . " Aurora stood behind me, her hands resting on my shoulders. "He's so in love with you."

I ignored her comment, still reeling from what Luca had just done for me. Again.

It gave me the push I needed to carry on because I wasn't alone in my torment. He was always there.

"Cut it." My voice trembled, sounding weak to my own ears. "Now."

The first snipe of the scissors echoed, my shoulders becoming rigid with every cut strand.

I hoped by the time Aurora was done; I'd feel like I had some sort of power back in my hands.

It was more than a haircut. This was something I could control, and I wanted to take back what was taken from me.

With every feather of hair that fell down my body and pooled at my feet, the tenseness in my body dissipated, a lightened feeling replacing it.

"All done." My best friend moved to stand in front of

me, grinning mischievously. "In case you didn't know, you're sexy as hell with short hair."

I grudgingly reached up and touched the even strands, letting my fingers get accustomed to the length.

My hair didn't define me, nor did my body or face. It was a hard pill to swallow now that my beauty was tarnished after having been praised for it.

I never needed the validation, but holding that power was mine. It had been my identity, and I couldn't blame myself for feeling lost. But this was a step forward.

"Thank you, Aurora."

We shared a silent moment of tenderness, understanding reflecting in her eyes before she hugged me close.

Another week had passed, and I felt myself slipping away. Luca was hurting me more than he knew and if he did, he wasn't acknowledging it.

His obsession with me was blinding him from seeing that I was suffocating.

I was shut out from the outside world, and I was slowly losing my mind.

The last rays of sun shined through the window when Luca came to the bedroom.

My heart went into overdrive seeing his appearance. He was covered in sweat and blood, his face harsh against the shadows of the room.

I clenched my teeth, pursing my lips before turning away from him.

Guilt speared through me for ignoring him, but if I

didn't stand my ground, then I was compliant in staying here.

The click of the door grated against my ears, the sharp slam of it startling me. Moments later, the sound of the shower occupied the space.

Was that his blood or someone else's? I itched to follow him inside and make sure of it myself, but my pride weighed heavier.

He came back to me in one piece, so there was that.

After a few more minutes, he reentered the bedroom with nothing but a low hanging towel around his hips.

No blood.

A sigh escaped me and damn him for invoking a tsunami of feelings in me.

Luca disappeared inside the walk-in closet before coming out with a handful of clothes.

With purposeful strides, he walked toward me, my pulse skyrocketing all over again.

He was too beautiful for his own good. Hard muscles, sharp features and a buzz cut that warmed my skin.

"Are you going to be difficult today?" His voice was rough, skating down my spine.

"Depends on whether you give me what I want." My voice came out raspier than I intended, causing Luca's eyes to darken.

"And what is it that you want, *piccola ribelle*?" His eyes held mine captive and I knew it would be undeniably easy to give myself up to him. To accept whatever he gave me, knowing I'd savor every second of it.

"Freedom."

One word, yet it held more meaning than just being held captive by these four walls.

He stilled, letting his hand fall limp at his side as he pierced me with a hard stare. "Raise your arms, Irina."

I sighed, following his order.

How the brute managed to piss me off and swell my heart with affection for him simultaneously, I'd never know.

He'd been changing my clothes for me ever since I told him I wasn't ready to see myself and even went as far as covering the mirror in the bathroom.

Nausea burned my chest at how weak I must appear, and I hated it.

Luca slipped the camisole over my head, replacing it with a long sleeve shirt. His gaze held mine the whole time, with an emotion I couldn't place.

My pants went next, and every stroke and stare left me breathless, proving the unprovoked effect this man had on me from the slightest attention.

When he put my boots on my feet, curiosity peaked. "Where are we going?"

He stood and walked back inside of the closet before coming out dressed in his signature outfit, jeans, and a white tee shirt under a leather jacket. With his neck tattoos, he was every woman's dream and nightmare all in one.

"Out."

Instantly, my mind went into creating possible escape plans. I didn't question him further, not wanting to sound too eager about finally getting out of here.

I stood from the bed, my body shaking from restless

nerves. If I succeeded in leaving him, what would happen then?

He grabbed his keys from the nightstand and walked toward me, stopping when the toe of his boots touched mine. "Make me regret this, Irina. I dare you."

The threat was clear as he nudged under my chin before opening the door.

Confusion weighed heavy on my conscious. "It was unlocked?" I could've left while he'd been in the shower.

"It's always been unlocked."

My head snapped in his direction as he leaned against the door, waiting for me to pass through. "What?"

"I never locked you out," he confirmed. "And you never checked either. . . well, besides that first night when you almost did."

I was going to be sick.

"I. . . I."

I had checked again though, right? My thoughts twisted together, trying to come up with a good excuse. Why would I willingly choose to stay here? He was lying.

A wave of panic threatened to grasp me, invisible hands curling around my neck, that familiar sensation threatening to pull me into the dark abyss.

"Breathe." Luca's sharp voice sliced through the black cloud, his hand grasping my jaw almost painfully, but it rooted me in place from sinking beneath the surface. "Breathe, sweetheart."

I inhaled a lungful of air, my vision clearing with every breath until I could see his distressed face looming over me.

He cupped my face, his deep honey eyes boring into me. "You *wanted* to be here because you felt safe."

I *wanted* to retort and tell him that he was wrong. That I didn't *want* to be here, but as the rest of his words registered, I couldn't help feeling angry toward myself.

Being with Luca gave me a different sense of security and I held onto that. He was attentive, aware of what I needed before I even did. And he'd gone out of his way to ensure that I was comfortable physically and mentally.

I was in denial of the depth of our relationship, and he was patiently waiting for me to acknowledge it the same way he had.

He hadn't trapped me.

I'd done that myself.

He placed a chaste kiss on my forehead, pulling me out of my stupor. "Come on. My sister wants to meet you."

Sister?

I didn't have time to regain my composure before we reached the ground level, where a young girl sat on a stool in the kitchen.

Light brown hair curled and not a single strand out of place, makeup done to perfection and a tweed skirt and blazer on her slim figure.

"Evangeline," Luca called to her, earning her attention.

If Luca was leader of the Camorra, then his sister was a Mafia princess, and it was clear she'd been brought up to portray a perfect image of herself.

She turned, a smile breaking across her face when she noticed me.

Pristine, elegant, and graceful. Yet, her green eyes held a different story.

"I've heard so much about you, Irina." With more

enthusiasm than I saw on anyone else, she walked toward us. "It's finally nice to put a name to a face."

If the scar across my eye unnerved her, she didn't show it as she beamed at me as if I was a treasure piece.

I gave her a small smile. "Have you?"

"She's lying," Luca was quick to huff out, glaring at his sister.

He was someone who exuded confidence, so it was amusing seeing him appear somewhat embarrassed at being exposed.

"No, I'm not." She smiled mischievously before gazing over at me again. "Although, I must say, his explanation of your beauty was an understatement."

Oh.

I caught Luca's eyes, his face passive, confirming that he really did talk about me to Eva.

Butterflies fluttered in my stomach as his pupils dilated, staring at me as if I was the only thing that mattered.

"Thank you." A genuine smile ghosted across my lips. "I could say the same thing about you." He hadn't told me a thing about her, but it seemed like the right thing to say.

Eva's eyes twinkled as she flushed pink. She really was sweet. Too innocent in a world full of wolves.

"We're headed out," Luca told her, kissing her head. "Call if you need me."

In a matter of seconds, he summed up their relationship with that one goodbye.

My heart swelled at his tender care. He was the most affectionate psychopath I'd ever encountered.

"I hope we get a chance to speak later, Irina."

I nodded hesitantly at her, not wanting to give her false hope in something that might not even happen.

The moment we stepped outside the house, Luca pushed me against the door, a firm grip around my throat before he slammed his mouth to mine, knocking the breath out of me.

He thrusted his tongue past the seam of my lips, claiming my own in rough strokes.

My brain short-circuited at the warmth of his intoxicating taste, and I couldn't think of anything else except for how to deepen his touch.

I wrapped my hands around his head, the short strands pricking my palms, fueling this heat spreading through my body.

I pulled him down while I went on my toes to feel him thoroughly destroy me and put me back together again.

Biting and teasing his bottom lip, I pulled it, relishing in the sound that escaped him as if he was restraining himself from completely devouring me.

He squeezed my throat, causing me to let go and gaze up at him. His eyes were pools of honey, desire and possessiveness swirling in its depth.

"What was that for?"

His thumb stroked the pulse on my neck. "For me."

He turned and walked down the pathway, leaving me to bring myself down from an adrenaline high.

The brute truly knew how to catch me off guard and tip me off balance.

I pushed off the door and followed him, watching as he pulled an extra helmet from the back of his bike.

"So," I started, feeling unsure all of a sudden. "You told your sister about me."

He closed the few steps between us before placing the helmet on me. "Is there a reason I shouldn't have?"

"Plenty."

He searched my eyes, the intensity of his stare enough to bring me to my knees. "None that matter."

"Does she know her brute of a brother kidnapped me?"

A smile touched his lips. "Something like that."

He grabbed my hand and helped me on the motorcycle, reminding me of how long it'd been since I rode my own.

When he settled in front of me, he reached back and wrapped my arms around his torso, holding my hands to his chest.

It wasn't something that should've made my breath hitch or my heart race, but the stillness of the night surrounding us caused me to lean forward until my cheek pressed against him.

I closed my eyes, savoring this moment because I knew once I had a chance to leave, I'd take it.

When the familiar field of Roman's property came into view, my insides churned.

Why were we here?

He passed through security, riding toward the manor before parking, and I didn't waste time getting off.

"What the *hell* am I doing here, Luca?" I

We both knew how Roman felt about me, and I doubted he wanted me anywhere near him or my brother.

So, what was his purpose to this visit?

He removed his helmet, narrowing his eyes at me. "Might want to lose that attitude of yours."

"Or what?" I laughed incredulously. "You're going to kidnap me again? Kind of moot, since you never let me go!"

"Why do you always do that?" He got in my face, staring down at me with pure rage as if I hit a nerve. "Assume the worst in everyone? *In me?*"

I gritted my teeth together, stopping myself from saying something stupid like how I'd never been given a reason to believe otherwise.

Luca had already crossed boundaries with me that no man had ever done before, and it ran deep into the crevices of my soul.

And maybe I was scared to open up to him because I knew this was a means to an end. Short-lived like everything else in my life and the thought of him being the next person to leave me was more painful than I cared to admit.

I sighed, exhausted from going in circles with him. "What are we doing here, Luca?"

His jaw ticked, and I knew he had more to say but didn't. "To see Nico." He brushed past me. "You're welcome."

I looked up at the night sky, trying to figure out how I ended up in this position.

I had a plan before coming to Italy, but the game had shifted, and I was losing.

With a churning twist in the pit of my stomach, I

followed Luca inside the house, where he waited for me in the foyer.

Without another word, he walked up the grand staircase with me in tow.

The house was quiet, void of any sound, but I knew better than to assume Luca came without informing Roman.

I wondered how he'd managed to convince him to let me see Nicolai. Or maybe I had it all wrong.

I knew I lost Roman's trust—not that it had been something I sought out genuinely—but he'd become a friend of mine, and I guess our feud didn't sit well with me.

He could pretend that he didn't care either, but if I was anyone else, he would've splattered my brains out on that dining table weeks ago.

Roman was never the enemy, but the moment he kept Nicolai from his position as the next *Pakhan,* he would be one to the Bratva.

The hall was glowing faintly as we walked past multiple doors before Luca pushed the one at the end open.

He waited for me to pass through before shutting the door behind himself.

The moment my eyes landed on my brother; I felt the heavy ache in my chest ease up.

He was awake, perched up on a bed full of pillows and blankets.

When he peered over at me, something between a laugh and a cry escaped me. "Nicolai. . . " I took a step toward him when another voice stopped me.

"That's close enough." Roman came out of the bathroom, his energy dark and full of venom, all directed at me.

"She's not going to harm her own brother." Luca leaned against the wall, causal in his demeanor but alert. His tee shirt stretched over his biceps as he crossed his arms. "Pipe it down."

"I don't take orders from you, Luca."

They were clearly not on good terms either, which made this visit even more uncomfortable.

I didn't like that I was most likely the reason for their drift. It was hard to witness, but I stayed silent, unsure of how to proceed in unknown territory.

Nico caught my eyes. The brown in his conveyed so many emotions at once, they were hard to decipher.

"Can you both leave the room?" he said, earning their attention. "I'd like to speak with Irina."

"Nic—" Roman turned toward my brother before he was cut off.

"Alone."

A silent conversation passed between them and as Roman raked through his hair in defeat, I knew he'd do anything for him.

"I'll be right outside the door." He pointed toward it before shifting his attention to me, his obsidian eyes glaring with unsaid threats.

For the sake of my brother, I chose to stay silent.

Roman grabbed Luca roughly by the arm and dragged him out.

I quickly crossed the room until I reached Nicolai and sat on the bed beside him. His chest was covered in bandages and flashes from that day came rushing back.

The sounds of his bones snapping. His limp body covered in blood. Me helpless.

"You should've never followed me that day," I choked, staring at him warily as I grabbed his hand before letting it go, remembering how he didn't like to be touched. "Are you in pain?"

His dimples appeared when he grinned at me. "Not anymore. I'm healing."

A relieved breath escaped me, and I slumped from the rigidness that my body had been in until now.

"I wanted to help you," I whispered. "So badly, Nico, that I'd have endured that over again if it meant you weren't harmed."

My chest ached from how true those words were. I never knew I was capable of harboring such love for someone I only met a few short months ago but he was my brother. I would've done anything to protect him.

"Don't." His pale blond hair was tousled and for once, he looked twenty-two. "I was there too, Irina. I saw what that man did to you. If you're carrying that hurt for me, then know that I feel the same way for you."

Tears spilled from my eyes, making a path down my face from the thick emotion in his voice.

The Bratva had their own agenda with Nicolai, but all I ever wanted was my brother.

"For what it's worth, you look badass with that scar across your eye." He grinned, attempting to lighten the mood.

My face became hot at having forgotten about it. "I wouldn't know. I haven't seen it."

He tilted his head at me, anger slashing across his stark features. "Don't give it the power to destroy you."

I pinched my lips together and nodded subtly.

"If Roman had found us sooner, then maybe this wouldn't have happened." He sighed, the dark rings around his eyes a contrast against his pale skin.

"What do you mean?"

"I have a tracker behind my ear." He tilted his head and moved his hair to the side. "It's beneath my skin."

The subtle dent of the chip was barely visible, but it was there. And suddenly, it all made sense. He hadn't been lying when he'd said he would get us out. He knew Roman would come looking for him.

"Why?" I breathed, not understanding the reason for it.

He stilled; his face unexpressive as he stared blankly in front of himself. "Roman is protective of me."

"I gathered as much." When he'd held a gun to my head.

He stayed silent, his eyes void and empty, and I knew there was more to it.

"Nicolai."

"Hm?"

"What's the *real* reason?"

"I asked him to." The answer left his lips as if it had been on the tip of his tongue this whole time, as if it was the first time he admitted the truth to someone.

I shook my head. "I don't understand."

"I don't want you to."

My stomach dropped, my blood running cold, and I hated that he couldn't talk to me.

Clearing my voice to stop the hurt from showing, I said, "Because I'm a stranger."

"Because you're my *sister*. And for once, I don't want someone to know my past and have it define me."

What happened to you? I wanted to scream.

We were the same in that sense. I didn't want Luca to know me in fear of how he'd look at me and Nicolai didn't want me to know him for the same reason.

"Is that why you followed me that night?"

"When we first met, I felt this sudden familiarity with you, and I didn't understand why or why I felt comfortable in sharing parts of my life with you." His forehead scrunched in vulnerability. "But then I found out you were my sister, and I couldn't let you walk away. I do want to have a relationship with you, Irina."

A watery laugh bubbled out of me as more tears unleashed. "Does this mean you'll come with me?" Hope rooted inside me as I leaned forward, waiting for his answer.

"What?" His face twisted in confusion. "No, that's. . . that's not what I meant. I'm not leaving Italy."

"But you just said-"

"I know what I said," he snapped and relaxed his tone when I inched back. "I want to know *you*. The rest doesn't matter to me. *He* doesn't matter."

"The *rest* comes with knowing me."

He leaned back against the headboard, saying nothing, yet everything showed in his gaze.

He was giving me a choice. Either I accepted his wish, or I didn't get to know him at all.

"You might've escaped your past, but you won't be

able to escape your future fate." I wasn't intentionally trying to create an issue with him, but he needed to know our father wouldn't stop until he succeeded. "But I don't want to lose you."

I hoped whatever came next in our story wouldn't hurt him in the process.

"Yet you're still leaving."

I scoffed. "I don't think Roman would appreciate me staying the night."

"That's not what I meant," he said, nodding his head at the door. "Are you leaving Italy? Luca?"

That nauseating feeling in my stomach came back along with the heavy weight in my chest. I wanted to tell him the truth, that I was, but if Nico knew this, I couldn't guarantee that Luca wouldn't find out. He'd chain me to his bed if he did.

I smiled at him even when my heart cracked in two. "I'll come visit you again when I can." With a kiss on his forehead, I stood up and made it halfway across the room when his voice stopped me.

"Goodbye, Irina."

He knew. *Dammit.* He knew.

"Goodbye, Nicolai."

CHAPTER 27
LUCA

Roman's anger was palpable as we waited by Nicolai's door.

Our relationship had taken a hit, and it was unusual for us to go this long on bad terms.

The only reason I was able to bring Irina to visit her brother was because I talked to Aurora and asked her to persuade Roman.

He could never say no to his wife.

My best friend leveled me with a stare. "I want her out of Italy. Away from *him*."

I leaned back against the wall, hands in pockets. "You know I won't agree to that."

"You're a fool," he spat out, eyebrows pinched in exasperation. "She's the daughter of the *Pakhan*, Luca. Do you understand what that means?"

That she was calculating in her steps and the Bratva would come after her and Nicolai. I understood.

"We'll be ready if the Bratva retaliates." My voice was dangerously low when I said, "But I'm not letting her go."

"Ready?" he scoffed, raking through his hair roughly. "You've hardly been useful as leader of the Camorra. What makes you think you could handle war when I've been picking up your slack?"

I chewed the inside of my cheek, knowing he was right. My mind wasn't fully in the right headspace and everything I did for the Camorra sent me into a spiral filled with wrath.

Carrying after my father's footsteps never sat well with me and if it hadn't been for torturing him almost every other day, it wouldn't have been worth it even a sliver.

"Even if you don't think so, you're still *my* brother," I said as he stared at me hard until he sighed and turned away. "I want *her*. Whatever it takes."

"Does she want *you*?"

"Did Aurora want you at first?" I shot back, walking toward him. "How is it any different from what I'm doing?"

"Because my *son* is now involved!" His obsidian eyes glowed with fury as he pointed toward Nico's door. "And I'll be damned if anyone tries taking him away."

My heart pounded against my chest, lost for words. It was the first time he admitted how he saw our youngest member.

"I would never hurt him intentionally." My voice was low and definite. "Irina would never hurt him."

"Irina." He chuckled, shaking his head. "I wouldn't be surprised if it was her people who beat him half to death."

I sympathized with him, but he was illogical in every sense. "Why do you act oblivious to Irina being in the same position as her brother? She was also there! Drugged and tortured."

"I blame her for all of it." His jaw ticked; face consumed with hatred. "And nothing will change that. If she had never come here, this wouldn't have happened."

"You're being unreasonable. You know she's not at fault for what happened."

"No, I don't," he strained out, getting in my face. "I don't know shit because whoever the fuck did this covered their tracks. They were strategic and clearly strapped with resources."

That's why he thought it was the Bratva. Aside from them being ruthless and intelligent, he had no other leads yet. Still, it wouldn't make sense to blame them when Irina was the *Pakhan's* daughter.

Unless there was a bigger play at hand.

"Wait." My mind tumbled, the pieces of the narrative coming together. "You knew Nico's background. That's why you were on the fence about affiliating with them when Viktor came to visit."

He pressed his lips into a thin line, the answer evident on his tired face. "I didn't think they'd known about him."

Irina's lies kept piling. I was almost certain Viktor wasn't an exporter and that he'd been in Italy for the same reason as her.

It was then that Nico's door opened, Irina storming past us until she disappeared down the hall.

"While you run after her, you might want to think long and hard about who you're risking everything for."

He waved his hand mockingly. "Go on, ask her about Viktor and why he was really here."

Then he disappeared inside the room, leaving me to follow the one person who would be my demise.

When I stepped outside, I saw Irina walk past the bike, her steps furious.

"Where the fuck do you think you're going?" I called out to her, frustration building inside me. With Roman's anger issues and Irina's chaos, I had enough.

"To hell!"

My own feet beat against the gravel as I caught up to her before lifting her off the ground.

Her legs kicked in the air as she beat her fists against my back, but it was futile. "Let me go!"

"Never," I hissed, squeezing the back of her thigh.

Making my way back to the bike, I dropped her on it, searing a look in her direction as she bared her teeth at me.

"What's wrong with you?"

"Me?" she huffed out before laughing hysterically, eyes watering in an ocean blue. "What the hell is wrong with *you*?"

She stood up and closed the space between us, face scrunching in irritation. "Do you have *any* idea what's at risk the longer I stay here?"

My jaw tightened at her tone before I gripped her collar, pulling her up to me. "I do but for the life of me, I can't find a good enough reason to let you go!"

"Why?" Her voice cracked, pressing her hands against my beating chest. "My father will come for me. Viktor will come for me!"

And there it was.

"What do you mean Viktor?" The bite in my tone made her flinch. "Why would an exporter come for you, Irina?"

"Because he's not an exporter," she whispered. "He's my cousin."

Motherfucker.

I let go of her and turned away, grabbing the back of my neck.

She *had* lied to me, and I aimlessly believed her.

It wasn't a coincidence that he'd shown up at the same time Irina did. He had been here to keep an eye on her—on all of us.

"Luca." She wrapped her hand around my bicep before standing in front of me. "Let me go. *Please.*" Her voice shook as she pleaded me with her drawn eyes.

My chest ached from her words. She was still in my vicinity, yet the mention of her absence was worse than her lies. It felt like shards of glass cutting me open.

They would come for her. And Nicolai.

"What does Viktor know?" I asked, the pounding of my heart painful against my ears.

"Everything," she whispered. "He knows I was supposed to be back in Russia already." The scar against her eye flashed more prominent under the moon. "Do you understand now? Their silence isn't acceptance. I need to get in contact with them before this escalates."

I searched her eyes, feeling myself drown in them and every rational thought slipped from my mind.

This wasn't obsession. This was a visceral feeling so raw that death seemed better in comparison than removing her from my life.

She must've seen something in my gaze because she stepped back, her head shaking in dismay. "It doesn't matter *what* I say. You *won't* listen."

"Get on the bike, Irina or I'll do it for you."

She held my stare, eyes narrowing as her body shook from rage. "I hate you, Luca Canaveri."

I leaned forward, a merciless smile curving my lips. "And I hate you." For making my heart attach itself to yours.

With nowhere to go, she grabbed her helmet and swung her leg over the seat, arms crossed over her chest in displeasure.

I'd find a solution and fast but it sure as fuck didn't include her leaving me.

She went rigid as I sat in front of her, and I waited for her to wrap her arms around me, but the warm press of her body never came.

I ran my hands up and down her thighs for a moment before reaching for her arms, uncrossing them with force and wrapping them around my chest.

Her fingers curled into fists, and I held them close until she spread them. Sighing in relief that I still had her; I started the engine.

It didn't take long until we reached my property.

The bike wasn't at a full stop when Irina got off, throwing the helmet to the ground before barging through the house.

The pent-up rage buzzed beneath my skin, and I had reached my limit.

I was over this hot and cold, this fucking push and pull between us.

Turning off my bike, I followed her inside the house. The lights were off which meant Eva had gone to sleep already.

Taking the steps two at a time, I reached my bedroom before closing the door behind me.

With adrenaline pumping through my veins, I shrugged off my jacket and tossed it on the bed.

The faint glow of the bathroom light seeped through the closed door.

The hinges creaked as it banged hard against the wall when I pushed it open.

Irina didn't react at the abruptness; her body hallway turned when I closed the space between us in quick strides. I grabbed her by the throat before slamming her against the shower door.

Her breath fanned across my face as she held my stare, fire simmering in her eyes. "Get out."

"Not until I fix that attitude of yours." Gripping the neckline of her shirt, I pulled it until the fabric ripped apart.

She was stubborn. Stubborn enough to not cover herself even when her chest rose and fell with quickened breaths.

With a delicate touch, I ran my fingers across her skin, feeling the raised flesh of her scars.

"You're crazy," she said, her voice low and wavering.

"You've made me this way." I fell to my knees, hooking my fingers on the waistband of her jeans. I held her gaze as I slid them down and removed it. "Remind me how much you hate me, sweetheart." I knew she deserved a far better man than me, but I was the only one she'd ever be with.

I leaned down, pressing a kiss to a scar on her thigh, hearing her inhale sharply. I continued my way up her body, kissing each mark until I was standing before her again. I pressed a lingering kiss to the scar above her eye. "Tell me."

Instead of pushing me away, she held onto my biceps, nails digging into my skin as if she wanted to draw blood. "I hate you." Her voice trembled as if she hadn't meant it at all.

I peppered kisses along her jaw until I reached her ear, grazing my teeth along her skin. "How much?"

Irina belonged to me as much as I belonged to her. If not more.

I pulled her chin down with my free hand until she let go of her lip, blood coating the bruised flesh.

Her face flashed as I dragged my tongue across the crimson color, tasting her—*hungry* for her.

She tasted like everything I'd ever need to survive.

"You try so hard to appear unaffected, but you forget that I know you better than I know myself." Leveling my gaze at her, I stared into the depths of her soul. "Now, tell me how much." I bit down on her cut lip causing her mouth to part in a silent cry before I soothed it with my tongue again. And because I was a glutton for her dominance, I said. "Please."

"I hate you," she repeated, voice thick and eyes glossed over in malice. "So much that some days it feels like I can't breathe."

The heated look she gave me thrummed beneath my skin.

My lips twitched in amusement before I angled her

face to me. "If that were true then why did it sound like the sweetest confession?" I captured her lips and slipped my tongue inside her mouth, feeling her melt against me. She met each ravenous slash of my tongue with her own. The kiss was sloppy, filthy, and painful. Exactly how I fucking wanted it.

I'd never get enough of her.

After a moment, she pushed against my chest until I was forced to pull back. She shot a glare my way. "Are you enjoying this?"

"Not as much as you are," I said, turning her around to face the mirror.

She instantly averted her gaze. "Arrogant much?"

I grinned, pressing her back to my chest. "Only because you like it so much."

Irina was silent and I knew it had everything to do with the position I'd put her in. "Look in the mirror, Irina," I whispered in her ear. "Look at how beautiful you are."

I knew she hadn't seen herself since the accident and it killed me inside to see her avoid her reflection as if she wasn't pure perfection.

Maybe I was an asshole for taking advantage of this moment, but I needed her to understand that she wasn't alone. Whether it was near or from afar, I'd be her shadow.

She shook her head, resting it against my chest as if she was passing on the weight of her pain to me.

"Trust me," I said to her.

Her breathing quickened before she slowly peered straight at the mirror.

"I want you to remember this moment every time you see yourself." I locked eyes with her. "That I'd willingly carry your pain and if that was all you ever gave me, I wouldn't hesitate to take it."

She reached back until she grasped onto my neck, her tear-streaked eyes roaming over her body. "Luca..."

"I know, sweetheart." I pressed a kiss to the top of her head, understanding that this was difficult for her. "You're ethereal."

My heart thrashed against my ribcage as she turned in my arms and stared up at me with vulnerability swimming in her blue eyes. "Thank you for this." She lifted her hand, tracing the angle of my jaw with a softness that would've brought any man to their knees. A crease formed between her brows as she ran her hand through my buzzed hair. "And this."

I caught her wrist, bringing it to my lips. "I would do anything for you, *piccola ribelle*."

Her face conveyed an internal war she was having with herself, and I had no idea what thoughts plagued her mind, but I'd wrench it out of her soon.

I'd taken her to bed shortly after we'd showered.

With her back to my chest, I wrapped my arm around her waist and rested my face into the crook of her neck.

I might've used my body wash on her, wanting my scent to linger against her skin—even though I'd stocked the bathroom with her addicting amber scent.

When Irina's breathing evened out, I thought she'd fallen asleep, but her voice broke the silence. "The nightmares started after my first panic attack."

I pressed her further into me to let her know I was awake. I'd waited for Irina to share parts of herself with me willingly, and I would've waited longer.

"In each one I'm trapped in a dark room, the walls closing in on me until I can't breathe." Her hand was cold as she set it atop mine, holding onto me.

I'd seen what her nightmares did to her, and it scared the fuck out of me.

I didn't say anything, giving her the power to continue at her own pace. I only hoped that my presence brought her comfort in her vulnerability.

"When I left Russia at eighteen, I never wanted to be tied to who I was before," she whispered, curling in on herself. "But when you're hidden away from the rest of the world for most of your life and you're finally free, it brings a different type of loneliness to a person. I couldn't escape who I was."

Envisioning Irina as a child, alone and afraid sent a fiery rage through me. It was hard to imagine her in that way when she was nothing like that person now. "Why were you hidden away?"

"A father's love can be suffocating." She turned around until she was facing me, a furrow deepening between her brows. "It's hard to despise him when all he ever wanted to do was protect me from our world."

Yet, she'd been hurt either way.

"But I felt so alone, Luca." The broken tone of her voice chipped away at my soul, and I held her a little closer. "For eighteen years, I had little to no communication with anyone outside of the manor." As if she needed validation for her own trauma, she added with a tight laugh, "It was hard to not let it affect me when the few people I talked to were on payroll. Aside from my parents, who were occupied most of the time with business, I was left to my own devices." A sigh escaped her. "I hadn't even gotten involved in the Bratva's business until after I left Russia."

It was extreme for her father to have done that to her but with being the leader of the Bratva, it seemed that he let his paranoia drive his motives and was too conflicted to see how it affected his daughter.

"I *see* you." I cupped her face, caressing her cheek with my thumb. "I *hear* you, sweetheart."

She grabbed my hand and leaned into it further as if it were her anchor to keep going. "The silence became unbearable, trapping me in my own mind and I didn't know how to stop myself from spiraling—to even explain how badly I was hurting right here." She pointed to her heart as her face twisted in agony. "I hid my emotions deep inside the hollowness of my chest where it festered. But then you came into my life." Her blue eyes searched mine, and I felt myself fall for her further. That's what happened when Irina set her gaze on me, she utterly consumed me in every way. "And it terrified me that someone could read me so thoroughly without knowing me."

From the moment I first saw her, I knew she'd be mine. One way or another I would've had her.

"At first, I avoided you because I knew you were trouble and my father would disown me if I was involved with an Italian." She shook her head, and a tear slipped from her eye. "Then I avoided you because I realized I didn't want to do that at all. The incessant feeling in my chest wouldn't go away. And I keep pushing you away-"

I cut her off with a kiss, taking her pain for myself. "The first time I pulled you out of a nightmare," I started, my heart picking up speed as I recalled that night. "I felt the same helplessness I did when my mother was killed in front of me. *That* was the moment I realized how desperately I needed you."

Her blue eyes misted over before she pressed her lips to my jaw, chasing away my demons with each tender kiss.

I gripped her neck, making her face me again. "You could never push me away, Irina. I'm right here. I'll *always* be right here with you."

CHAPTER 28
IRINA

My lips twitched as I stared down at Luca. He was still a heavy sleeper.

I pressed my forehead against his, breathing in his scent as the words I wanted to say vibrated along my tongue.

But if I said them, I wouldn't be able to let him go.

Nausea burned my throat as I held onto him. This scene felt all too familiar, and it was because of me. Again.

I couldn't keep hurting the people I care about, most of all him.

"I have to let you go," I whispered, my heart bleeding for him. "I'm so sorry."

I clicked the button on the intercom near the gates until a beep sounded. "Tell Roman that Irina needs to speak with him."

The static went dead, the silence of the night being my only company before the gates slid open.

I took a deep breath and walked toward the house as Roman's long frame appeared at the front door.

"You're alone."

"I am."

Curiosity shown in his gaze, but he caught on fast. Luca wasn't with me which meant he was unaware of my whereabouts.

"Is there a reason you're on my property at three in the morning?" he asked, his features strung tight, eyes darker than the sky above us.

"There is. Can we go inside and talk?"

If he wanted me gone, he wouldn't have let me through in the first place. It was wishful thinking, but I had a suspicion he still cared for me enough to hear what I had to say. Or I was completely off and any second he'd aim his gun at me for the second time.

He pursed his lips after a moment and stepped aside, leaving room for me to walk through the threshold.

The house was faintly lit as I followed him down to his office, and he only spoke again when we stepped inside. "Aurora doesn't know you're here."

"I know." There was no way he'd have woken her up because of me.

A sort of calmness had set over me and maybe it was the exhaustion finally reaching its peak or the acceptance of defeat, but I was done.

"I'm going home, Roman." I clasped my hands in front of me, feeling a slight tremble in them. "To Russia."

He leaned against the desk at the center of the room. "Then why come here first?"

I held his gaze, searching for an ounce of warmth in his eyes but they were void, glossed over with disappointment.

He knew if I managed to escape Luca, I could've used the opportunity to leave Italy.

"When I was younger, I had this skewed image of family. While hidden behind the walls of our manor from society, I only yearned for my parents' attention."

Roman stayed silent as I continued sharing with him what I hadn't even shared with Aurora.

"In the beginning I understood their reasoning. I knew my father had enemies, and I was isolated for my own protection." I laughed at how ironic it was. "And then some time passed, and that understanding turned into resentment."

My chest felt sore from the heartache that never dissipated from all the grief it held.

"He may have protected me from the outside world, but he couldn't protect me from the damage that was happening here." I tapped the side of my head, my lips trembling.

"Irina..." A hint of emotion strung along my name as his brows furrowed.

"I don't hate them for it." I gave him a watery smile. "I might not agree with my father's actions, but I still love him." I turned my head and stared at the clock on the wall. "Maybe that makes me naïve."

"It doesn't," Roman said, bringing my attention back to him. The cold exterior he had shown me the past few weeks had begun to thaw.

"I don't need your pity." Even though it was Roman who I was speaking to, I hated when men thought of me as weak. "That's not why I'm here."

"I know."

An understanding passed between us as we stared at each other from across the room and it gave me the courage to say what I needed to.

"When I learned of Nicolai, I felt hope for the first time in years." The mention of my brother's name had Roman stiffening. "I was hellbent on finding him even if it meant serving my father's agenda." Dimples. Freckles. Glasses. "But then I met him and realized I loved him too much to sacrifice his happiness for my own." The sting of tears burned the back of my throat "So, I'm letting him go."

I didn't know when or if I'd see Nicolai again once I left Italy, but this was the closure I needed and I knew Roman was capable of protecting him when the Bratva retaliated. And they would.

"I don't know what'll happen next, but I'm sorry for-"

"Roman." Aurora's trembling voice cut through the air, bringing our attention to her. She stood near the door with her hand atop her stomach, green eyes wide against her pale face. "My water just broke."

The second the words slipped from her lips, a loud explosion reverberated in the air.

CHAPTER 29
LUCA

When Roman woke me up by calling and texting repeatedly that Irina was at his house, I didn't hesitate before rushing here.

I turned my head in the direction of where the sound came from, my pulse racing.

And now I had no idea what I'd just walked into.

With steady strides, I made my way toward the sound, unease swirling in the pit of my stomach.

I'd made it past the main stairs when hushed voices reached me. Unfamiliar voices.

I hid behind the nearest wall and waited, cold sweat sliding down my spine.

Something wasn't right. I could feel the eerie tension in the air as I peered around the corner.

A group of men walked down the corridor, strapped in guns and covered in what appeared to be bulletproof vests.

I pulled back, pressing myself against the wall, my breathing turning shallow at the clarity of the situation.

Fuck. I didn't know how it was possible with the extensive security Roman had around his property, but whoever these people were had managed to breach them.

The house had gone quiet, too quiet but there was no chance that Irina and the rest hadn't heard the bang minutes ago.

I needed to find them and fast.

Careful of my surroundings, I went up the stairs with ease, watchful with my gaze until I landed at the top.

Irritation toward my best friend brewed. Did the bastard really need to have an abnormally large house? Where the fuck was I supposed to look first?

I started opening doors, each room empty, causing my heart to speed up with adrenaline.

The floorboard creaked beneath my feet, the hairs on the back of my neck rising when I felt the presence of someone.

I'd never been wrong when it came to my intuition, even now as I shifted around, coming face to face with one of the men.

A fist came flying toward my face, but I dodged it, ducking to the side before gripping their head and twisting it in a quick motion. The crunch of bone brushed against my palms. I laid him down on the floor, peering around to see if there were any others before I removed the gun strapped to him.

I'd gone through the other rooms without being spotted but when I opened the last door, my heart stilled.

Irina's eyes whisked to me, widening a fraction as if she were silently telling me to leave.

I shifted my gaze to the other side and saw why.

Without hesitation, I lifted my arms, taking aim at the fucker.

"You shoot me," Viktor said, his voice slicing through the air as he gazed at me while taking the safety off his gun. "And it'll only take a second for me to put a bullet through her pretty little head."

The last thing I expected to see was Viktor holding his cousin at gunpoint, but it only made me believe that he'd be true to his word.

"Drop it."

I peered at Irina, adrenaline strumming through my veins from her vulnerable position. If I could divert Viktor's attention, I might be able to disarm him.

"Now!"

"Alright." I slowly set the gun down before raising my hands and stepping further into the room.

"Why are you doing this?" Irina asked, her tone laced with disbelief.

"You know why." Irina shook her head, and his face turned an angry shade of red. "Yes, you fucking do," he seethed.

"No, I don't." A strike of her fiery temper peeked through as she stared him down. "Why would I know why my cousin is threatening to kill me!"

Viktor barked a laugh, keeping his darkened gaze on both of us. "Did the torture null your intelligence, princess?"

Cold sweat ran down my spine as the meaning of his words registered. My jaw strained when I looked over at Irina. She had gone still, a sickening hue coloring her cheeks.

"That was you?" I asked through gritted teeth, narrowing my eyes at Viktor.

"I would've gotten rid of her and that undeserving bastard she calls brother if you hadn't shown up." He snarled at me.

"Why?" Irina's voice cracked, and I internally screamed at her to not give him the satisfaction of seeing her break.

"I was the next heir to the Bratva." Viktor answered her as if it were the most common knowledge. "*My* father died yet *yours* replaced him and now he wants his bastard son to take his position as *Pakhan*." He spit on the floor in disgust.

"Your father made that decision, and you know it."

As if she struck a nerve, he paused for a brief moment, an eerie sensation crawling along my skin.

"On second thought, I'll kill him first." Viktor changed direction, aiming his gun at me before pulling the trigger.

The bang ricocheted off the walls, and I waited for the impact but the bullet never struck me.

My ears rung, my feet threatening to pull from under me as I watched Irina fall to the floor.

No.

"Irina?" Her name fell off my lips in a rush, my eyes deceiving me, and refusing to accept what she'd just done. I fell to my knees beside her, turning her into my arms. "What did you do sweetheart, huh?" My voice cracked as tears blurred my vision.

Her gaze landed on me, blue eyes slowly dimming as she bled out.

My heart thrashed wildly as I pressed the wound in

her chest to stop it from bleeding further.

"Perhaps I won't kill you after all." I'd forgotten Viktor was in the room until he spoke again, fury surging through my veins. "Watching you suffer as she dies is far more satisfying."

He kept talking, but I couldn't register anything beyond the woman dying in front of me. The woman I loved.

I *loved* Irina, and she was dying.

"Why did you do that?" I whispered, pressing my forehead to hers, trying to keep her awake when all I felt was her slipping away as the seconds ticked by. "You shouldn't have done that."

"Luca. . . " The pain in her voice as she said my name brought out a guttural groan from me.

It was hard to breathe, and I knew I wouldn't survive this. "If you die, Irina, I'll never forgive you."

I pulled back and saw tears pool in her eyes, emotion softening her features.

"Don't do this to me, *il mio piccola ribelle*. Please." My own tears fell on her cheeks, each one carrying a piece of my broken heart because if she died, she'd take me with her.

An audible sigh escaped her before she opened her mouth to speak but instead of words, blood sputtered out.

Fear grasped me in its claws, and I held Irina closer, my sanity threatening to shatter.

Yet, she never looked more at peace. The corners of her mouth lifted and for the first time, she genuinely smiled at me.

"That's right, sweetheart. Just keep looking at me like

that," I cooed, sniffling as I pushed stray hairs out of her face. "I'm going to get you help."

It didn't matter what I said.

Her eyelids drooped halfway, and I shook her, palming her jaw as I became frantic. "Hey! You're not dying, you hear me?" A single tear streaked down her cheek and fell on my thumb. "Don't you dare fucking leave me."

"You motherfucker." A pair of hands grabbed me by the collar, wrenching me away from Irina but I couldn't remove my gaze from her limp body to see who. Until their fist hit me in the face causing me to stagger backward.

I turned my head and my body tensed as I came face to face with Ivan Morozov. Viktor nowhere in sight.

Cold sweat raced down my spine. He thought I did this to his daughter and even though I could, it would be useless to prove otherwise.

I was running out of time.

All I could focus on was Irina and holding her in my arms again. "Please." One word yet it held more meaning than any other.

The bullet hit me hard and fast, knocking me to the floor next to Irina.

I waited for the pain to consume me, but I was numb as I stared at her across from me.

"Irina," I whispered, tears trickling down my face. I needed to say those three words to her. Words I should've said weeks ago. And even if she couldn't hear me anymore, I needed to say it aloud. In some tragic way, I wanted her to know I loved her in this life, and I'd love her in the next.

"I love you."

CHAPTER 30
IRINA

That's the irony of time, it doesn't wait for anyone.

And as I lay beside Luca, our hands reaching but never touching, I realized my mistake.

It didn't wait for me to say those three words back.

It was too late.

CHAPTER 31
LUCA

A soft caress on my jaw caused me to blink away the tiredness from my eyes.

"I knew you were a heavy sleeper, but don't you think it might be time to get up?"

I shot upright at the sound of Irina's voice, a sigh of relief escaping me at seeing her angelic face.

"You're here?" I asked, pulling her on my lap, the press of her body easing the heaviness in my soul. "You're really here." I kissed her everywhere I could reach to remind myself that she was safe in my arms.

"Where else would I be?" She chuckled, a dull ache forming between my ribs. I wanted to hear that sound forever.

"You wouldn't believe the nightmare I just had," I breathed, inhaling her amber scent. "But it doesn't matter now. I'm never letting you go."

"Luca?"

"Hm, sweetheart?"

"It'll be okay."

I froze. "What do you mean?"

But as I pulled back to look at her, another voice punctured the space between us, and I felt the vision fade as I was thrust back into a reality I wanted to escape.

"He's been sitting like this for weeks, Roman," Eva whispered, as if I couldn't hear her conversation with Roman. "I'm so worried about him."

"Your brother will be okay."

"You promise?" The hope in her voice chipped away at what little was left of me.

"Have I ever broken my promises?"

"No."

I was grateful that Roman had stepped in for me and looked after her.

It seemed that he'd been doing that for me more than once and I owed him.

When her soft footsteps faded away, my best friend came to sit across from me in the library room.

"You know I can hear when you both talk about me, right?"

"Yes." He appeared unfazed as he leaned his elbow against the armrest, fist beneath his chin. "How long are we going to do this, Luca?"

Cold dread flooded my stomach. "I don't know what you're talking about."

"Pretending as if you're okay."

"I *am* okay." I stared into his obsidian eyes, hating the expression on his fucking face as if I was broken.

There was only one topic that would interest him

enough to divert the attention off me. "How's Aurora and the baby?" I asked.

She'd gone into labor the night of the invasion and Roman was forced to birth their child in the house.

It was a fucking miracle they survived under those circumstances. I'd given shit to him about his abnormally large house, but I was grateful for it now in keeping them hidden.

Roman sighed, catching onto my obvious attempt at changing the subject. "You know you could come and see them for yourself."

When I'd come out of surgery, he'd told me to keep what happened to Irina a secret. It wasn't hard to do when I'd gone days without speaking after that night, let alone capable of being near others.

I knew if I saw Aurora, I'd break, and she didn't deserve to see this fucked up version of me.

Aurora didn't know her best friend had been shot, and I *couldn't* be the one to reveal that information. How could I when I'd spent the last several weeks blocking it out myself?

All she knew was that the Bratva attacked us, and Irina managed to stop it before going back to Russia.

"Not yet." I tapped my finger against my thigh. "Is she still calling her phone?"

Aurora had found it suspicious that her best friend hadn't contacted her since but she had kept her optimism, believing that Irina had a good reason for being silent.

He nodded.

My jaw tightened in aggravation. That nod was the same answer as always. It meant Irina hadn't picked up the phone because she wasn't there. It meant that Aurora was waiting on a call back that'd never come and I was waiting on my fucking forever.

"Luca."

The glass shattered against the floor before I could process what I'd done.

It didn't dull the rage inside me and all I wanted to do was rip my own heart out with how painfully it beat against my chest.

The scattered pieces triggered the part of me that wanted to forget, and it all came rushing to the surface.

My vision blackened as the room fell apart. Tremors racked through my body as I smashed everything near me, the sounds of shattering glass and wood echoing in the otherwise silent room.

The torment of living every day without Irina had consumed me, and I wanted it to end.

I fell to my knees, panting as tears clung to my lids. "I'm not okay," I whispered, my throat tightening. "Because the woman I love took a bullet meant for me."

My body shook as the agony took over, robbing me of the wall I'd built up to avoid the unbearable truth.

Irina was dead.

A guttural scream tore from me as I punched the floor over and over again until my knuckles split open, blood coating them.

Roman wrapped his arms around me and pulled me back. "That's enough."

"It hurts, Roman." Lifeless blue eyes pulsed at the forefront of my mind. The image of Irina dying burned into my soul. "I can't go on without her," I choked. "I can't."

"What happened. . . "

I looked up through hooded lids to see my little sister run into the room, her face turning pale as she took in the scene.

Humiliation whirled inside me, and I couldn't stop myself as I said, "Get out." She didn't need to see me this way, let alone be surrounded by the chaos I came with. Hurt rimmed her round green eyes, but she didn't move. "Get out, Evangeline!"

My sister had always been a fragile soul since she was a child, more so after our mother passed away. She didn't have anyone to rely on except for me and while I was far from perfect, I tried my damn hardest to raise her.

It didn't matter that we had maids for every minuscule thing. She never looked to them once, but as we grew older, that changed.

I knew what it took to be a Mafia princess, and I hoped I hadn't been too late to save her from that burden.

Eva faltered in her step at the harshness of my tone before she ran out of the room.

I let my head hang between my shoulders, trying to even out my breathing, but it was no use. The raw ache had intensified, and I felt completely lost, suspended in the space where Irina once was.

She'd left and taken my heart with her.

CHAPTER 32
LUCA

I tossed and turned in bed, praying for sleep to take me under.

It was the only time I could be with Irina and pretend that she hadn't left me in agony.

Facing the empty space next to me, I gripped the bedsheet, my fingers trembling from the loss of her presence.

I didn't know how long I stayed like that when my mind conjured up an image of her.

My heart shattered all over again because I knew it wasn't real. She was a figment of my imagination.

"Is this how it'll always be?" I asked, gazing at her. "I don't know how to go on without you, Irina."

She smiled sadly, her blue eyes sparking with a warmth that I couldn't feel.

The moment I reached out to touch her, the image scattered away, leaving my hand suspended in the air where she had been.

I cursed myself as I ran a hand down my face and got up from the bed.

I walked downstairs and into the living room to find my best friend sitting on the couch, his eyes glued to the baby monitor in his hands.

He carried it with him everywhere.

"I told you to go home, Roman." He looked up at me as I sat across from him. "I'm sure Aurora needs you more than I do right now."

"She was the one who told me to stay." His obsidian eyes darkened as if he had more to say.

"What?"

He pursed his lips, contemplating his words before he said, "She told me to tell you that Irina loves you and that she would never leave you behind on purpose, even if that was how it seemed."

My gut twisted, bile rising in my throat. I didn't deserve Aurora's concern when I'd been selfish in not visiting her these past few weeks. She was family and I cared for her, but I couldn't face her. My pain was raw, the torment of living every day without Irina visible to anyone who set their gaze on me.

I couldn't hide it. I *didn't* want to hide it. It was the last feeling she left me with and if this grief no longer existed then I'd have nothing.

We sat in silence for some time, the air thick with a strange tension.

My thoughts were chaotic, scattering in all directions until it became difficult to grasp and I found myself asking aloud, "What if we were wrong?"

Roman sighed, glancing at me briefly. "We've been through this before, Luca."

"Then why do I still feel her in here?" I pointed to my chest, a sharp pang striking through me.

I refused to accept that she was gone. Accepting it would mean that our story had ended before it even begun, and I'd *never* be done with Irina Morozov.

"Because you loved her." He came to sit beside me, setting a hand on my shoulder. "But she's gone, Luca."

Shrugging him off, I stood and turned to face him. "I'm going to Russia."

The crease between his brows deepened, something he did when he was stressed. "Don't do this to yourself."

"She's not dead." I had deluded myself the past few weeks when I should've gone after her. What if I'd been wrong?

No one had told me what I wanted to hear when I'd woken up in the hospital. Irina's body wasn't in the house when I'd been found, which led me to believe that her father took her.

"Irina was shot in front of your eyes," Roman said, grabbing my head between his hands as if he was trying to snap me out of my thoughts. "You saw her die."

"She's not dead," I repeated, anger spiking through me from his inability to understand what I was telling him. "I'm going to bring my girl home, and no one can stop me."

Maybe my sanity had finally shattered into pieces, leaving my mind in ruins but I couldn't repeat another day like this.

Ivan Morozov might've shot me and presumed I was dead, but I knew he'd never let Irina see the same fate.

If she was truly gone, the tender place between my rib cage where my heart beat only for her would've dissipated.

I wouldn't let the memory of her dying be my last.

CHAPTER 33
LUCA

"Am I going to regret sending you off without security?" Roman asked, stealing one of my cigarettes before lighting it.

I'd fought tooth and nail with him until he accepted that I wasn't going to change my mind. I needed to do this alone.

"This is my choice and mine alone." Either way, I'd be with Irina. Whether that was in life or death, the outcome would be the same.

The sun beamed against my face and for the first time, I appreciated the warmth it brought me.

"You're a crazy son of a bitch, Luca."

I exhaled a puff of smoke, side eyeing him. "You took me as I am."

He chuckled softly. "That I did."

A sleek black car pulled up next to us before Nico stepped out and walked toward us, his strides purposeful.

"I'm going with him," he said, his words directed at Roman.

"No." Roman threw the bud on the floor and crushed it beneath his shoe. "You're not."

"I have the right to know who I am."

"The answer is no, Nicolai."

The air stretched tight as neither one of them backed down from their stance.

"Irina is dead." Nico's voice carried a slight strain, and I could see grief coating his brown eyes. "I owe her that much."

I'd been so caught in my own self-destruction; I didn't think about how he must've felt after that night.

"She's not dead." I took another drag, savoring the addictive burn.

They both turned to look at me and their silence was enough for me to know that they didn't believe me. I could feel their pity radiating toward me with a sickening hold.

They must've thought I reached the brink of insanity and fell into a delusional state of mind.

You're delusional.

I closed my eyes and smiled as Irina's words pierced my thoughts. It was easy to imagine her staring at me with that same fiery spark she always carried, but it was hard to imagine her gone.

So, fuck them and their pity.

My Irina wasn't dead and soon, she'd be back in my arms.

I pushed off the car and slipped my sunglasses on. "I'm leaving."

"Great. Let's go." Nico walked toward my car, but he

didn't get far before Roman grasped him by the neck and pulled him back.

"Go the fuck home. *Now*."

Nico shrugged off his hand, the vein in his forehead pulsing from restrained anger.

No matter how difficult or irritating my best friend could be, the little shit Nicolai had never disrespected him.

If anything, this was the closest he'd gotten to doing it.

"Get in the car, Nico." My patience was running thin, and I didn't have all day. "Watching this back-and-forth is tiresome."

After a few tense beats, he rounded the car and sat in the passenger seat, his expression drawn.

The nervous energy Roman exuded put me at unease and I knew he was a second away from becoming manic.

I caught his arm. "He'll be with me. Besides, I doubt the heir to the Bratva will be in danger."

"Unless Viktor is six feet deep into the ground, I'm not taking any risks."

Hot fury scorched through my blood as I thought of Irina's cousin and how he'd betrayed his own, all for a position that was never his to take.

It would've been a courtesy to inform the *Pakhan* that he had a traitor in his organization of Russian mobsters, but I'd do one better.

Viktor's blood would be shed but by my hands only.

"I'm sending security with you, after all." Roman's voice brought my attention back to him, his dark eyes set on Nico.

As if the tracker he implanted in his ear wasn't enough.

"Shocker." I rolled my eyes. "You know he's not a child, right?"

He grunted in annoyance. "I know."

Yet his actions contradicted that.

"I'll call you when I land."

"You *call* when you need me, you hear?" He embraced me in a hug—a rare occurrence for us. "I'll always be here, brother."

I hugged him harder. We might've drifted apart because of my relationship with Irina, but no matter where we stood in our friendship, he'd never left me behind. That's the kind of man Roman had always been.

CHAPTER 34
IRINA

The first thing I felt when I woke up was the ache in my chest.

And it wasn't from the phantom pain of the gunshot wound.

"*Printsessa.*"

I slowly peeled my eyes open until my father's face came into view. He looked terrible, dark circles beneath his hollow eyes as if he hadn't slept or eaten in days.

"You've been out for some time," he said, stroking my face affectionately. "I've been so worried."

My stomach sank. *How long?*

As if the emotions harboring inside my chest needed a breakthrough, it finally rushed to the surface in an unbearable release.

"*Papa,*" I sobbed, fear paralyzing me as I clutched my chest. "Please, please..." I cried harder, my voice failing me as images flashed through my mind. "Please, tell me he's alive." My vision blurred as tears soaked my face. "Tell me you didn't kill him," I breathed, pulling at my hair to feel anything but this suffocating torment.

"*Irina.*" His arms came around me, stopping my movements.

My body shook restlessly, my lungs caving in from the loss of the person I wanted most. "I love him," I chanted, curling in on myself.

The confession washed over me in blinding anguish and I felt like a little girl again, trapped with four walls closing in on me.

I hadn't realized I'd passed out until I felt myself come to consciousness again as my father's voice pierced through.

"*Irina*, can you hear me?"

I wanted to scream and tell him I wished I didn't, that I'd rather die than face whatever this was, but nothing came out.

"I'm sorry." My father's expression twisted into guilt as he stared at me with regret. "I thought he was the one who shot you."

I turned away from him, staring at the white wall in front of me. It took me a second to realize it was my old bedroom.

I was in Russia.

"Is he dead? Are they all dead?" I held my breath, my heart pounding as I waited for his answer.

One. *Breathe.* Two. *Breathe.* Three. *Breathe.*

"I don't know."

A lone tear slipped from my eye. "I'd always thought I'd never find a place to call home and the one person who made me feel as though I did, you took him away from me."

I couldn't look him in the eye after what he'd done to Luca, to *me*.

"I've stood by your side in everything, *Papa*, even after the isolation I endured when my mother was alive." If there were pieces of me to break and shatter further, it would've happened in this moment. I loved my father, but it wasn't enough anymore. "But I cannot forgive you for this."

"*Irina*." His Russian accent was strong, thick with emotion.

"Please, leave."

After a few beats of silence, the soft click of the door became my only comfort.

I wept into the soft fabric of my pillow, the heartache reaching far into the depths of my soul, crushing me from the inside out.

If something bad happened to Aurora, Nicolai, Roman. . . Luca. Oh, God, I wouldn't forgive myself.

I'd never felt so alone in my life, existing in a space of nothingness.

I'd lost time, yet it felt like none had passed at all, reliving a memory that would forever leave a scar.

Shutting my eyes tightly didn't get rid of the scene when Luca was shot. It only became more vivid, sinking into the broken pieces of my mind.

It felt as though I was being whisked away, floating in the abyss, and if this was death, it was far less comforting than I expected.

The pain in my chest intensified when the echoing sound of another gunshot reverberated in my ears before a loud thump hit the floor.

Luca stared at me. His caramel eyes filled with such regret, I wondered if he knew how deeply that look would haunt me forever.

He'd fallen beside me, our hands mere inches apart, and I couldn't do anything to feel him—to save him.

"Irina," he whispered, and it was the first time I had ever seen him cry.

My tongue was stuck at the root of my mouth, forbidding me from speaking.

"I love you." His words drifted toward me in a soft caress that ended all my suffering.

I shot up from the bed in a heaving mess, my skin slick with sweat.

Luca loved me and not being able to say it back was killing me.

He had to know, right? He had to know that he succeeded in capturing my heart and soul for himself. That I couldn't think past who I was before he barged into my life.

Pulling my knees up to my chest, I cried some more. This feeling was far worse than the empty void in my chest that I'd been carrying for years. And the one person who had been capable of stopping it was gone.

I died that day in Roman's house and what I was living now was a cruel nightmare.

My thoughts plagued me, clouding my judgment from reality and fiction.

"I love you." I rocked back and forth on the bed, my face crumpling as I forced my mind to tumble back into my happiest memories. Back to Luca. "I love you."

CHAPTER 35

LUCA

It was easy to drive through the Russian streets and find where the *Pakhan* lived—that wasn't a secret to anyone—but it would be difficult to pass through the property.

As Nico directed me toward our destination, my mind wandered to Irina. For a split second, I wondered if this would lead to a dead end, and I'd deceived myself astray in believing she wasn't gone.

Stop.

The ache in my chest weighed heavily, washing over me in an indescribable feeling that would only ever cease when I saw her again.

"Whatever happens, I've got you," Nico said, pulling me away from deteriorating thoughts. He stared at me with understanding flickering in his brown eyes and I hadn't noticed how heavily he resembled Irina until now.

"Only one thing will happen." I gripped the steering

wheel harder. "I'm going to get my girl and bring her back where she belongs." *With me.*

His sigh was audible as he peered out the window. "Okay, Luca."

"You don't believe me either."

"I never said that."

"You didn't have to."

"It doesn't matter." His tone was sharp, as if the controlled barrier he'd presented to everyone was shattering piece by piece.

He was young when Roman brought him in and sometimes it was hard to not see him as a child anymore

"It *does* matter." He'd conditioned himself to always be composed, and he could only keep up the charade for so long before he broke. "You're allowed to be angry."

"Angry would mean I left with Irina that first time she asked me to and avoided the attack. Angry would mean I stopped you and her from getting shot. *Angry* would mean I could stop. . ."

"Stop what, Nico?"

He rested his head back, peering out the window. "Nothing. Turn left here."

The conversation died down after that, and my nerves were too strung out to continue it.

After driving up an empty road for an unnecessary amount of time, we were met with a large metal gate at the end.

There were four men dressed in combat standing guard, two on either side.

"You can't even see anything beyond the gates,"

Nicolai said, pushing his glasses up with his middle finger. "How massive is this place?"

"Guess we'll find out." I opened the door and stepped out of the car.

Nico followed after me, his blond hair striking against the sun. "Maybe if we had security this extensive, they wouldn't have been able to ambush us."

"Did you just make a joke?"

He shrugged, walking down the gravel road.

The situation was dire, yet a grin peaked through at his less than amusing comment. I shook my head and walked beside him.

We hadn't even reached the gates when the guards pointed their rifles at us. *"Dostatochno blizko,"* said one. It was hard to differentiate between them when their build was the same.

"I'm here to see Ivan Morozov." I could've easily spoken to him in Russian, but if they were ignorant to my knowledge of the language, I could use it as an advantage.

They laughed among each other before another asked, "And who is asking?" His accent was as thick as my urge to rip them to shreds for wasting more time.

"His son." My gaze snapped to Nico, shocked by his admission. "Tell Ivan that Nicolai is here to see him."

The air stilled with a brewing intensity, the tension stretching thin under the weight of his words.

Even the guards' smiles faded.

One of them turned away from us, speaking quietly into his headpiece. After a moment, they all took their stance again, staring ahead.

Nicolai and I glanced at each other, confused by the oddity.

The sound of an engine could be heard in the distance, increasing as it came closer before a car neared the gates from the opposite side.

A second later, Ivan Morozov stepped out of the vehicle. The last I encountered him, I'd hardly taken a glance at him before he struck a bullet in me.

His face was sharp yet rough around the edges, as if he'd seen things in his time that no one should. When he strode toward us, the gates opened in his favor, allowing him to pass through.

Ivan removed his sunglasses, his blue eyes landing on me for a split second before they cast toward Nicolai.

Protectiveness rushed through me, and I stepped slightly in front of him, tilting my head in challenge.

I might've agreed to letting Nico come with me, but I wasn't stupid enough to let my guard down, even if it was his father.

Ivan flicked his attention back to me, his mouth turning upward. "I shot you," he said casually, as if *that* was fucking normal.

"And what a poor aim it was, considering I'm still standing." I patted my chest where the bullet had hit me. "I'm doing much better, by the way. Thanks for asking," I remarked sarcastically.

"That explains your delay."

I stood frozen, confused at his civilized manner. This was the same man who'd thought I shot his daughter.

My eyes narrowed at him. "You know why I'm here?"

"Alexei." Ivan caught my stare. "Take him to Irina's room."

My world tilted and suddenly, that was all I could focus on. Silence stretched between us, but my ears were blaring with the need to know. To know it wasn't all in my head and that *she* was alive.

My heart thumped against my ribcage, and I felt myself ignite with desperation. Maybe I was walking into a trap but I didn't seem to care.

Everything blurred from then on, my warning to Ivan, my caution to Nico and the path toward where Irina grew up.

It felt as if I was spinning, tipping over through my consciousness up until the guard stopped by a white door.

Planting my palms against the door, I dropped my head between my shoulders and breathed in.

I needed to get a grip on myself.

I opened the door and slipped inside the room, the air thick with the same grief I'd been carrying for the past few weeks.

In the low-lit room, I could make out the shape of the only woman who had ever been capable of bringing me to my knees, winding me so tightly around her finger, I'd become a part of her.

She was alive.

My chest squeezed as I approached the bed where she slept, and it took everything in me to not break down right then and there.

I lifted the blanket and slid in behind her, careful not to wake her, but it was hard when I'd been deprived of my reason to live until now.

Wrapping my arm around her waist, I pulled her to me as I leaned into the crook of her neck, letting her amber scent embrace me.

A helpless tear escaped my eye as Irina's body molded into mine. I could finally breathe again.

She was my home.

It wasn't until I felt her tremble against me that I realized she was awake.

"Luca." She choked on a sob and the broken way she said my name told me she wasn't questioning my presence, but haunted by it.

"I'm here, sweetheart." I turned her around and when my gaze caught hers, I knew without a doubt I was completely done for. "I'm here."

"You're really here," she whispered as she reached up and traced my jaw with her fingers, sorrow lining the pout of her lips. "I'm sorry." The hurt in her tone slid down my skin along with her palm, landing against my chest—where I'd been shot. "I'm *so* sorry for everything."

Seeing Irina distraught cut me open and for some reason, her apology didn't sit well with me. She'd always been unapologetically herself and I loved that about her.

I reached for the buttons of her shirt, holding her gaze as I undid each one. She didn't stop me as I parted the shirt, revealing her naked chest.

A long scar ran above her breast. The result of death nearly taking her away from me.

I placed my hand on it, her heart thumping against my palm. "I'm okay now, Irina." I searched her eyes, willing her to understand that as long as she was fine, I was too.

She leaned up abruptly, causing me to move back until

we were sitting up. "None of this is okay. It's my fault the manor was attacked that night." Her blue eyes darkened with self-loathing, and I wanted nothing more than to snuff it out.

"You couldn't have known." I took her hand in mine, squeezing gently. "Besides, I'm not innocent here either." I'd kept her to myself, knowing it would've ended badly.

"It doesn't matter." She scoffed, relentless in taking the blame. "I'm as guilty as my father by jeopardizing the lives of everyone I love in the first place."

"Everyone is safe," I said slowly. "Roman, Aurora, the baby. . . they're perfect."

A whimper escaped her as she pressed the heels of her palms to her forehead. "I should've never agreed to any of it. I was so blinded by my need for a *real* family that I didn't think of the repercussions."

No matter what I said, she wasn't hearing me, battling her own demons from the guilt.

"Look at me." I grabbed her wrists and pulled them away from her face. She looked so small and vulnerable; it sent a sharp pang to my chest. "You have me. *I'm* your family." Our knees touched as I closed the space between us. "And *I* love you."

Her tears framed her cheeks as she closed her eyes and when she opened them again, a watery smile split across her face. "I love you back."

Her confession hung in the air, and I held my breath, afraid she'd take them back.

"I love you," she repeated, every syllable shooting straight into my heart. "With all the broken and scarred parts of me, I do. You stopped the hollowness in my chest from consuming me."

Wrapping my hand around her throat, I tilted her head back, holding her stare with an intensity that would burn me alive. "How can you be broken when you've made me whole?" I pressed my lips against hers, pouring everything I am into that one kiss.

CHAPTER 36
IRINA

Luca was it for me. My person. And I loved him. Devastatingly.

I had hidden parts of myself to the world for far too long, but I wouldn't hide what he meant to me. Not when I'd experienced the worst few weeks of my life without him, even if I was unconscious for all of it.

He had come to Russia for me despite not knowing what he'd find, choosing to believe that somehow, I'd survived the gunshot wound. Now it was time for me to show him how far I'd go for him.

Luca squeezed my hand as we walked down the corridor of my childhood home.

Everything appeared the same—as if no time had passed at all.

I glanced up at him, soaking in his beauty as butterflies fluttered in my stomach. I'd never get over him.

"You alright, sweetheart?" he asked, his caramel eyes full of warmth as he held my gaze.

I leaned up and placed a kiss on his cheek. "I already am."

It felt right to be with him, and I couldn't believe I tried convincing myself otherwise. There was a lightness in my chest that had only ever been present when he was near.

I followed the sound of hushed voices until I'd reached the living area, my breath catching in my throat.

"Nico?" I couldn't believe the view of my brother and our father in conversation.

What was he doing here?

He stood up, his mouth falling open as if I'd stunned him. "Irina."

I'd crossed the room and almost lunged at him before stopping mid-way.

He saw my hesitancy and surprised me by catching a hold of my wrist, pulling me into his chest. He wrapped his arms around me tightly. "I'm so glad you're alive."

"Me too," I whispered, clutching his shirt, my heart soaring.

It would've been one of my biggest regrets not getting to know him.

I stepped back and glanced at my father before catching Nico's brown eyes. "What are you doing here?"

"You were right before." He shrugged, running a hand through his disheveled hair. "I can't escape my fate."

I blinked at him, hoping he wasn't planning on doing what I was thinking.

"I've decided to stay in Russia."

Panic rose in my throat, and the sudden emotion felt uncalled for when this had been the plan all along.

"Did you have something to do with this?" I asked, narrowing my gaze at my father.

I had been wrong before. Nicolai could escape his fate; he could alter it. If he didn't want to be the next *Pakhan,* then he could say no. It had only taken a gunshot wound to the chest for me to realize I also had choices.

"Yes, because I'd been *so* successful in my endeavors before." Sarcasm laced my father's tone, but the underlying steel peaked through, reminding me of who exactly I was dealing with.

Ivan Morozov was feared by all and for no other reason than being a vicious leader who did as he pleased without considering others.

Yet he never let me be on the receiving end of his wrath, let alone raising his voice at me.

He stood from his seat, hands behind his back as he regarded me with the same shade of blue eyes I had. "He wants this, Irina."

"Roman won't like this," Luca chimed in, crossing his arms over his wide chest.

"I'll deal with him," Nico replied, his expression drawn with distress.

Luca pinched the bridge of his nose. "I'll never hear the end of it from him," he muttered to himself.

I caressed his arm soothingly. When Roman finds out, I'd no doubt that they'd be at each other's throats.

"I'll be here whether you want to pursue this path or not, Nico." I gave him a small smile to reassure him that he was stuck with me.

His dimples appeared as he returned me a smile and I knew after all this chaos was settled, that we'd be fine.

"Where's Viktor?" I stood toe to toe with my father, a vicious rage searing through me from his name alone. "If my brother is staying here, I want him dead."

I hadn't seen him around, but I'd no doubt he fed my father a story that would cover his ass.

"He did this to me." I pointed at the scar on my face, the rage bubbling over. "He tortured Nicolai and was the one who shot me." Tears threatened to release when I thought about how much he'd stripped from me. "All because of a title he was never deserving of in the first place."

My father leaned forward and cupped my face, pain flashing in his eyes as if he felt my hurt, if not more. "And he'll never do it again. No one will, for that matter." He wiped a fallen tear from my cheek with his thumb. "He's also floating somewhere in the Moskva."

What? "He's dead?"

"Did you think I'd let him live after what he did to you?" he asked, anger lining his forehead.

My pulse raced, cold sweat running down my neck. "How did you figure it out?"

"After the bullet was extracted from your chest, I asked to see it."

Realization dawned on me. The bullet was Viktor's, which meant it had the same symbol as my own gun had.

Had he been so careless, blinded by his revenge that he didn't realize he'd set himself up or had he assumed my father would never question his loyalty.

"I'd taken my time drawing out his pain until he begged for death," my father continued, a crease forming between his brows. "As my nephew, I'd trusted him blindly and I shouldn't have."

"At first, I thought it was quite stupid to give engraved bullets to specific people in the Bratva, but I stand corrected," Luca inserted his opinion per usual, and I could tell it irritated my father with the way his demeanor changed.

"What's this motherfucker talking about, Irina?"

"Nothing, *Papa.*" I definitely wouldn't tell him I had lacked all judgment whenever the brute next to me was near and had figured out who I was before anyone else did.

"Is this where you apologize for shooting me falsely, *dear father-in-law*?" Luca kept riling him up, his voice full of arrogance.

My father's face became red, and I knew he was a second away from lunging at him, but I was frozen in place.

Father-in-law.

My heart fluttered in my chest, and I felt myself growing faint. Luca wanted to marry me?

"I should've shot you in the head instead," he spat out. "And *don't* call me that."

"What? Father-in-law?" His grin was wide, and it was so infectious, I couldn't help but reflect it. "Doesn't it have a nice ring to it, though? Sort of like the one I'll be putting on your daughter's finger."

Before I had a chance to react, my father was on him, his hand wrapped around his throat. "Not unless I kill you."

Luca barked out a laugh, not fighting back. "You tried that already."

Nicolai grabbed our father before he followed through

with his threat, pulling him back with a force I didn't think he was capable of.

Luca shifted his gaze to me with a longing that made my heart nearly give out. "I'm not joking, sweetheart. I will marry you."

He wasn't asking me; he was telling me, and his possessive side drove me insane. Heat warmed my face and for the first time ever, I was lost for words.

"Great, you've traumatized my daughter with your unsolicited confession. She can't even speak!"

"No," I breathed, holding Luca's stare, knowing exactly who and what I wanted. "He hasn't." Tears clung to my eyelids as a thick emotion cascaded over me. "He saved me."

The truth would've brought me to my knees if it wasn't for my father, who had firmly grasped my elbow, stealing my attention.

"All I've ever wanted was to protect you," he said, his voice sounding distant—almost haunted. "But I see now how I've suffocated you in the process. I should've never gotten you involved in this world, either." He pulled me to his chest, wrapping his arms around me. "I'm sorry, *Printsessa*. For everything."

I sighed against him, letting him carry the weight of my hurt for once. He'd loved me in the only way he knew how. Even though he'd been too blind to see how his actions took a toll on me, a part of me couldn't fault him for it. I still loved him.

"I forgive you," I whispered.

He squeezed me tightly as if he was afraid to let me go before he spoke over my head, his words directed at Luca.

"You made it evidently clear that you love my daughter that night but if you make me regret letting her go, I'll personally slice your limbs and feed it to my hounds."

"By the hands of the *Pakhan* himself? What a true honor," Luca snidely replied as he pulled me to him by the back pocket of my jeans until I was facing him. "Besides, love is too vague of a word for what I feel for her."

He smiled down at me, his eyes crinkling at the corners, and I knew with everything that I was, I'd never regret him.

I'd found Nicolai alone in one of the studies a few days later. He was standing in front of the window, peering down at the guards littered across the front lawn.

I leaned against the door, clicking it shut before striding toward my little brother.

"Nico."

He didn't turn around, merely hummed in response as if he wasn't surprised by my presence.

"Can you look at me?"

With his hands clasped behind his back, he angled his head at me.

I searched his brown eyes, the light in them nearly gone. "Why are you doing this?"

"This?" He quirked a brow.

"Why are you staying in Russia? And don't give me that bullshit excuse of not being able to escape your fate."

He looked back out the window as silence stretched in the taut air.

"I ran into our father that night he attacked the Mancini manor." My ears rung as that night resurfaced in my mind. "I plead with him, Irina, for him to stop his soldiers." His voice carried a dark edge, a bite in his tone. "We were outnumbered, and I couldn't lose. . . " He stopped and cleared his throat. "He agreed."

The room swayed beneath my feet as his words echoed against the walls. "At what cost?" I asked hoarsely, but I'd already known the answer.

"Take his place as the *Pakhan*."

"No. . . " I shook my head, moving to stand in front of him. "No, you don't have to."

"Yes, I do." His face was drawn, exhaustion lining his features. "I want this."

"We both know this isn't what you want." I held my hands to my chest, feeling the weight of this burden he'd taken upon himself. "Don't sacrifice your happiness."

"I'm a man of my word, Irina. I'll survive just fine."

"Surviving doesn't mean living."

He stared at me for a long moment as if my words were true beyond this conversation.

"What about everyone back home?" I asked, a feeling of loss washing over me. He'd be here, and I'd be in Italy.

"I'll visit."

His words were sharp and blunt, but I knew him better than that. I knew it was killing him inside. He'd given up his life to save us that night and now he would be paying for it.

"I'm talking to our father." If he wouldn't put an end to this, then I would. How could they both have lied to my face?

"You will not!" Anger marred his features, the intensity of his gaze prominent beneath his glasses. "I'm serious, Irina."

"*Why* are you so hellbent on taking this role?"

"Isn't this what you wanted?" he asked exasperated. I wanted to scream at him for acting so callous. "Wasn't this the plan all along?"

"I was wrong!" My body shook from frustration because I knew this was a losing battle.

"I've made a decision, and I won't be changing it."

"Nicolai. . . " My voice broke and before I had a chance to say anything else, he wrapped his arms around me, reassuring me with his touch that he'd be okay. It all felt wrong. "You don't owe him anything."

"No, but he owes me." He pressed a kiss to my temple. "Don't be mad at your father. This is between him and me."

I let out a shaky breath, feeling his shirt dampen beneath my cheek from my tears. "This isn't goodbye."

"Never."

It made sense why Roman had said everyone had a soft spot for Nico.

Leaving Russia was bittersweet.

I hadn't listened to Nicolai and naturally blew up on my father until Luca pulled me away.

Of course, he had nothing to say, reassuring me that my brother would be safe but that's not what I was worried about.

The argument had escalated until Nicolai intervened, disappointment wrinkling his forehead as he stared at me.

It had taken another few days to relieve the tension, and I was torn and resigned. There was nothing I could do.

On my last day in Russia, my father was done giving me space and barged into my room, refusing to let me leave until we had made amends. He swore that he wouldn't let anything or anyone harm Nico while I was gone. And I chose to believe that because whether I liked it or not, I knew I could trust him in that regard.

After all, Nicolai would be the next *Pakhan* of the Bratva.

And now Luca and I were back in Italy, our first stop to the Mancini household.

Roman had opened the door for us, his murderous gaze settling on Luca immediately before grasping him by the neck and forcing him into a room.

I guess Nico shared the news with him sooner than I expected.

Walking past the foyer and down the hall, I'd reached the living room.

There was a sort of melancholy being back here and after all that happened, I couldn't quite pinpoint it.

I stopped near the entrance, almost afraid to see my best friend. The last time I'd seen her, she was in early labor.

"Are you done hogging my nephew?" Enzo's voice drifted toward me, and I peered around the corner to see him take the baby from a scowling Evangeline.

"It wouldn't kill you to ask nicely," she replied back before taking a seat on the couch.

"It might."

Enzo was as bitter as ever and it could only mean one thing, Sofia was still in rehab.

"Irina. . . "

My head snapped to the right, heart dropping when my gaze landed on Aurora, her mouth parted in shock.

A whimper fell from my lips as I rushed toward her, her cinnamon scent relieving me of all the heartache as I hugged her tightly.

"You left without telling me," she whispered against my neck, her voice cracking.

Confusion set in at her accusation.

Unless no one had told her what really happened to me that night. It made sense if they didn't. Relief flooded through me, and I smiled to myself. The last thing I wanted was to stress her out more than I already had.

"I'll never do it again." I pulled back and caught her green eyes. "I'm sorry."

"Good because I really want you to meet Aro." She half sobbed, half laughed as she grabbed my hand and led us inside the room.

"Oh God, Irina." Eva clung to me as if my absence had jarred her. "I'm so glad you're alive," she said to my ears alone.

"Thanks to your brother," I replied. Even if that bullet had taken my life, I'd felt more alive with Luca than I ever did before him.

She peeled away from me; her expression filled with sympathy I didn't deserve.

"Survived death once again I see," Enzo said with a hint of amusement.

I nervously looked at Aurora, hoping she wouldn't decipher the meaning behind her brother's words before Roman walked in my direction with Luca in tow. "Don't be dramatic, Enzo," Roman chided before reaching me. He leaned forward and placed a kiss atop my head. "Welcome home, Irina."

Instant affection flooded my chest. I'd been seeking for the love of a family all along when it already surrounded me, and it was all I needed.

"And don't speak of death near my child." Roman took little Aro into his arms and stared down at him with the same devotion that he'd only ever shown to one other person. His wife.

"Not your turn, husband." Aurora swept in and stole their son from his embrace, and her voice rose a few octaves as she said, "You ready to meet Auntie Irina?"

I hadn't even held the little one yet and the urge to cry was extreme. *What the hell was wrong with me?*

Aro was fast asleep as his mother passed him to me. I stared in awe at the bundle of joy whose nose was as cute as a button and had more hair than a newborn should, black waves covering his head.

I pressed a kiss to his forehead. "You're beautiful."

Large hands settled on my hips before Luca leaned down until his lips grazed my ear. "I can't wait to make you the mother of my children."

Flutters took flight in my stomach. "How about that ring first?" I teased.

CHAPTER 37
IRINA

The weight of sleep held me under, warmth seeping into my skin from the body pressed against my back.

A deep voice drifted to me, whispering sweet promises into my ear and pulling me out of my drowsy state.

I couldn't help the grin that spread across my face when his arm wrapped around my torso, pressing me further into him—if that was even possible.

"I'm having trouble breathing here, you brute."

Luca's rough chuckle slid along my spine as he moved me around as if I weighed nothing and set me on top of him, my knees on either side of his hips. "I'm sorry, sweetheart."

He placed my hands against his chest, giving me balance as a high spiked through me.

I caught sight of the bullet wound scar on his chest, guilt gnawing at me.

With a finger, I traced over the surface before pressing

my lips to it until I found myself kissing every single visible scar.

Luca grabbed me by the hair—stopping my exploration—and brought my face close to his. His gaze bore into mine with an intensity that could set me on fire. "What are you doing?"

"Appreciating your beauty." My smile widened as his forehead creased in confusion as if he was appalled by the concept.

He flipped us over, so I was under him now and a giggle escaped me. Deep whiskey eyes held me captive, pupils dilating and consuming me in its darkness.

"I think that's my job," he said, kissing the scar across my eye before playfully peppering kisses along my jaw, mouth and nose causing my laughter to grow.

Happiness. He was my happiness.

Waking up in Luca's arms was one of my favorite things ever. It was the best way to start my day, easing my anxieties before they even had a chance to arise.

So, when I'd woken up for the second time this morning without the warmth of his body cuddling me, I sighed in disappointment.

I sat upright, reaching for my phone to check the time and froze.

I couldn't have missed the gleaming diamond even if I'd tried.

He didn't...

As I brought my hand up to my face—inspecting my ring finger as if it was a foreign object—the door opened.

My heart thrashed wildly against my chest when I caught Luca's heated gaze, his caramel eyes darkening in satisfaction as it dropped to my hand.

"What is this?" I asked, glaring at him as I lifted my hand in the air.

He strode into the room with ease and took off his leather jacket, exposing the white tee shirt he wore underneath, the fabric hugging his muscles deliciously.

I felt my resolve fading by the mere sight of him. *Damn him.* I was a weak, weak woman.

"When I told your father I'd put a ring on your finger, I meant it."

"Usually, you get on one knee and ask an important question, no?" I scoffed, unsure why irritation was an emotion I was feeling when I wasn't surprised by his actions at all. "Or, I don't know, maybe waking me up first?"

The brute had the audacity to chuckle, the sound rippling across my skin. "The end result would've been the same."

"Bold of you to assume I'd say yes." I didn't back down from his stare, even when he'd rounded the bed to my side.

Instead of sitting down as I expected him to, he kneeled on the floor in front of me. He grabbed my hips and turned me toward him until my feet touched the cold floor. "And now you don't have a choice."

His snarky replies usually grated on my nerves, but as he looked up at me with such tenderness, all I could think about was how I didn't want anything more than I wanted Luca Canaveri.

"You saying you don't want to marry me, Irina?" His question came out in a hoarse whisper, pulling at my heart strings.

I caressed the back of his head, the short strands of his hair pricking my fingertips. "Never." Leaning down, I pressed my forehead to his. "I'm yours. I've only ever been yours."

His mouth split into a sweet smile, the broadest I'd ever seen before he pulled me into his lap, kissing me senselessly.

"Irina Canaveri," he chanted between each peck, and I completely melted against him, never wanting the feeling of falling for him to go away.

EPILOGUE
IRINA

One Year Later.

I'd never get used to this.

It wasn't because of the blaring sound of the crowd or the adrenaline pumping through my veins.

It was Luca purposefully letting himself get hit to rile up the crowd in his favor. Only this time, he'd taken it too far.

I widened the rope and slipped through the ring, my gaze narrowing on Luca, who smiled at me with bloodied teeth.

"Fiancée!" he called out, coming down from a bloodthirsty high with the way his eyes were glossed over.

Oh, for fuck's sake.

I reached him and grabbed his face, anger rippling off me as I assessed the cuts. "What the hell is wrong with you, Luca Canaveri?"

He circled my waist, pulled me to him and planted his

lips on mine before the audience erupted into a deafening volume.

"Nothing that you can't handle, Irina Canaveri," he whispered against my mouth.

Oh, he was *good*.

"You never let them hit you more than twice." I pushed back the sweaty strands of hair from his forehead.

"You should see the other guy," he mused as he stood up and towered over me. "You're adorable when you pout, sweetheart." He nudged under my chin and signaled toward the back.

I irritably followed him but at least there hadn't been random women waiting for him in his locker room since the last time.

When he'd shut the door behind us, I laid out the supplies I needed to clean his wounds.

Luca knew how to do it himself but if it was up to him, he'd slap a Band-Aid over it and call it a day.

He sat on the bench, wiping the sweat off his torso before throwing the towel aside. "My sister once asked me who takes care of me."

I paused my movements, turning to glance at him.

"I had always been the one to care for her after my mother died so one night she asked me, 'and who takes care of you, Luca?'"

My heart clenched tightly at the tenseness of his tone. I knew he had been close to his mother and with her gone, he felt like he had no one.

As I worked on the cut above his brow, he continued. "It wasn't until I met you that I thought maybe it wouldn't be so bad to let someone in."

I could feel his eyes on me as I worked on his cheekbone, savoring his words and understanding them.

Luca had always been there to stitch my wounds, internally and externally. And I would spend the rest of my life doing the same for him.

He had read me like an open book that very first night in the museum. He believed in us before I ever did and even though it nearly killed us, I would do it all over again if it meant he'd be mine each time.

I leaned down and pressed a kiss to the corner of his mouth before patching his last cut.

Once I finished, he grabbed my waist and pulled me down onto his lap, his thick thigh flexing beneath me.

I tilted my head, searching his caramel eyes and feeling myself fall more in love with him.

In the confined space of my heart, it was just us two, nothing more and nothing less.

"You thought right." I kissed his chest—where not only his but my heart resided—expressing everything I needed to. "I'm yours in every lifetime, Luca. Thank you for letting me see all of you."

The sounds of laughter erupted throughout Enzo's house, and I basked in it.

With everyone preoccupied with their own lives, I'd missed our family gatherings.

Even Nicolai was here. Although, he'd become broodier with each visit, I hoped the Bratva didn't change him for the worse.

Highly unlikely.

"Dinner will be ready shortly," Aurora said, joining us in the living room. She'd been insistent on cooking tonight, told us Gianna taught her a new pasta recipe. "Enzo, go get Sof. I've no idea what's taking her so long to come down."

Aro squealed and clapped his little hands at the sight of his mother before waddling toward her. Roman held him upright, smiling at his attempt to walk.

Their little family made my heart melt.

"You're staring too hard."

I turned my head to the left where my soon to be husband leaned against the armrest and pinned me in place with his heated gaze.

"At your best friend?" I teased, biting my lip as his eyes darkened. "I don't know, he's kind of. . . "

My sentence ended on a gasp as he pulled me by the throat, my face mere inches from him. "What was that, sweetheart?"

My pulse spiked at his public display. "Luca. . . "

"I'll mark you right here if you need a reminder that you're mine and mine alone."

And he would do good on his threat despite our audience.

A smile split across my face at his unwarranted jealously. It was almost too easy riling him up.

I put my left hand up between us, showing him the ring he'd put on my finger a year ago. "I don't think that's necessary."

"When it comes to you, I'll always want more," he rasped out, brushing his lips against mine. "You are the scar that's engraved into my soul, *piccola ribelle*, so even in death, I'll feel your presence."

The meaning behind his words drifted down my skin in a soft caress until my throat thickened with emotion.

He'd shown me that my scars weren't something to hide or be burdened by. I'd always found his beautiful, and he had proved to me that mine were too.

"Have I told you how maddeningly in love I am with you?"

His grin was sinful as he nudged under my chin. "Couldn't hurt to remind me."

Brute.

"I love you," I said, stroking his jaw. He leaned into my touch, his expression conveying all the ways he'd reciprocated that feeling, "So much that some days it feels like I can't breathe."

"Ya tebya lyublyu." And this time, he stole my next breath, not only by capturing my lips in an all-consuming kiss but the Russian that rolled off his tongue.

I melted against him, almost forgetting we weren't alone until an ear-piercing scream echoed against the walls.

We pulled away, the abrupt sound bringing us to our feet along with everyone else.

My heart raced as we stared at one another, the air still with cold anticipation.

"Enzo. . . " Aurora breathed, her face turning pale.

THANK YOU FOR READING!

WHAT'S NEXT?

If you enjoyed reading Stolen Seconds, please consider leaving a review!

Next up is the story of Enzo

ACKNOWLEDGMENTS

To my family: Thank you for supporting me on this journey and being my rock. I wouldn't have gotten this far without you.

To my friends: Thank you for listening to me hours on end talking about the same plot repeatedly and being excited as if it was the first time. You know who you are.

To my editor: Thank you for being patient with me, despite my midnight messages. My grammar has never been better.

To my supportive readers: This wouldn't have been possible without any of you. I hope you fall in love with my book as much as I did writing it. Thank you, infinitely.

ABOUT THE AUTHOR

Gheeti Nusrati began her writing journey in 2022. With a strong love for reading, she discovered a passion for creating stories that invoke strong emotions. She hopes to continue this journey with the support of her amazing readers.

instagram.com/author_gheeti

goodreads.com/gheeti

tiktok.com/@gheeti

Made in the USA
Monee, IL
29 December 2024